Mine to Spell
Book Two of the Mine Series
by
Janeal Falor

To learn more about this author, please visit: www.janealfalor.com

Cover Art by Rainbow Danger Designs

For Rae

Who makes me laugh and isn't afraid to tell it like it is,
which is exactly what I need.

CHAPTER 1

Cynthia

Seventeen today. It should be a birthday like no seventeen-year-old Chardonian girl ever had before. Waverly made a cake I actually get to eat, and father isn't here to beat and hex his wrath on anyone. The dining room is crowded with my sisters, mother, and Waverly. The only warlock present is Zade, who's nothing like father. But the spell which just zipped in the window, and floats in bold over the table for all to see ruined the perfect day.

Stephen's daughter, take control of your property or we will do so for you.

PROPERTY MEANING ME. The words are glowing, bright and yellow with flecks of crimson, hovering above that perfect birthday cake. Waverly says that in Envado they have candles on cakes. Why they would do such a thing, I'm uncertain, but after this fiery display, it's not something worth even attempting. It's too much like the threat of a hex, burning hot, and ready to slam into me.

Zade zaps the spell with a flash of blue, but not quickly enough. Even the youngest girls know something is wrong. They hover together with their eyes wide. Even though they are only courting and not officially engaged still, Zade puts an arm around Serena as if it will protect her. A twist of longing aches in my chest for someone to care for me that much.

Though Serena may be feeling differently. Her chin is tilted up the way she does when she's determined. She's probably thinking on how to deal with this newest threat, but I'm doubtful it will solve the true problem. Me.

This birthday means I'm eligible to be sold to a warlock husband. Most girls don't get tested for magic on their birthday, but they at least have plans to even if it's a couple of years in the future. But the only plans here were cake and kindness. Obviously that didn't work out so well. Living in a society where only warlocks control everything and only they do magic was bound to ruin my day no matter how much I wanted it to be different.

"The property is protected," Zade says. "Nothing more than harmless threats can get in."

Probably true, but the way it cracked the joy from us only moments ago—it's not exactly harmless.

"Can we please return to enjoying the festivities?" Serena folds her arms like she's trying to keep herself together.

I'd do the same if I thought it'd help. Instead, I thread my fingers through my necklaces, keeping a neutral expression tightly in place.

"Certainly." Zade motions to Waverly. "Would you like to cut a slice for everyone?"

"I'd be happy to." She bounces over to the cake.

"Zade and I will be in the study," Serena says. "Please carry on and enjoy yourselves."

The girls giggle happily now that the spelled words are gone and cake is coming, easily covering Zade and Serena's exit. I wish I could so easily forget, but instead, I go on pretending as usual. Despite being adept at it, I rather despise it.

"What an exciting day." The words are all too cheery spilling from my lips. "The only other time I've ever seen so many treats in one place was the tournament last year."

"Did they make a cake as pretty as Waverly's?" Sally asks.

I don't even recall if they had cake. "No one could make a cake as pretty as Waverly's."

"Only because I cheat." Waverly acts as if nothing has happened. She slides the first piece on a plate and passes it over to me. "Happy birthday!"

Her voice is a little too perky, but I chime back just as happily, "Thank you!"

Her smile becomes softer at the corners, less forced. At least my pretending appears to be good. Even if I'm faking my happiness, it's still satisfying to boost another's mood. The girls receive their treat, starting with the youngest.

Next, she serves mother, who's gained quite the sweet tooth with this pregnancy. The last thing father left us before the Grand Chancellor took him in to custody was another sister to be born sometime in the next several months. Mother seems to be taking this pregnancy like all the rest, but I can't help but wonder what will the baby's life be like never having his cruel influence in it?

My bracelets jangle as I force myself away from such thoughts to eat some of the white cake with pink frosting. Any other day, the rich sweetness would be fantastic, just not now. Instead, it sticks to my mouth like a giant gob of honey, and my throat wants to clamp shut, refusing admittance to its passage. That's just perfect.

I shovel in the bites regardless, not wanting to hurt Waverly's feelings, and take a big swig of milk after each one. At least that's easier to swallow. By the time I finish my slice of cake, my mouth and throat ache from forcing them. I never want to eat cake again. But it's done, and I've pretended long enough to make a getaway.

"Thank you again, Waverly." After pushing myself to my feet I say, "I'm going to wander around some."

"Check to make sure that Serena knows we're running low on sugar," mother says, clueless as to my real intent. Probably due to exhaustion. This pregnancy seems to be harder on her than I remember the others being.

But Bethany, the third eldest sister, and Waverly aren't as clueless.

"It will work out," Waverly whispers as I brush past her.

Bethany gives me a look that says she knows exactly what I'm doing. Not that it matters. As long as the little girls aren't worried, and mother's content, I can do as I wish. It's the first time my birthday has ever been celebrated, after all. Even if it's no longer much of a celebration.

"I'm going to make certain it does," I tell them.

I stride down the hall toward the front of the house, not bothering to knock when I reach the study. It's a simple thing to nudge the door open. It may be wrong, but catching Serena and Zade making lovey eyes at each other sends a giddy thrill through me. They'll both go red and start stammering, but won't lose the happy glow that they must get from each other. My sister is finally happy. Only when the door creaks open this time, neither of them has a glow to lose.

Zade is pacing one side of the study while Serena is on the other, rigid in her chair and staring out the picture window. The painful knot in my stomach tightens as I move into the room. It's worse than I feared.

I shut the door behind me and say, "I believe I should be included in this discussion."

"Who says we are discussing anything?" Serena retorts.

"You said we were going to do birthdays different now that father is gone, and I could have things the way I want. Well, I want to know what's going on. It's about the latest threat, isn't it?" Still neither says anything. "The threat was because of me. I deserve to know."

Serena jumps to her feet. "It wasn't because of you. It was because of me."

"Clearly, I'm the one whose blood should be tested to see what warlock wants to buy me, so of course it's because of me." Anger bites my words more than I meant to let out. I clench my teeth to trap it back inside.

"There's enough to fight out of this room, let's not bring it in here," Zade says before going to Serena. "She does have a right to know."

She bunches her fist. "My freedom was supposed to enable us to make choices for ourselves, not keep us locked up and scared."

"I know, but things take time. Hopefully, they'll get used to the way things are with you now," Zade says.

"But they aren't getting used to it fast enough," I say. "That's the seventh threat we've had this week, and by far the most foreboding. Most hinted about my coming of age and being sold, of which we've had no intention of following their expectations. The only other thing we could do is return to class, and that isn't an option. You remember what it was like. What they teach about women subjecting themselves to warlocks." And how I spent most of the time convincing everyone class was right where I wanted to be. At least it kept us safe, like we need to be now. Too much danger haunts my family.

Serena collapses back into her chair and rubs her temple. "I know."

The silence, thick with worries, doesn't last long before the door opens and Bethany slips inside, closing the door behind her. "Mother wasn't feeling well again and went upstairs to rest. Waverly's taking care of the girls. What's going on?"

"We're discussing the threats," Serena admits.

"Which are about me," I add.

Serena glares at me. No matter that it upsets her; it's all too true.

"What can we do?" Bethany asks. "It's not like we'll return to the ownership of a man."

Unless the council somehow forces us to. The way things are going, it seems rather likely.

Serena says, "We'll figure something out."

"How much time do we have left to figure something out before these threats become more than just threats?" I ask, trying to keep my emotions from flying.

By the tightening of her mouth, I know I've hit onto the real problem. What started as us staying around the house out of uncertainty has become us being caged out of fear. The servants, or Zade, bring everything we need, and even they are cautious. Yet regardless of this, there are a few who have ventured to us, like Councilman Daniel and his wife Annabelle who helped Serena at the ball, but mostly we are avoided.

"We can figure something out." But her repetitive words are as small as her voice.

"We can." I hesitate a moment but not long enough to really let the fact of what I've been considering doing since the threats started sink in. "I will enter the marriage pool."

Gasps sound from the girls, and Zade stares at me in shock.

Once she starts to breathe again, Serena says, "You can't!"

"Are you going to stop me?"

Her lips press into a thin line. The command not to place myself for sale is right there, waiting to tumble from her. I can see it in her eyes, but it goes against everything she's tried to do as an owner. As my master.

"No." Her words come out harsh, but firm. "I won't stop you as an owner. But as a sister, I'm pleading with you not to do this." I open my mouth to reply, but she plunges on. "Please, please don't do this. You know what they're like. How they'll treat you."

"I've always enjoyed the company of warlocks more than you

do." Her face crumples against my words. My true words. Just not true for the reasons she suspects.

"Perhaps, but being owned by one isn't what you want. I know it. You've reveled in the freedom more than any of the other girls. You've taken your own room with glee, enjoyed spending time alone and getting up in the middle of the night without repercussions. If you go back to being owned by a warlock, those are only a few of the things that will end. Much of your life will grow a great deal worse."

Exactly what I've been trying not to think on. With those big, begging eyes, it would be so easy to give into her pleading, so I switch my gaze to the person in the room most likely to side with the safety of my family. Zade. "If I enter the marriage pool, do you think it will ease some of their fears? Do you think it will help show them that Serena can... *handle* her property?"

His eyes stay perfectly trained on mine, and I have to wonder if he's struggling not to give into Serena's pleading as well. "I can't guarantee anything. You understand that, don't you?"

"I do."

He rubs the back of his neck. "It would probably go a long way toward helping. It would give those supporting us something to help prove that Serena isn't different from other warlocks. It would show people she's in control and willing to follow society's ways, which is something hard to dispute and fight against. Though there will still be those that are unhappy just with the fact that she's a woman."

He moves closer to me. Most of the time I forget that as an Envadi how much taller he is than me but at a moment like this, with my neck tilted back to look up at him, every inch of his height is a stern reminder of the seriousness of the situation. "You know if you enter the marriage pool there will be little we can do to prevent your ownership by a warlock. From when I checked before, we know the magic in your blood is more potent than Serena's, and there were many who tried for her hand. There will be many applicants, and she will have to choose one. I'm sure she will let you pick which one you'd like, but you'd still be giving your ownership back to a warlock."

Even though I already know all this, somehow his statement rages through me more than Serena's threats. But what will happen to my family if I don't show compliance to society's ways? It's not something I want to dwell on. My mouth is dry, making my reply harder to get out than it should. "I understand."

Serena moves next to Zade, somehow bearing down on me even more than he is, despite being my height. "Are you certain you do?"

I nod, even though the ever-growing desire to never have started this conversation builds. I almost wish I had never come to the study after them.

"They'll not only use you as a breeder to make powerful warlock babies, but they'll want the magic in your blood for themselves. It's too strong for them not to."

"I know."

"And you still wish to do this?"

I push past the choking in my throat, letting my words come out clear and strong. "It will help our family. I'll be happy to do my part."

Serena wrenches me into a hug. "We can find another way."

But we can't, and even if we could, would we discover it in time to help? Doubtful. I pull out the facade I spent years wearing, the one I hoped I would never need to use again. "Don't worry yourself over it. You know how I enjoy all the attention from warlocks." About as much as I enjoyed punishments from father, but I give her my winning smile, as if it will be the best thing that has ever happened.

She scrutinizes my expression, probably looking for some hint I'm faking this all. But she won't find it. Cracks don't happen.

"Are you certain? Absolutely certain? There'll be no changing your mind."

"Of course I am. I'll ready myself to go to the testing center."

Her eyes grow wider. "Right now?"

"You heard Zade. We can't let them doubt you any longer."

She gives a jerk of a nod and with a voice calmer than I expected, says, "I'll call the carriage."

"Thank you," I choke out, struggling to rein in the building frustration and loss so it doesn't come screaming out.

I turn to hurry from the room, but Bethany stops me. Her eyes are bright with unshed tears. She gives my hand a squeeze, a silent show of support and longing, and then moves to clear the way.

I saunter through the hall, past the kitchen, toward the stairs like I have some happy purpose, trying desperately not to let myself race to my room as I wish. The younger girls call after me, but I can't let myself do more than give them cheery hellos and hurry on. Vaguely, I hear Bethany saying something to them. She probably followed me out, anticipating such a thing. I step faster, up the previously forbidden stairs, down the empty hall, and into my room. My very own.

Serena was furious when she discovered there were enough rooms in father's house for each of us girls to have her own, and still have extra rooms left over. If father were around, instead of in a prison somewhere, I'm sure she would have knocked him out with her gun again. I felt the same. After cramming together in a couple small rooms our whole lives, realizing there was more than enough room to spare sent us both into a fit. But even if it wasn't a surprise, it was one more thing that we had no control over.

Apparently, there's still much we have no control over, even when I try to pretend otherwise.

But now we each have our own rooms, and she was kind enough to let me pick the one I wanted first. The choice has made it much easier to keep secrets.

I close my door, working extra hard to have it make the slightest click when it latches and not to slam it. After it's closed and locked, it doesn't take long to secure my room. It's almost without thought the motions come to me. Sally often likes to hide under my bed or in my closet which I double check for. Once I'm sure the room is clear of sisters, I draw the thick curtains, even though a tree thick with foliage is right outside my window, making it difficult to see in.

When I'm positive nothing that takes place in this room can be seen, I do one of the few good things I ever learned from father. I feel the power in me, the eager glow inside me flaring to life, yearning to respond to my will. I seize hold of it and launch it in a clear, save for a few crimson streaks, barely visible spell straight at my throat. It wraps around my voice just as I demand, blocking all sound. Then I scream.

CHAPTER 2

I stare at the stack of papers on the kitchen table, which looks large enough to wallpaper my room with. But it's time. Time to make a choice. I'd much rather faint in front of everyone again, as I did when I saw my blood during the testing. At least that part is over.

Waverly entertains the younger girls with her antics outside while Bethany prepares dinner in the kitchen. Serena and Zade are sitting at the table, trying to be helpful, though they have yet to be so. Still, I wish I could switch places them, or with any of the others. Or go back to my room, cast the silencing spell, and scream some more.

"I didn't think there would be so many." The stack is just so large. I knew there would be a lot of interest in me, but this much is unfathomable.

Serena and Zade exchange a look but say nothing. I'm too busy trying to keep myself together to figure out what the look is even supposed to mean.

"This is good." Not really, but I press on. "We'll be able to find a worthwhile warlock with so many options." There has to be at least one. Please be one.

Serena places her hand on mine. "Not we. You. We will aid you as much as we can. However I won't make the decision of who will own you next. If I could decide anything, you'd be gaining your freedom instead."

Freedom. A word more magical that any spell I can cast. And yet, even if I were as free as she is, I wouldn't be really free to do what I love most. Magic.

What would happen if they knew I could cast spells? If the warlocks knew? The council? Or, Master forbid, the Grand Chancellor? It goes against everything society wants, what the council and Grand Chancellor want. Everything they talk about and feel. Freedom wouldn't bring the ability to do magic. No. Trying to make us appear as if we're still a normal family, a family that complies with their expectations, is what they want and what will keep the girls safe.

Waverly bounces in the back door, short of breath. "Your sisters are wild. I can't keep up with them. Presha is watching them while I take a break."

"They weren't wild before you came along." And it makes me smile, a true smile, like nothing else has since my birthday. Everyone in the house has grown happier since Waverly started spending much of her time with us.

Serena laughs. "Now you have more sisters than you know what to do with."

Waverly returns the laugh as she heads to the wash basin. "It's true. I do, but I'm not the only one. Zade has his hands full of them, too." She gives him a sly look. "Maybe he wants more sisters permanently."

Serena and Zade both blush and pointedly look anywhere but each other. Usually their antics are endearing, but now it just reminds me I'll never have anything like that unless I can find a miracle in this stack.

I skim another application, but the words mush together after the first line. All my choices are the same: Will give lots of money for my purchase; Will restore some honor to the family name; Have great magic to join with mine in passing down to their sons. As if I want that to happen. None of the options are remotely appealing, but the thought of having a son with one of them is enough to make me vomit. Or hex each and every one of them.

Yet, thinking of all the magic makes me wonder about something I've wanted to know for a long time. Something only a warlock outside Chardonia would know. One who just happens to be sitting at the same table.

"Zade," I say, "do women in Envado do magic?"

The room goes horridly quiet. It's as if father cast a silencing hex on everyone and everything. I shouldn't have let the question slip. Except I want to know. I can't be the only woman in the world that does magic, can I?

No, I can't possibly. There have to be others like me somewhere, only where are they? Why am I so alone? Envado seems like a good place to start looking for answers. Or at least I thought it did until the already awkward silence keeps pounding on like a beating that will never end.

I focus harder on the application before me, trying to pretend the answer doesn't matter. Though the longer the stillness permeates the air, the more I change to pretending as if the question was never asked.

Serena finally says, "What a strange question. You know only men do magic, which is just as well. Even if there are good things done with magic, there's too much hexing involved."

Her words singe me right at my hidden desire to be known for doing magic and to be accepted for it, yet it's not as if she's aware of how personal a question it is. I risk glancing at Zade. A strange look is on his face, one that's impossible to decipher.

Those at the kitchen counter aren't any better. Bethany's eyes are innocent and wide with shock. Waverly is frozen with a glass of water partway to her mouth. She's the first to come out of her trance, taking a sip of her drink before putting a big smile on her face.

"Really, Serena?" she says. "Magic isn't that bad. I thought you liked what we did with the ball."

"True," she concedes. "Zade did a great job with everything."

Waverly's smile dims some but doesn't disappear entirely. "Yes, Zade did."

I scrutinize her, searching for a deeper meaning.

"Honestly," Serena replies, "it's not that I didn't enjoy it. I did. Yet, it's hard to forget the consequences that followed. Zade's life almost ended, and he was injured. You were knocked out. Luckily there were no lasting effects from that. Nathaniel's fiancée was killed. That is what magic brings."

But it doesn't always.

Not that it matters. It doesn't. At least not to the well-behaved, boy-crazy, family-saving girl I'm pretending to be. Back to acting as if I didn't ask, and putting all my focus on which warlock will be my next owner.

Blast. Just the thought makes me wish I'd never gone through with this, but there are too many others depending on me. I can't abandon them when I've finally grown brave enough to help. There hasn't been a single threat since I was tested, and I'm not about to take that relief away. Not that I could anyway.

Zade pops out of his trance, bolting to his feet. "I think I'll go see if any of the girls want another shooting lesson."

He strides from the room, boots pounding across the floor. The silence that follows manages to be more awkward than before, even without my asking a forbidden question.

We pretend to work at our tasks, none of us looking at each other. At least I'm still pretending. Perhaps Serena really does find the pattern of the table interesting, Waverly enjoys staring at half-empty glasses of water, and Bethany thinks her vegetables a prize worthy of staring instead of chopping.

Serena runs her hand across the table, drumming her fingers

a few times before saying, "I didn't mean his spells were bad."
She stares after his long-retreated form. "Perhaps I should assist
him."

"I'll help with the girls so you can talk," Bethany says. "If you
don't mind taking over for me, Waverly? Or would you prefer to
distract the girls?"

"I'm still recuperating from distracting the girls last time.
They're always more energetic than I expect. Why don't you go
ahead, and I'll finish up here?"

Bethany nods and coaxes Serena out the door.

My question broke things more than I expected. The guilt
brings a sharp sting to my eyes, leaving the applications too blurry
to read. I blink away the pain, wondering if they'll sort their
differences.

Waverly works on the vegetables, the snap of her knife familiar. Though she's occupied with the task, she keeps an eye on me
as I muddle through the mess of papers. And what a mess it is. I
don't know what to do with any of them, strewn as they are
across the table.

What do I look for in a potential new owner? How much
money they're willing to pay for me? How much clout they have
in politics and with fellow countrymen? How each one says
they're the best choice out of all the candidates? The one thing
that doesn't sway me: how much magic they will pass on to our...
sons. I grip the seat of my chair until my fingers ache.

"Maybe you should make piles," Waverly suggests. "Stacks of
men who are no good, okay, and maybe. Something like that.
Then you can look closer at the better options."

Why didn't I think of something like that? It seems so simple.
"That would make it easier."

Yet, I still can't do anything but stare. The words just won't
come into focus.

"What if I helped? These vegetables are about done anyway
and won't need my attention while simmering. I could help go

15

through and take out warlocks I know you won't want, the ones who are obviously rude and condescending."

The tears want to come again but not with stinging, more like soothing relief. It's the best thing someone has said since I plunged into this crazy scheme. "That would be fantastic."

In less than ten minutes she has a growing pile for me to go through and an even bigger pile set aside for fire starter. I've never been so grateful for assistance before, or so enthused to start a fire.

Looking through the applicants still brings on a headache, but at least I can focus. Once I get into a rhythm, I stop thinking about what the papers are actually for, what they mean, and it gets easier to toss them where they need to be. I divide them into more piles, as Waverly suggested, for sorting later. No decisions have to happen now, only narrowing the options.

Together we work, making progress on the requests. After some time, she says, "Why were you wondering about women using magic?"

My fingers tighten around the paper they're holding. I try to shrug nonchalantly except it feels more like a jerk. "The thought just crossed my mind."

The papers rustle, filling the room with their shuffling. I should let it go. Not say another word on it, but I've wanted to know most of my life. With the changes coming to my life, I yearn to know more than the usual, but caution urges me toward the silent survival route.

Quietly, I ask, "Do women use magic?"

I pretend to focus on the paper in front of me, but really I'm paying heed to her every move. Not that she's moving. She's still again, like the first time I asked. Everything seems to depend on what she says next, but she's not speaking. She lowers the paper to the table as if it's a sleeping baby being laid down in its cradle before studying my face. Not just looking, searching.

Whatever she's hoping for, she must come to a decision. "Even if they did." Her words are so faint they can barely be heard. "Chardonia would never allow it. Especially not the council and the Grand Chancellor."

I swallow past the sudden thickness in my throat. We return to sorting, but her words don't leave me. All afternoon they ricochet around my head, more pressing than the warlocks, one of whom may become my future owner.

Perhaps whether or not other women can do magic shouldn't be my question. My real question should be: What will the Grand Chancellor do if I'm caught?

* * *

WHEN SERENA and Zade return several hours later, they stand close together. Yet, something is off. Both are stiff, as if they're afraid what will happen if they relax. Perhaps afraid of what will happen if they let their words loosen too much and bring trouble again. I don't know. It's hard to comprehend the type of relationship they have. It's nothing like mother and father's, and that is the only relationship I know. Not for much longer, though. The pile of acceptable applicants is small. Too small.

Serena takes the chair next to me while Zade sits across from us.

"So," she says. "Have you made any progress?"

After giving my necklace a tug, I randomly pick one of the three choices I've narrowed it down to. At this point, there's nothing different about any of them. All are rich warlocks offering much for possession of me but say little else. Any warlock who said anything more always said something distasteful. "Contact this one. And make sure he pays for me before you sign anything."

"You're making the decision so soon?"

There's no holding back my emotions any longer. This isn't something I want any more than she does, but there's a part to play. I focus all my negativity into cheer. It comes out in a squeak of giddiness. "Naturally I did, Serena. I can't wait until I'm with my new owner. Excuse me while I go embroider a handkerchief with his name on it."

The stunned look on her face makes an apology want to tumble from my lips, but there's no saying the words. I spring from the room like I'm the happiest woman in Chardonia, not the one returning to a world full of hexes and beatings and warlocks. A world where my own spells will have to be even more hidden. A world I despise.

CHAPTER 3

The next day it takes a concentrated effort not to let sparks fly. Literally. I try to spend my time alone in my room with the curtains drawn, wondering why I didn't pick one of the other three applications it had come down to. One who wouldn't insist on signing the engagement contract the day after I accept it.

The spells that flare out of me are hot and angry, once even triggering a fire. I throw a blanket over it and put it out quickly enough. The charred coverlet is now hiding at the bottom of my trunk. At least the smell was easy to chase out by opening a window.

When I leave my room, not only is it hard to keep my frustration from showing, but it's extra difficult to pretend I'm excited to be sold, to be owned by some man who will treat me like father did for years. It was easier to pretend interest in men when I was only watching them for their spells. Now even that sounds unappealing.

Soon, I'll be officially owned by a warlock again, instead of having the freedom of Serena owning me. Learning a few new spells is pointless in comparison to that. Why learn new spells if it's near impossible to cast them?

It's likely I've made the wrong choice.

The study where we're sitting, waiting, is dreary. Not because of the weather outside the picture window, but for what's brewing in here in the midst of forbidden books, a desk, plush chairs, and my dark secrets. I can't stop my fingers from moving from my necklaces to my bracelets before twisting my rings and doing it all again. My face paint is thick, a heavier reminder of how I'll have to return to wearing it all the time now as society expects.

Serena breaks the silence. "May I ask something?"

Please don't. But I force a cheerful face. "By all means."

"I've been wondering, why did you choose Edward as your owner?"

"He seemed like he might be good. There wasn't anything aggressive sounding in his application."

"Yes, but…" She bites her lip. "He didn't provide much information save for the basics."

I shrug like it doesn't matter. Because it doesn't.

"It's only…" She hesitates a moment then hurries on. "If this is truly the choice you wish to make, I'll support it, but he was one of the highest bidders. And, well, I want to make certain you made the choice because you thought he would be the best for you and not because of the money. We have enough for our needs from my own sale. And I'm sure Zade would assist us with anything should a need arise."

"It's not the money." Or at least not wholly. I figure if one option looks the same as another, she might as well have more coin from my sell. I force all my frustration to come out as excitement. "He'll be fantastic. I'm certain of it. And I'll get to have Katherine design an engagement dress, and then a wedding dress. It'll be fantastic."

"Awful lot of fantastic." Her mouth bunches as if she disagrees but is trying not to say so. Not that I blame her. I disagree as well. "Well, if it's what you want?"

"Obviously, it is. I'm happy." So fakely happy. "And eager to meet him when he gets here." Which should be much too soon. When Serena sent his acceptance, his reply was swift and his desire to see me even swifter. For good or ill, he's coming. At least it's here at home and not at his house like Serena had to meet Thomas.

Zade enters and, without a word, begins pacing the room. Serena watches a moment before staring out her window, her hands knotted in her lap. Waverly and Presha are entertaining the girls so we won't be disturbed and so Edward won't see how wild they've become under Serena's care. Laughing and playing as if they were boys. It's difficult not to be jealous of what they're gaining while I sacrifice.

Yet there's no undoing the past. The only thing I can affect is the now and the future. The future holds nothing bright, except keeping my family safe. Nothing but standing happy yet aloof, wishing I could spell myself out of this. But the only thing I can spell away is my voice when my frustration can no longer be bottled.

It's difficult to determine how much time passes as we wait. It's long and cold. No forcing of enthusiasm or mindless chatter. I must save all my energy for when Edward arrives. My new owner.

"Zade," Serena interrupts the silence. "Do you know anything of this Edward?"

"Very little. He's never been in a tournament, doesn't do much publicly, and is very wealthy, keeping almost as many servants and tarnished as the Grand Chancellor."

It's difficult to think of him having tarnished. At least servants are paid or are working off debts. The tarnished are already forced to be bald, barren, and have their face not only tattooed but the tattoos spelled to glow a different color every month to make certain they're checking in with the council. Can't have them breaking any rules. It makes me sick to think of people treating someone like my close friend Katherine that way. But maybe

Edward is like Serena. Taking in as many tarnished as possible and treating them well.

Serena looks at me before glancing back out the window. Perhaps it's something I should have thought to ask before. What will he be like? I don't even know his age. Some applicants included it, but it wasn't a requirement. What if he's as old as father? What if I'm his fourth wife, soon to be tarnished with the first girl I bear? Other than having a child, this is the preferable option.

It'd be difficult to be tarnished, especially with the ever-growing restrictions placed on them, but at least I wouldn't have an owner. Katherine would surely take me in and help me learn the ways of the tarnished. How to deal with someone keeping track of my movements. Of being filled with unbearable agony if I leave an area I'm supposed to be in. Of having that pain kill me if I don't return to where I'm supposed to be. I swallow past the growing tightness in my throat.

Dearest Katherine, ever since they changed the law keeping tighter control over the tarnished, it's been strange seeing her tattoos glowing a different color every time I see her. It's impossible to imagine what my appearance would be if I'm thrust under the same conditions.

The clattering of a horse coming up the drive pulls my attention to the present. My magic feels as if it's surging inside me, struggling to be free. It wants to cast a spell. Any spell. Something to relieve the pressure shackled within me.

A few moments later, there's a knock on the front door. Serena rises to her feet and nods at Zade. He pecks her cheek with a swift kiss before leaving, though he won't be far. Close enough if we need him, but out of sight.

A moment later, Bethany enters. "May I present Edward Stafford?"

I give her a flicker of a smile before she moves aside to let my new owner in. My owner. My erratic magic suddenly stiffens, my pulse dropping to nothing.

The man who steps in is younger than I expect—mid-twenties perhaps—dark, thick hair, long nose, and a blank expression.

Serena recovers before I can decide what to feel about this first impression. "I'm Serena. Please have a seat."

Without a word, he sits at the desk. A bit presumptuous, yet I suppose even if Serena has the status of a warlock, it would be hard to change a lifetime of habits. He still hasn't looked my way. Not that I want him to, but does he even know I'm in the room? Does he care where his soon-to-be property is? What I look like? Who I am? Thomas didn't want to see Serena before he signed the contract. Perhaps most warlocks are this way.

Yet the thought that I made the wrong choice nags at me.

"May I introduce you to Cynthia?" Serena must be wondering the same thing.

"No need. Just show me the paperwork."

I press my lips together and try not to let his words upset me. What did I expect from a man who barely filled out his paperwork and offered an obscene amount of money? His bid for me was one of the highest: that must have been all he had to offer.

Perhaps it's a good sign. If his conversations are always so short, I won't be lectured as much. Father always did talk too much. Maybe I'll be able to find a sort of freedom, not the type I have with Serena, but something in my own way.

"It wouldn't take long to introduce you," Serena persists.

"We'll meet soon enough." He smiles in a manner most charming.

"Very well." Her tone is stern, like she's trying to bite back everything she wants to say. Her movements appear stilted and forced as she hands him the paperwork that will bind my sale. An urge suddenly strikes to burst it into flames as I did the blanket, but I contain myself.

He skims it and flashes a black and silver spell at it. His signature. I've never seen anything quite like it, but it happened so fast, I couldn't catch much. Most spells happen too fast for me to learn much even though I'm constantly trying.

I expect him to say something to Serena about her not being able to spell her signature or demand to spell it for her. Instead, he silently watches as she uses the special pen Zade spelled for the occasion since she doesn't do magic herself. It has to be sealed with magic as well as a signature. I didn't get to see him cast that spell, but the pen flashes an emerald green at the tip as she writes.

The moment her pen lifts from the document, he whips the paper in front of him, scans it, and stares right at me, a hungry grin on his face. The change is so sudden and jarring, there's no time to fake anything. My pure shock must be showing.

I hurry to exchange the surprise from my expression for something more pleasant. Despite the itch to, I don't move or fuss under his stare, yet neither do I look down like I should. Might as well start my new ownership off with the expectation of defiance, even if I'm pleasant about it. It doesn't seem to bother him, though. Another good sign?

He stands and heads for the door. "Come."

Is he speaking to me?

"Would you like us to join you somewhere?" Serena's voice sounds as confused as I feel.

He whirls around and sneers at her. "Not you. I've no further use for you, wench. I was speaking to my property."

The condescension in his voice makes me want to hurl a hex at him. What have I done?

Serena slowly rises, her back as straight as when she would face father for punishment. "Where are you taking her?"

"She and her whereabouts are no longer your concern."

As if summoned by his words, the clopping of more horses sounds outside. Does this mean he's taking me with him? Now? That can't be. The engagement ceremony isn't for another month. I need time to plan, to think.

The room suddenly seems very, very small. Everything's too close. Cramped.

"You can't take her now," Serena persists. Her voice sounds far away.

"Why not?"

"Because no one takes a bride before the wedding."

His smile slants up one side of his face. "Ah. But you know better since you were also taken before the wedding."

Her fist tightens in her skirt. I must do something before this morphs out of control. This was supposed to help them, not make things worse. If I don't go, things will be much, much worse. And whatever consequences might befall Serena, I will mostly likely be forced to go anyway.

Zade's certain to have heard all of this and be on his way. I have to act before he gets here. I shake the hold that's frozen me and force my legs forward. Edward reaches a hand out to me and snakes it around my shoulders the moment I'm within reach. It takes all my willpower not to pull away and pulverize him with a hex. Only a lifetime of practicing saves me from following instinct.

I can't look at Serena. Can't face what this must be doing to her. That I'm walking into what she always protected me from. He's not going to be as bad as father, though. I'll be fine. Everything will be fine.

Except I can't convince myself of that enough to give her a forced smile.

"No," Serena says.

Edward yanks me toward the door, but Zade stands in the way, blocking every inch of the opening and then some.

"Where are you going?" Zade's voice is low, threatening.

"I'm taking what's mine. No different than what you did, only I won't be stupid enough to give my property away."

It takes all my willpower not to flinch.

"I'll pay you to let her stay longer."

For a brief moment hope kindles, but Edward's cold chuckle extinguishes it. "Didn't you see how much I paid for her? Money is nothing to me. She is everything."

A chill rushes through me. Why am I everything? Why do I matter so much? I'm simply a girl who's trying to help her family. That should mean nothing to a Chardonian warlock. My magic then? But it's not everything. Is it?

This can't be happening. Yet somehow it is. Zade doesn't move. I can't let this escalate any further. Serena protected me for this long; it's my turn to be the protector, even if it is the last thing I ever wanted to do.

"Please step aside, Zade. I'll be fine." My words come out sure and steady, like I mean them to be, not like the fearful quivering overwhelming my insides.

Zade's eyes dart toward me, narrowing like he's going to contradict my words. But thankfully, he moves aside. Edward grips my upper arm and strides toward the hall.

Suddenly, Zade reaches out to Edward. "If you mistreat her—"

"You'll what? There's nothing you can do. She's my property. Any interference will constitute you breaking the law. I'd hate to see you lose your Chancellorship over something so trivial."

Anger flames at the insult. If anything, the last year has taught me that no one is trivial. But now isn't the time to fight. I will Zade to leave it, but he doesn't get my silent message. "The Chancellorship may be important, but she's more important. Don't forget it."

Zade's words and stance warm me, yet are also enough to make me want to cower even though I'm not the one he's threatening. Edward only laughs, this time big, happy and loud, crowding the small space further. "Oh, I won't forget how valuable she is. You can be assured on that count."

He yanks me forward, digging into my arm so hard there will be a bruise later. I clench my teeth to keep from crying out.

"At least let me get her things," Serena calls out.

"The only thing of yours allowed to enter my house is her. And she is no longer yours."

The words are sharp against my ears. Part of me is aching to struggle against this, but most of me is still attempting to process it. This was just supposed to be a meeting to sign me over to him. Nothing more.

He continues jerking me forward, out of the house and into the carriage. I tumble onto the wooden bench as Serena calls out something I can't make out. Edward slams the door shut, and I'm left in darkness. Alone.

CHAPTER 4

When the carriage finally stops, and I'm allowed out, night has fallen, replacing daylight with heavy clouds. The house appears to be big, though it's difficult to discern in the moonlight that attempts to peek from behind one of those clouds. Whatever the building's exact size, it rivals Zade's house. There are no servants or anyone around except us. Even the horses and carriage have been led away by servants I didn't see. I shiver, my thick skirts not enough to warm me.

"Follow." Edward strides toward the house.

Left with no other choice but the one I've forced upon myself, I do so. He leads me inside where there are a few dim electric lights on, but it's almost as dark as it was outside. The scent of fresh air trails in with us, yet as we go along, it's replaced with the musty smell of disuse. Where is everyone?

The further we twist through the halls, the stronger the urge to run back the way we came grows. Shouldn't there be at least one servant here? Someone to greet him? To take care of his needs? Zade said he had lots, but where are they?

Edward turns down yet another hallway. Still no one in sight. What can he possibly have planned? Is he going to brand me tonight instead of waiting for the engagement ceremony? Leave some sort of tattoo on my neck that claims me as his forever unless tarnished?

I can't keep quiet any longer. "Where are we going?"

He spins around so fast I almost trip into him. "Shut up."

Without another word, he hurries down the hall. Fine. I can shut up. I can also stop following him.

Between his erratic behavior and the lack of people, I don't dare discover what his plan is even if it means severe punishment for trying to escape him. Blast. This isn't helping my family, and it certainly isn't helping me.

I turn to retrace the path out. Except, which way is out? Not only is this place massive, and we've twisted through much of it, I was too busy wondering about unimportant things to pay attention. Foolish act.

A moment later he realizes I'm no longer following. "Come. Now." His tone is the same as before but with an undercurrent that sends a streak of fear darting through me.

Slowly, I angle toward him. Though we're about twenty paces apart, the stone coldness of his words demand obedience. These are the orders of a warlock who is always obeyed. My body knows those orders so well, trained to follow them from birth. It leans forward to surrender, but I can't do it. I can't.

I've brought myself far enough to keep my sisters out of trouble. They shouldn't have any problems now if he's the one that is supposed to control me and not Serena. I won't suffer myself to be led toward whatever doom he has waiting for me. Not just sneaking away. It's too late for that, but openly defying him. The instant the decision is made must show on my face because at that moment he strides toward me. So I take the only option left. I turn and run.

His footsteps are heavy on the floor behind me, closing in. It won't be long before he catches me. I push myself faster, wishing I'd worn breeches regardless of having to meet him this morning.

When I come to a cross-section, I randomly dart down a hall, willing it to be the correct one. Before I've gone two steps, a hand wraps around my arm. Caught.

He snatches me to him, anger narrowing his dark eyes. "Don't run again, or there will be punishments."

His words mean nothing. Father used to say and do much worse. Yet his grip, vice-like around my arm, means there's no choice but to comply. I struggle anyway, jerking away from him.

A powder blue spell shoots from him, straight at me. It's weaker than anything father ever threw at me but still enough that I float up in the air a few inches, drifting in a sort of bobbing motion behind him as he continues on. I flap my arms and legs every which way but continue floating after him. All my struggling is useless.

My anger brews my magic into a storm worthy of capsizing the entire house. But it's entirely useless. I punch my fist in the air and give a growling scream. Edward doesn't even bother to acknowledge it.

We turn again, but this time into a room. Its grandeur is dimly lit by electric lights showing a space crammed with books, all of which seem to have titles related to magic. Chairs and a sofa dot the room, all matching the velvet red drapes.

He directs the spell holding me to the far wall, away from all the books and chairs. I wobble over against my will. As much as this makes me think of father, being around a new spell is distracting. Rarely do I get to see a spell so close for so long. In spite of its obvious lack of power as it struggles to keep hold of me, it's fascinating. I'm studying it, wishing I always had more of a chance to see spells like this one. When I'm not the object of its hex.

Then I realize, not only has it distracted me from my anger—but from Edward. He's only a few paces away, a wild look shining in his eyes.

Distraction flees. There's nothing left save for bludgeoning fear. His face, which was so deceptively bored before, has grown excited, eyes wide, mouth slightly open like he's thirsty for something. And the only thing around is me.

Serena's experience with Thomas last year at the tournament flashes through my mind. I kick and thrash as hard as I can toward him, but nothing changes about my predicament. His eyes only grow hungrier as he steps closer. I scream for help, but his crooked smirk silences me.

"No one can hear you. Even if they could, they wouldn't step in the way of what belongs to me."

Fear tightens my throat, but I force words out. "You can't. The law says—"

"That I own you. I won't wait for the engagement ceremony for what I want."

The engagement ceremony? Not the marriage ceremony? The unexpectedness of the comment rattles me a moment. And that moment is enough for his spell to propel me toward him. I steel myself to fight, to bite and claw and thrash, but instead of him grabbing for me, he pulls out a knife.

Fear closes my throat tighter, but I can't lose my words—not now. I need them to save me.

"What are you doing?" I sound calm. Reasonable. Not at all the frantic girl screaming inside me. I've never been so thankful for the tightness of my true emotions. Perhaps I can convince him to stop whatever has been planned.

Or perhaps not. His answer is to bear his teeth in a hungry jeer which rids my remaining control. With one fluid motion, he slices my wrist. My blood immediately flows, red and bright. The world sways at the sight. I struggle to hold on, to figure out what's going on, what he's doing, but focusing is growing harder.

My blood wells until it starts to drip. Instead of reaching the ground, he catches it with a powder blue spell like the one he's using to hold me. Then he does something even stranger. He slices his own wrist open. He uses the same spell to stop his blood seeping from his wound.

The dizziness from all the blood helps to chase away my fear but also muddles my thoughts. I only know that this is bad. Very, very bad.

Yellow streaks grow throughout the spell holding my blood. The spell pulls my blood toward him. And something else starts to tug, something deep inside. My magic. He's taking my magic. Panic claws at me.

As the strongest wave of dizziness attacks, I know I have to do something before it's too late. The world is darkening around me, trying to force me to succumb, but it hasn't taken me yet. I slam a spell at him. I'm so far gone, I don't even recognize what spell it is, but it flings him across the room and plasters him there.

I crash to the floor. Without him hovering, there's no spell keeping me or my blood in place. The blackness creeps further over my vision, but I can't give in. Not now. I hold whatever spell I'm using on Edward steady and focus a second spell toward closing my wound. I push my power into it, willing the blood to return into the wound and heal quickly so I can deal with the issue that is Edward. And a much bigger issue: exposing my long-kept secret to one of the worst people possible. My master.

I open my eyes and discover no blood in sight. The wooziness remains, but at a manageable level. And he didn't manage to steal any of my magic. After several deep breaths, I pull myself together enough to stumble over to Edward. He's bound against the wall, whimpering, my bronze spell forcing him in place.

Blast. I didn't mean for that to happen. Then again, I don't know what I meant to happen. His grin has been replaced by wide-eyed shock. Well, the plan to become his possession is ruined far beyond repair. Might as well go all the way.

I gather my eager magic for a spell father always used on Serena when she was younger and would try to run. The spell ripples from me and surges straight toward him. Its golden flare is streaked with red, hot and fiery, as it encircles his wrists. They are almost like an extension of me, feeding off my fear, tightening around him so he can't hex me again.

He lets out a whimper as I use the spell to lift his hands above his head. He struggles against it, attempting to shove his wrists free, but they hold. A silvery spell darts from his hands. It bites into my chain spell, trying to weaken it.

The weakening is tiny, barely anything at all. Yet if it continues, will it be enough to get through? How long can I hold this spell anyway? I don't know enough to stop him. But if I cover his hands, sort of bind them, maybe that would stop him? It's worth trying. If I don't do something, I'll end up back under his power, and my magic will mean nothing to me and everything to him.

And worse—what will the council do to me? To my sisters? Will the council think they are involved? I have to fix this.

The red streaks flare brighter as I propel the spell out harder, making the bands thicker and heavier until they are big enough to wrap around his hands. My folly may be the undoing of my sisters. This will be enough to keep him from sneaking free. It has to be.

He struggles again, faint flashes appearing from his fingers beneath the gold and red, but nothing happens. It seems, for now at least, he can't do anything other than grunt and squirm about. Feigning a confidence I don't feel, I lean over until my face is inches from his.

"This is what we're going to do. You are going to release your ownership of me, just like Chancellor Zade did with Serena and I will go free." He starts to say something, but I interrupt him. "You made it clear earlier you know all about it. There's no escaping this. Do you have servants?"

He doesn't respond.

"Do you?" I yell, fear sounding so much like anger.

"Yes," he croaks out.

"How many?"

"I don't know, lots. Over fifty."

Thank the magic. "We're going to gather them all together and you will tell them of my freedom. Then after I leave, you will tell everyone you know, *everyone*, that you changed your mind. That you didn't want me but didn't want to tarnish me because I'm just so nice." His eyes tighten, but I press on. "That you gave me my freedom and no one is to bother me."

He starts to shake his head. I tighten the already snug spell on his hands and wrists, emphasizing my control.

"You will do this. And then you will never, ever speak to anyone about what I can do, or I will make sure they all know, with vivid detail, how easily I overtook you. Do you understand?"

His face goes pale and finally he gives the slightest of nods.

"Good." I hope. If my threat doesn't work, I don't know what fate will befall me and my family. "Take us to your servants. And if you make one wrong move, we'll be right back here going over this again. Only next time, I won't be so kind."

Once more he nods, his lips giving a strained twitch. I release him from the chain spell but keep my hands up, ready to clamp them back in place.

He shrinks away and without a word leads me through the house. I follow, not trusting him, but having no other choice. If he should do anything contrary to what I asked, I'm ready to act however may be needed. Even if it means being harsher than a chain spell. At least I think I am ready.

We move from one hall to another, to another. How anyone can stand living in such a labyrinth is beyond me. I've no idea if we're going anywhere useful or not. Though, perhaps that is the point. Wandering does afford plenty of time for thinking. Or rather, worrying. Mostly about what a terrible mistake I've made. What if he doesn't keep quiet? What if he tells others about me? What will happen?

There's no way to know. Besides, what other choice did I have? He was trying to take my blood. Thinking about it is making my head spin again. My thoughts are jumbling, piling up in a mass of worry. I need to focus on getting out of here. Then I can figure out what damage my actions caused, and if there's anything that can fix it.

After a while of walking and turning down halls, we finally stop. He has led me to the kitchen. Makes sense. There's always someone in the kitchen. It's larger than I've ever seen, with an unfamiliar-looking electric cooktop, long counters, and two sinks. Six servants turn to him, their heads, whether the tarnished bald or not, lowered. They were all hiding in here, I suppose.

He addresses the closest servant—a male, lower class. "Gather everyone here as quickly as you can."

Though Edward doesn't sound as confident as when he was at Serena's house, if I hadn't hexed him myself, I wouldn't have any idea what he'd just been through. My threat may be enough to make this happen with the servants at least.

The retainer scurries away, presumably to tell the others the latest order. The others return to their task. We wait in silence, me standing a little behind him, ready to bolt or cast a spell as soon as it's needed. Every so often, one of the servants shifts or grabs another cooking utensil, but they don't do much, either. They must be frightened of him as well.

When no one returns, I start to wonder if he somehow tricked me. Did he give some sort of signal to the servant and I didn't notice? Something that said for him to bring the closest law officer? And do what to me? I don't know. However I do know I don't want to find out. I was watching the entire time.

While I'm hesitating over what to do, one of the doors opens. I jump and bend my knees to run. But it's not a law officer. It's a tarnished servant. I relax some, but stay ready to run.

The servant is out of breath but hurries to the center of the kitchen and stands with his back straight, arms at his sides, head lowered. It's the fact that he's out of breath that finally clues me in. This house is big. Of course it's going to take time for everyone to gather together. From the way the servant is acting, it would appear they're coming as fast as they can. I'm such a ninny.

Still, I don't let down my guard.

Servants continue trickling in, slowly at first, but soon the kitchen is crammed full of them. Yet, somehow they manage to give both Edward and me a large berth. They're pressed against each other so tightly, it's a wonder they can breathe. Where were they all when I first arrived and so desperately wanted to see another human?

Finally, the original servant he sent off says, "We're all here, master."

There are so many of them. More than Zade has running his home, and he has a lot because he tries to protect and help as many lower class and tarnished as he can. This is what I need to hope that Edward giving my freedom will be accepted—a room full of witnesses. The biggest relief doesn't just come in their numbers, but that most of them are lower-class men. Their word will be accepted more than the women, and especially the tarnished.

But gossip will spread from everyone gathered. Hopefully, across town or wherever I travel to. I don't even know where I am, let alone where to go. There's no time to panic about that now. I have to finish dealing with this first.

"This is my latest acquisition, Cynthia." His voice sounds strangled. I'm no longer hexing him, so why is he so agitated? "She is—That is to say, I am going to…"

He looks to me with a sort of begging look on his face. What is this for? Does he really believe I'd succumb to that? He must be a complete dunce. There's no chance I'm not taking my freedom. I scowl at him. It's then he does something a warlock never does,. He lowers his head.

"I am going to set her free." His voice cracks. "I don't wish to own her but don't wish to tarnish her. She shall be as free as any warlock, just as her sister Serena." It almost sounds as if he is in tears as he turns toward me. "Now get out."

I want to remind him to keep the second half of my demand, but I don't want the servants to hear. That would be worse than saying nothing at all. Instead, I nod and move to leave. Only I have no idea where the entrance is. I'm lost. Of all the times I've been grateful I've perfected faking my emotions, none have even come close to this moment.

I smile at the closest servant, a man with a thin scar on his right temple. "Would you please show me the way out?"

The servant looks startled, then turns toward Edward for permission, but my owner of not even a day has already departed.

Once the servant realizes the master is no longer here, the uncertain look leaves his face. With a most solemn expression, he says, "I'd be honored."

The rest of the servants must also feel it would be an honor as well, because as I'm shown out, they all follow. All of them. It can't be easy or comfortable traveling after me through such a confined space. Still they come. Quietly, yet gently moving with me through the maze of the house.

When we reach the entry, the only area familiar in this place, the servant I asked for help says, "I would offer you a carriage, but…"

"I will manage. Thank you." I face everyone. "Thank you all."

They nod, eyes bright as they watch me leave. With my head held high I step out of the house, walk down the lane and out onto the road. Once I'm out of sight of the mansion, the reality of what just happened slams into me. I'm free, free as any warlock. The dirt is hard beneath my shoes as I do a running sort of skip down the road that would make my younger sisters proud. I'm as light as air, and happier than I've ever been.

I break out in a full run, pushing myself as fast as I can. The stretch and burning in my legs is as good as casting any spell. Then my foot slips in a hole. Suddenly I'm falling, down, down,

down—I slam into the packed earth. Pain splits up my knee, hands and face. I lay on the ground, letting the pain eat into my reality.

What am I doing? It's late at night, and I'm alone, running in the middle of the road because I don't have an owner anymore? It almost sounds nice until the other side of that freedom crushes in on me. I have nowhere to go, nothing to wear but this dress, which is probably torn and dirty, though it's too dark to see for sure. I've nowhere to eat, nowhere to sleep. This freedom came with a price I didn't even know I would have to pay.

I roll onto my back and stare mindlessly at the stars above me. What did I just do? What have I done? Naturally, I want to be free, but I should have thought about the consequences of my actions more. Not only am I left with nothing, but I haven't any idea whether or not Edward will stay true to his word. If he calls for law officers to retrieve me, will it matter if a group of servants saw him release me? Even if there were so many of them?

What's worse is not what may happen to me, but what I've done. I wrap my arms around myself. I'm just like father.

The thought makes me ill. What I did to Edward is exactly what father would have done. If I had done something wrong and Serena stepped in to save me from punishment, he would have punished her. Perhaps he would have taken it further, but the concept is the same. How can I be just like him? My stomach roils until I'm scrambling to the side of the road, heaving.

Once finished, I pull myself up and limp down the road. I can't stay where there are only thoughts of how like father I am, where I could be captured at any moment. I don't know where I'm going, but I need to get farther from where I am. From who I'm becoming.

CHAPTER 5

I spend all night trudging along. Walking and walking, yet unsure if it does me any good. For all I know, Edward lives in the countryside without another soul for miles. Or perhaps he lives right next to town, but I went the opposite direction. Blasted windowless carriages. I'd hex them all to be burnt to charred ash if I could.

Night deepens. My legs and feet ache, each step makes the pain expand, tearing into my muscles. My stomach growls, mouth dry. It's like father's here punishing me, once again locking me in the basement for two days, but there's nothing to be done for any of it. Perhaps there's some spell for conjuring food, but I've never seen or heard of one. I know of nothing to aid this insane mess I've thrown myself into.

I shove on. There's no other choice. I must find someone, or somewhere, that can help. I don't want to escape a life of being owned only to die of thirst and starvation on an unfamiliar stretch of road. Walking becomes a mind-numbing journey. Can't allow myself to think or feel. Dirt and rocks beneath my feet, dark abyss all around.

Finally, there's a light off in the distance. The closer I get, the more the light multiplies. It's a town. For a brief moment, the weight pressing me down lightens. But then it's back, heavier than ever. Without knowing what awaits me there, I can't be glad. It's not home. The carriage ride to Edward's was much too long for me to have reached my home on foot, and that's the one place that would make me truly happy. If I'm fortunate, maybe I can find some food and avoid being apprehended.

Fortune is not my friend.

As I enter the town, I keep to the shadows. The houses are mostly dark, but a rare few have the glow of electric lights and several have the softer glow of candlelight. Stepping lightly, I try to stay in shadows of houses without any light.

It must be past curfew. Though I may have my freedom, there's no way to prove it. Besides, it's doubtful most warlocks would care even if there was proof. Since gaining my freedom wasn't public, as Serena's was, no one would notice or care if I disappeared. At least no one with the ability to do anything about it.

There are so many houses here. More than I've ever seen in one place. They vary more in shape and size as well. Some are tall and skinny, while others sprawl across the land. The further into town, the more the sprawling ones give way to the tall, skinny ones. No sign of food anywhere. From houses to the few shops scattered among them. With so many houses, there must be a lot of people in them. Where do they all get their food?

It doesn't matter. My limbs can barely move. I stumble around like someone who drank too much wine. My eyelids droop. I'm worse off than a toddler at nap time. As I'm searching for a place to hide and rest, loud laughter echoes down the street.

I press myself against the closest house, pulse drumming through me. Several young warlocks are wandering down the street, playfully pushing each other and casting spells, though it's difficult to tell what type. It's not important right now anyway. Fool of a girl, I can't be trying to learn when their presence means danger.

40

I slink along the edge of the building, trying not to draw attention to myself before I reach the corner and slip to the other side. Inch by inch, I grow closer to my goal. I'm almost there, almost there. I'm going to make it without being spotted! My foot kicks a rock. The resulting crash is loud, too loud. I freeze.

My hands flex, magic pulsing through me. But the warlocks continue cajoling each other as if they heard nothing. I relax the back of my head against the wall behind me before slinking along again, this time paying extra attention to what my feet are touching.

A few more steps and I'm around the corner. As I enter the alley, I let out a sigh and hurry away. Except I'm not safe yet. Their raucous laughter is growing closer and I'm still visible from the street. I rush to the other end, hoping their noise covers mine. Only the other is a dead end. A brick wall.

Panic claws at me as their sounds come closer. I shove it away as I struggle for a solution. The only things here are garbage bins. Disgusting. But not so vile that I would risk getting caught instead of hiding. Holding my breath, I dart behind them.

I close my eyes and make myself take shallow breaths as I listen to the warlocks, hoping they pass by my alley. They ignore my silent plea. Their teasing gets slowly louder and closer. I wrap my arms around my legs, squeezing myself into a ball as they near the alley.

"Where're you going, Saban?" one calls out.

"Need to take care of something."

"What? Down there?"

Down there? As in down here? Please, no, no, no!

"Old Grayson could use a little extra something. He's always so rigid."

One of the voices is getting closer, and the footsteps. Blast! They crunch against the pebbles and dirt, heading straight for me. If he comes close enough to the tins, I'll be seen, and there's nothing to be done about it.

Well, there is something. I've always kept my magic secret until yesterday, but if it comes to either my being caught and punished, or using magic, I could hex him. Possibly. But would this be one more thing to make me like father? Would it make me more like the rest of the warlocks? Their cruelty is something I never, ever want to emulate again. But to protect myself, perhaps that is acceptable as long as I don't become overzealous. My hands shake as I hold them up, ready to defend myself.

The footsteps move closer. The shaking grows more violent, the energy inside me trembling with it. Suddenly, there's silence.

"Hurry it up, Saban."

"There are some things you can't hurry," the closer voice shouts back.

The boys laugh. What are they talking about? Is he trying to slowly sneak up on me? Purposefully making a mess of my emotions before dragging me out of the alley? If so, it's working. Though the strain on my nerves makes me feel like my magic will erupt at the first sight of him. It's not a consequence he'd expect. However, as bad as my hands are shaking, my aim would be ineffective.

I take several slow, steadying breaths like Zade taught us to do when shooting. There's a strange sound. Like something I should recognize, but don't. Like a spray of water landing on something hard? Oh, filth! Is he taking care of his personal business in public? Revolting!

The sound trickles on for much too long before finally stopping. I'm so shocked and dismayed that the shaking in my hands has lessened at least. But as his footsteps sound again, the shaking returns. Until I realize the sound is fading away. I let my shaking hands fall to my lap as he and his friends leave, laughing over his crude manners as they go. Still, I don't relax until there's no sound left.

Once it's silent for a minute, I start to lean back against the wall. The thought assails me of what that warlock just did. My back goes hexed straight.

Ugh. How incredibly foul. The only place that would be worse to be right now is back at Edward's. As exhausted as I am, there won't be any relaxing this close to where someone relieved himself. I just can't.

I stand, brush myself off, and walk toward the street—this time keeping far from the walls. Not far enough, though. My skin itches with the need for scrubbing. I brush myself off again, but it does nothing to ease the feeling. When I'm to the street, I cringe and creep toward the wall, though I don't touch it. Only the need to stay safe and hidden is keeping me here.

I peek around the corner and examine the street. No one is coming. When I'm sure no one's there, I slink out and hurry away from the tainted alley. The extra energy coursing through me after almost being caught wanes. I pass several alleys before I finally pause in front of one.

This isn't where I want to hide. What makes this alley different from the last one? It could be just as tainted. My eyes drift closed as I try to find a solution. My body sways out where anyone could see. The realization means it doesn't matter if the alley is tainted or not. If things stay like this, I will be caught.

I enter, taking my time and carefully sniffing. It doesn't smell pleasant, like mildew and kitchen waste, but at least it doesn't smell like a water closet. I make my way to the back and hunker down behind the bins. The stench of waste is stronger here, but at least I'm out of sight.

I shift around to make myself comfortable, but it's impossible to gain any sense of comfort in this place. I give up and simply huddle tight with my eyes closed. The swirling drift of coming sleep quickly follows.

A drip wets my face. I jolt awake, fearing someone is now using me like the previous alley. But there's no one. Just another drip and another. Coming faster and thicker. It's raining. Of course it is.

It's cold and wet. All. Night. Long. At least my gloves supply warmth, little though they add. And my thick skirts protect me some, but still manage to get soaked through.

Morning comes just as wet and cold. My stomach aches, reminding me the elements aren't my only problem. I need to find food, and hopefully better shelter than I had last night. There's much to fear from wandering about, like what will happen to me if someone should recognize I'm unchaperoned, or worse, Edward's recent purchase in need of punishment followed by a swift return. Yet, if I continue like this, there won't be anything left of me to punish.

I peek around a bin. There's no one in the alley, though two warlocks pass by on the street without glancing my way. I jerk back. It's not so bad being cold, wet, and hungry. Telling myself that doesn't work as well as I think it ought.

Suppose I'll have to pretend to myself as well as everyone else. The only things I have are the clothes and jewelry I'm wearing. When father was my master, I used to keep food hidden on me somewhere, a habit I should never have given up, even if things seemed safer. I sigh and comb my hair back with my fingers before returning it to a bun, letting my magic smooth it down.

Once I'm feeling a little more prepared for what may await me, I stand and plod to the street. No one is paying me any mind—yet. I step out and move along as if this is exactly where I belong, keeping my face lowered, and pretending like I'm following someone even though no male leads me.

People wander around, walking down the street, going in and out of shops. Mostly males, but occasionally a woman accompanies one. I make my way to an empty area and stand next to a building, out of the way, not knowing what to do or where to go. What I need is information. And food. And shelter. A bath would be nice as well. But where does one go to discover any of that? It's not like I thought this through. If I had—no, if I had thought it through, I would have done the same thing. Except to perhaps make a plan for what to do afterward. Then again, maybe not. Plan making isn't a skill I've ever excelled at.

For the most part, I'm ignored. Save for one man, with an umbrella protecting him from the downpour, hiding his features from me. Every time I peek down the street he's still there, hovering. The only reason he'd have for watching me isn't good.

He's thin but in a strong sort of way. The way his coat hugs his frame speaks of trim muscles, not the bulge so many warlocks carry. He's short, at least short compared to Zade, though probably just taller than me. I can't know for certain without him coming closer. And he is coming closer. Blast.

Pretending a nonchalance I don't feel, I head away from him. My legs throb with the desire to move faster, to race away, but I force myself to stroll. Slowly, I increase my pace until I'm going as fast as I dare. Is he following? I can't look back. Which is safer? Stay on the main streets or use a side street? If I take a side street, it could be another dead end, but the main streets have warlocks who will side with him.

My stomach rumbles, growling with a gnawing pain as if I needed to be reminded of one more problem. I'm hungry and dirty and tired, sloshing as fast as I dare through the mud, without any idea what to do.

Suddenly, the warlock is at my side, strolling next to me as if this was planned all along. Except I don't even know who he is. He's perhaps a year or two older than me, my height as I suspected, with dark skin just like the way I make a cup of chocolate with a dollop of cream stirred in. It tugs at a memory of others having darker skin at the tournament last year. Deep-brown eyes hiding behind the framed windows on his face also stir memories. Those like him wore red at the tournament, I believe.

There's a faint smile teasing his lips that, despite its size, seems to radiate joy. Probably not the type of joy that will bring me any happiness.

"Can I help you, miss?" His odd request drawls out in a slow, lazy sort of way.

My pulse is pounding so hard it almost hurts, yet I don't know what's making it faster this warlock or my quickening pace. Probably both. I'm careful to keep my head lowered and voice submissive. "No, I don't think so, sir."

The statement doesn't deter him from continuing on, nor does it stop him from staring at me. Not that I expected it to, but things would have been easier.

"Are you certain? You look lost."

This statement does the strangest thing to me. Tears build, stinging for release. But it's a feeling I know how to suppress. What's harder is suppressing the fear. "I'm fine."

He gives a small snort as if he doesn't believe me, then gives my neck a not so subtle glance. "Is your owner around?"

My unbranded skin says I should still be under my father's control. I cover it with my hand, but it's too late. Should have stayed in my cold, little alley. Might as well hope the truth can save me before something drastic is needed, like a spell. "The only owner I have is myself."

His eyebrows rise. "Serena?"

Her name startles me into looking straight into his rich, brown eyes. It's only for a brief moment before I remember myself, yet it's enough to prove my willfulness. Of course warlocks know her name. Am I going to spend the rest of my life having my status compared to hers? "No."

His eyebrows crinkle together, creating a thin line between them. It makes me want to look at him full on instead of out of the corner of my eye and discover how true of a reaction that really is as he answers. "But she's the only Chardonian woman who isn't owned… Unless you're not Chardonian?"

"I am." Unfortunately. The way he keeps staring at me makes

me wonder what he's planning that he doesn't want to let me out of his sight. At least it gets rid of the desire to look at him closer. He is the enemy, I remind myself. All males are except Zade.

"My status is newly acquired." As in, so new I don't know if Edward has told anyone else yet like I'm hoping he's done. Like he must do if I'm to survive.

"Ah. I see." His smile widens. "Is that why you look so lost?"

I have an urge to ramble a reply, one that would likely turn into my life story if I started. This man is making it difficult to keep myself in check. Why doesn't he just do whatever it is he's going to do to me? Why do they always have to turn it into a game? "I do not look lost."

His smile shifts to one that says he doesn't believe it, but he'll humor me. Like the type of smile one would give to a small child who doesn't know better. "Forgive me if I misinterpreted your standing out in the rain, watching everyone go by with big, hungry eyes like you don't know what to do, as lost."

I scowl at him. Has he been watching even longer than I thought? And then I realize that my emotions are slipping through. Again, apparently. What is it about him that is making me lose control? It's not him. It's the situation. I've never been in one like this before, and it's making me break. I grasp my emotions back tightly within while keeping my head lowered.

"Thank you for your concern, but I assure you, there's no need for your assistance."

"Hmm." He nods his head like he finally understands what I'm saying, but instead of leaving like I hope, he says, "Then I imagine you'd turn down an offer to share my umbrella?"

I most definitely don't want to share an umbrella with some warlock. Warlocks are trouble. Not only trouble, but also harbingers of tarnishings and death. Besides, I'm already soaked. Nothing will change that now. Not even a kindly-offered umbrella.

"That would be a correct assumption."

"What about my coat then? Would you take it?"

Why is he so persistent? Does he have to leave one of his things with me as a way to prove I'm doing something wrong to one of the local law officers? Or is this just the way foreign warlocks behave? At least, I'm assuming he's a foreigner. "Truly, I'm fine."

"But you're shivering."

The cold had left my mind until he pointed it out, but I really am shivering. I don't remember the last time it was this cold. And sometime while we've been talking, my rapid pace has slowed. Though the season is starting to warm, at any time spring could turn even worse than it is now. Tonight. What am I going to do? Whatever it is, I can at least keep from completely freezing.

"I believe I could accept it."

His grin morphs into a winning one, yet still manages to stay small and warm. It's a smile like I've never seen before. He hands me his umbrella before taking his coat off. I try to keep the umbrella over him, keeping the rain from dripping on him. It's heavier than I expect, and my arm wavers. The umbrella tilts to the side. Before I can right it, the water pooling on it falls, splashing on his head, drenching him.

I brace myself for a hex that never comes. Perhaps the mistake didn't bother him as much as I expected? Who knows what this strange man thinks. At least his coat was already off and stretched out toward me so it's still fairly dry? Perfect way to treat the person saving me from freezing to death.

"Sorry." Did I just apologize to a warlock? One day I'm hexing a warlock, the next I'm apologizing to another. It's unprecedented. And not to be repeated.

He laughs. "Didn't really want to stay dry anyway. Rain is refreshing."

Refreshingly cold. Such an odd male.

He leans away from me and shakes the water from his hair, droplets spotting on the strange framed windows in front of his eyes. The short, dark locks glisten over those now water-sparkled eyes. It's hard to concentrate as he helps me into his coat, first one sleeve then, after switching the umbrella to his now free hand, the other.

As he reaches out to take the umbrella back from me, our hands brush. I snatch my hand away and pull the coat tighter. It's warm from being wrapped around him and smells faintly of something sweet and spicy. My shivering abates somewhat only to be replaced by my stomach growling again.

His brows raise again. I glance away, willing my cheeks not to pick this moment to heat and give me away.

"I will be on my way then, miss. Unless there's something else I can help with?"

Still having a hard time believing the only reason he stopped me was to give his coat, I shake my head.

"Very well then," he says as if he expected my silent response, and turns.

As he starts to walk away, I call out, "But your coat. How will I return it?"

"Keep it," he calls over his shoulder and rounds a building.

Keep it? As in, it belongs to me now? I pull it tighter around me savoring its warmth but also trying to decipher what it means to have something of my own. Not just something father purchased, and is letting me use, but something truly mine. Perhaps my first thoughts of him giving it to me to use as some sort of leverage with a law officer were correct. It doesn't make sense though. A warlock doesn't need such evidence. The fact I'm out here all alone and claiming to not have an owner is enough for punishment to be dealt.

So then why give me his coat?

CHAPTER 6

A while later, much past time for lunch, I'm still wandering through the town. I've become so turned about; I'm not sure how far I am from where the man gave me his coat. At least I'm warmer, but it only does so much good. What I need is some sort of information and help from someone I can trust. Food, shelter, communication with home. But there's nothing.

There's been no tarnished to attempt to get help from. They're the only ones I trust, and even then I don't know how far my trust goes. I spotted one, and followed her to a house, but she slammed the door so fast my words were good for nothing but banging on the wood. I don't blame her. Talking to me would probably only lead to her getting in trouble.

Which brings trouble. If my being around causes trouble, I shouldn't go home. Not that I know where it is anyway, but I had hoped. Perhaps I can still send a message to Serena and she could at least send me a few clothes along with enough money to do… well, something.

The longer I wander, the more my stomach feels hollow and angry. When was the last time I ate? I've had water, but food? I don't even remember for certain. Back at home, there was a small roll for breakfast before Edward came, though with my nerves it was difficult to eat. How long ago was that? Over two days, I think. The pain in my stomach makes it hard to think.

The rain makes my hair soggy, something my spell has dealt with before. It feels as if it's slipping from its bun, but I don't dare fix it in public. Even if I were to dart into an alleyway, there are too many people and someone may follow. There's nowhere safe from prying eyes. It can't be expected that my hair remain perfect in such weather. Naturally, they can and will, but I don't know how women manage it without magic. I do my best to smooth it, and hope it's enough to draw any unwanted attention away from me.

Suddenly, I realize a warlock is striding in my direction. Not just any warlock. Black breeches, orange shirt, baton hook at his side. A law officer. My hands go clammy. Is he coming for me? Have I finally been caught? What's to become of me if I am his intended target?

I cross the street. He crosses as well. My pace quickens. So does his. My heart races, magic banging about inside me, but I keep my outward appearance in check. This can't be good. I glance behind my shoulder and he's almost to me. I pick up the pace so I'm almost running.

"Stop," he calls out.

Which is worse: to stop and listen, or to run? Neither are likeable options, but I stop. Running can come later if needed, with a hex to give me a head start. Only it'd better not come to that. Perhaps he only wants to tell me to fix my hair and leave it at that. Unlikely, but I can pretend to myself as well as others. I have options. Just not good ones. I keep my head down and my back straight, not letting any other reason for him to find fault with me to slip out.

"Where's your owner?" he demands.

A few people on the street stop to watch. I don't know

whether it's good or bad they look on. I do know this is a bad, bad situation.

"He's just…" Not a he, he's a she who's me. Blasted words. If I'm confusing myself. He's not only going to be confused, but bring more trouble for thinking I'm untruthful.

As if to prove my fears just, he pulls out his baton and smacks it against his hand. "Where's your owner?"

A beating. That's what he has in mind for me. My gaze can't tear itself away from his baton, which slaps against his hand several more times. It will be painful. Not what I want, yet something I can handle. What comes after the beating, though? Why did I think coming to a town full of people and law officers was a good idea?

I open my mouth to say something, though I'm still trying to formulate what, but before I speak, a voice with a drawl says, "Do you have a problem with this woman?"

Coat Man. Without his umbrella now and more soaked than ever. What is he doing here? And why is he interrupting?

The questioning warlock scowls, his crooked teeth bared. "And just who are you?"

"A friend of her owner."

My owner? Does this mean he's claiming to be my friend, Edward's friend, or Serena's? And why, exactly, would he claim such a thing?

"Doubtful," the warlock scoffs. "With your looks and accent, you're not from around these parts. More like someone who needs to be shown their place."

Coat Man shrugs, nonchalant-like. "Whether you believe it or not, I'm watching over her. And as for showing me my place, I'm here from Chryos preparing for the tournament. Your country so graciously invited me to come."

Chryos? Tournament? That explains so much. If men from Envado, like Zade, are different, why wouldn't men from other countries be courteous as well? Do they do things like offering their coats to cold women without another purpose? Though claiming to be a friend of my owner is a little farfetched and watching over me?

"Your country may have the coal the council wants, but it doesn't mean the rest of us are gracious about anything." The crooked-toothed warlock spits. "Best stick with her. You wouldn't want your friend in trouble because she's wandering alone and doesn't look as she ought."

"Point taken, sir. Thank you for your help."

The warlock glares at Coat Man and then at me before storming off. Relief drenches me, easing my magic but not my posture. The gathered crowd dissipates once the law officer is gone, though with many backward glances. The Chryon lingers, thumbs hooked in his pockets.

Once the listening ears are far enough away, I say, "Watching over me?"

"It's not a lie." Though his words are defensive, his hands remain in his pockets, as if he's relaxed.

"Yes, it is. You don't know me or my owner."

"You are wearing my coat."

The statement sends an irrational amount of embarrassment flooding through me, but I don't let that show. "A coat doesn't make you friends with my owner. Besides, you said I could keep it, which makes it mine."

"You've got me there." He leans in a little closer, and suddenly my mouth feels dry. "But I did give it to you."

My mind is blank. I can't think of a single response. Nothing that would bring any sense to this situation. I can't even reach my usual fake smile that everyone falls for. Yet he grins, his small yet powerful grin, like he knows it.

What is wrong with me? This is a warlock I'm thinking about. There's not a single, valid reason I should be turning into the puddled mess I'm always pretending to be around warlocks. I jerk away. His smile dims and for some reason it makes me want to lean back in, which only makes me angry with myself. I divert my gaze back toward the ground where it should have been the entire time.

"It is true that I was requested to watch over you," he says.

This pulls me out of my ridiculous thoughts and helps my stoic face regain its facade. "Oh? And who ordered that? Edward?"

"Who's Edward?" He sounds so genuinely puzzled that I have to believe Edward truly didn't send him. Except then, who did? He continues, "Whoever he is, I'm helping anyway. What would have happened just now if I hadn't?"

I have no idea, but just thinking on it sends my magic spiraling madly again. "Do you know? Being a foreigner, it's not as if you know the customs here."

He rocks on the balls of his feet, yet says nothing. Perhaps I'm mistaken. He could know. Perhaps they're even harsher to their women in Chryos. Maybe doing kind things like giving women their coats when it's raining is a way to lift them up so when they're punished, the women have all the farther to fall. I have farther to fall.

In any case, his point is correct. Whatever happened wouldn't have been good. Very well. He wins. For now. But I'm not admitting it aloud. I cross my arms in front of my chest and stare him down.

"I have a friend who's good at helping with situations like yours," he says.

A friend? That's not cryptic. "How do you even know what my situation is?"

"Please. You've been outside, in the rain I have to add, since sometime before I went to the bakery this morning. Chardonia women never do that. And, though it's not very gentlemanly of me to mention, your stomach keeps growling."

I want to cover my stomach. I want to, but I don't. His mention of the bakery only makes the sounds louder. Still, I keep my arms crossed, not lowering them even an inch. I don't even give him the satisfaction of a reply.

Though my cheeks are hot, which is reply enough.

"So we're agreed your situation could use some, ah, aid," he says.

"I implied nothing of the sort."

He ignores me as if I didn't say anything. Which I shouldn't have. Why do inappropriate things keep spewing out of my mouth?

"My friend thinks we may be able to help. He's actually making his way here to check on another situation close by, and said he'd stop by and help with yours,\ as well."

Great. Two warlocks shoving their way into my situation. Just what I need.

"I know you probably don't want to trust me, but Za— my friend really is a good guy. He'll do what he can."

"Zade? Chancellor Zade? Is that who you were going to say is your friend?"

"Possibly," he hedges. "What if he is?"

"That would change things."

"And what if he isn't?"

"That wouldn't change things."

He sighs and pushes the strange window things farther up his nose. "Fine then. It's Chancellor Zade. You've heard of him?"

Heard of Zade? If this wasn't so dangerous, I'd laugh. This has to be some sort of joke or, more likely, a trap. I put on my hard, no-nonsense expression disregarding the worry quivering through me. "What is it you want from me? Do you work with the council? Are you going to drag me somewhere no one will be able to find me? Are you here to punish me? To tarnish me? To kill me?"

"So you are in trouble?"

How am I giving too much away again? "I'm done speaking with you." I stride off.

Of course, he follows after. "Please, let me help. We can go to a restaurant and wait for Zade there. It's a nice, public place. I'll buy you something to eat while we wait."

Being in public doesn't mean safe. Yet his words keep tumbling though my mind. I stop, the boardwalk creaking beneath my feet. Zade, come here? It's a trick. It has to be. Zade should be with Serena, or doing whatever else it is he's always disappearing to do when it's not a council day. But if it is Zade, my problems would be a lot more manageable. If.

Even if it's not Zade, I'm hungry. This isn't going to be a chance I'll have again. I can claim a need to use the water closet and slip out when no one's looking. Because of father, I had a lot of practice with that. I'd even distract them with some sort of spell if I had to.

"Fine."

He says, "I really don't want to pressure you, but I think you should come—wait. Did you just say you'll come?" This time I'm the one to raise my eyebrows at him. "Right. Let's go."

Hopefully, this isn't as bad of a decision as the rest of the ones I've made lately.

I follow him into a restaurant. There are no tarnished eating at this one, unlike the only other restaurant I've been to. The tarnished are only servers. Most everyone else is a warlock, and very few women dot the place.

He leads me to a table in the back corner. As we weave past the other tables, I hunch in on myself trying to become small, unnoticeable, with my head down as I remain a step behind. It feels as if everyone's eyes are on me, boring into me and learning all my secrets. I wish he would have picked a table up front so at least we wouldn't have been paraded through them all.

Once seated, everything changes. Coat Man sits with his back to one wall, and I've got mine to the other. Having my back to the wall already lends a sense of security, even if it's only a small sense.

We have a good view of the entire room without making ourselves conspicuous, but most of the room has a harder time looking at us without straining their necks. And soon they forget about us anyway, going back to their meal.

Or at least they appear to forget about us. I don't trust that their unprying eyes mean unprying attitudes. I keep a close watch on them, the door, and the man I'm sitting next to. I can't forget he's brought me in out of the rain and is buying me food, though it doesn't change the fact that he's a warlock who hasn't proven himself unwarlock-like. His coat is still warm, wrapped around me, and dripping on the wood floor.

The waitress bustles to our table, a disgusted look on her face directed at me. Outwardly, I don't let her scowl bother me, and I stare right back at her, but inwardly I want to crawl under the table and hide. It's not like I want to be wet, dirty, and making a mess everywhere.

Finally, she looks away from me and I feel like I've won some victory, though in reality the only thing I've really managed is to drip more on the clean floor.

"What would you like to eat?" Her voice is much more pleasant than expected.

"How about two bowls of stew, milk, and as many rolls as you can bring us." Then he turns toward me. "If that's good with you?"

I struggle not to gape at him. He's asking my opinion? Perhaps he truly does know Zade. He's been the only warlock to show concern over my preference. "That would be acceptable."

Honestly, it's more than acceptable. At the moment, I'd eat anything.

"I'll have it right out." Before the waitress goes, she glances at me again, but this time with a questioning look. Probably the first time she's seen a warlock care about a woman's preference. What sort of thoughts will it put into her head?

In the silence that follows, there's only the low hum of other patrons conversing and my dripping. Well, not just my dripping.

I'm also attempting to watch Coat Man without giving away that I'm doing so. It flickers to my awareness that he's wet and dripping as well. Not only that, but because of me, he doesn't have a coat. His arms are crossed as if he's trying to keep his heat in.

I pick at the hem of the sleeve on the coat he gave me, feeling like I should return it, but all too aware of how cold it was last night. Cold and wet. If I give it back, I'll have nothing to protect me from that. He said I could have it, and I need it. Yet, it's hard to remember when he's shivering.

"If you don't mind," he says, "I think I'll be more comfortable if I dry off."

Apparently, I wasn't so subtle in my staring at his dripping state. But what does he mean by dry off? It's not as if there is a towel or blanket nearby. And then he does something that has me gawking.

He casually flicks his wrist, a sky blue spell, tinted with a darker blue, glides from his fingertips. The light brushes against him, leaving everything it touches dry.

I try not to be too blatant in my staring, except I've never seen anything quite like it. It's difficult not to be wide-eyed. Warlocks are rarely casual with magic. I want to study it, to see if I can discover how to duplicate it. But he quickly dries and no longer has any use for the spell. The light is extinguished before there's much time to examine it. That's how spells always are. Tiny glimpses, which leave me aching for more.

"I know it's not something causally done in Chardonia, but if you don't mind..." He runs a finger across the side of his framed windows a few times leaving me wishing he would just say what he wants to say. "I could dry you off as well."

The words are more than I hoped for. Not only showing me the spell again but helping me not be soaked? Please! Yet I mustn't sound too eager. I think of how Serena would answer, the slight disdain for magic still hasn't left her tone after all these months and the few spells Zade has shown us. "I suppose."

"I don't have to if you don't want me to."

Perhaps too much disdain. "It would be nice to be dry."

His forehead wrinkles, but he casts the spell. This time it's not just sky blue, but has red twirling around it. It moves much slower toward me than it did with him, a lazy floating as if it doesn't have the entire restaurant of warlocks as an audience. Perhaps he's trying not to frighten me off, except I'm anything but frightened.

The colors, heat, and flow of light are fascinating as they creep closer and closer until they brush my skin and clothes. The spell doesn't linger against my skin, not compared with how long it took to reach me. It feels as if a gentle breeze has picked up everywhere it touches, drying me. The red parts from the blue, seeping even closer, warming me.

When the spell pulls away, all too soon, I'm feeling much better. Warm, dry, and, though I didn't suppose it could be, even more eager for the coming food. Plus, there was a spell that wasn't a hex, which just lingered near me. That never happens. A swell of giddiness envelopes me, making me wish I was alone to work on figuring out how to replicate the spell.

The coat is stifling now that I'm warm and dry. I keep it wrapped around me, nervous over losing another barrier between me and the world, but the heat grows. It's hot, making sweat bead on my back. This is ridiculous. I'm no more or less in danger without the coat on, only more uncomfortable.

I take it off. And though I don't want to return it, with how things are going so far, I can't keep it either. He's been much too generous for that.

I hold it out to him, my grip refusing to be anything except tight on its collar. "Thank you."

"You're welcome, but I meant it when I said keep it. I don't need it."

I grip the coat even tighter, not believing he doesn't need it. It's not like I couldn't see him shivering before. But if he's going to insist, I'm not going to refuse. I drape it on the back of my chair, arranging it so my back presses against it. Every so often I let the back of my arm brush against it, reminding me that it's there. "Thank you."

"You already said that." His smile grows. "But you're welcome again. I'm happy to help however I can. I'm Lukas."

And here I've been calling him Coat Man, not that he ever need know it. It's a good name, like Luke. Familiar and different all at once, like he is. I'm still trying to process what the rest of what he said means when the waitress brings our order. She sets a steaming bowl in front of Lukas before placing one before me. As soon as the food is in front of me, it's a struggle not to gulp it down.

She places a basket of rolls in the middle of the table. "Is there anything else you need?"

"No. Thank you," he tells her.

And I feel guilty because the spoon is already filled and in my mouth. I pretend as if this was my plan all along. Women usually don't speak much around warlocks anyway. Though, they also usually wait for their owner or other warlocks to eat before starting. I own myself, though, and that's good enough for me, even if she doesn't know it, and he probably doesn't believe it. Yes, that was my plan all along.

The thought spurs me on faster, though I still use my manners as I devour my stew. The food is so good. Hot and savory. I don't know the last time I ate something so delicious. Or perhaps it's because I haven't eaten anything in almost two days. Before I know it, the soup is gone. The empty bowl is depressing, but of course I don't let it show. Instead, I grab a roll and, now that my appetite is somewhat suppressed, daintily nibble on it.

"You must have been hungry," he says.

I shrug as if my behavior is normal.

He chuckles. "I'll order you another bowl when she comes back."

Part of me feels as if I should protest. Why is he being so nice?

What does he want? I can't pay with money, yet this must mean something— the question is, what? Whatever it is, if things get too intense and threaten my freedom, I have a plan.

"Another bowl would be welcome."

His grin grows, but I don't understand how exactly. The size stays the same, but something in his expression is happier. Eyes brighter or smile lines deeper. It's hard not to study his face to identify exactly what changed.

When the waitress returns a few minutes later, Lukas orders another bowl of soup, which doesn't take long to arrive. Soon I've finished two bowls of soup and an absurd amount of rolls. My stomach feels much better but knows hunger won't be far off.

Remembering this, I sneak a roll into the pocket of my dress while he's staring at the door. Yet another reason to thank Katherine and her clever clothing designs. If I ever see her again. I might not. It's a sobering thought. There's room for three more rolls, which I quickly stuff in.

The wait without eating is more awkward than before. The noise of warlocks speaking is a pointed reminder that we aren't talking. And that all their deep voices are nothing like my high one. There's only one other woman here who isn't serving, and she is doing well at keeping her head down and mouth shut. I can't follow suit.

"How much longer are we going to have to remain here?"

He shrugs like it's no big deal, but the line of his jaw is taut. "It shouldn't be much longer before he gets here."

Or Zade isn't coming at all. I twist the ring on my index finger, no longer hungry. Food is stashed away for later, and I'm dry. Perhaps I should go now instead of waiting. The likelihood that Zade is really going to be the one to walk through those doors is slim.

It's still raining out. Guess the staying dry part won't last for long. Yet it can't be helped. I pull the coat off the back of the chair and stand.

"Please wait," he says. "He'll be here soon."

"You said that. It's time for me to go."

"Sit for just another five minutes. If he doesn't come, you can go. No questions asked." I don't trust him, but it is still raining outside, and I do have a plan. "Please. People are starting to notice."

And he's right; the warlocks are paying more attention to us again. If Lukas really wants to stop me, he'll have all the help he wants. I sit, letting the attention drift away so I can have a clear run to the door. And if it's not clear enough, well, I pull my magic close by for quick use. At least the coat is in my lap now and easy to access without alerting him I'm about to escape when the time comes.

"You don't trust me," he says, yanking me from my escape plot. "I'm sure you have good reason not to. But I really am only trying to help."

Foolish words that tug at me, making me want to believe him, even though I know I shouldn't.

"Why do you wear those strange windows on your face?"

His eyebrows lift. "You don't know what glasses are?"

"Glasses?" Sounds like something you drink from, except they are on his face.

"They help me see. When I don't wear them, everything looks blurry." He takes them off and holds them out to me. His eyes are even a deeper brown without them on. "Try them. They'll make things look different, not clear like they do for me, but you can still see what they're like."

Without them, he looks as if he's missing something. As if the glasses are a part of him. I'm staring again and he's waiting for me to take the glasses. I snatch them out of his hand and shove them onto my face.

The world looks... strange. Tilted almost, and a little nauseating. And the person who just walked in the restaurant looks familiar. Like I know whoever it is, but stretched funny. Zade. I pluck the glasses off my face as he comes striding toward us.

If it wasn't for all the warlocks around, I'd jump up and give him a hug before he could make it two steps in the room. It's actually him! Though the fact that I was wearing Lukas's glasses makes me feel as if I've been playing some bizarre sort of game instead of desperately needing help. I hand back the glasses as if it's the most natural thing in the world but as quickly as I can.

The business Zade was checking into, was that me? If so, at least I'm making things easier for him and not harder, not one more thing to add to his list. Except, it's as if I am the entire list. One created of my own ineptitude, trying to help and instead making things worse. As anxious as I was for his help, I'm not sure I'm ready to see his response.

The tension in his jaw lessens enough that it's still evident even from the corner of the room, though the way he stomps over brings a pit of chaos to my stomach. His long legs make quick work of getting to us, all eyes on him, except for Lukas, who's leaving some coins on the table.

Zade doesn't bother sitting. "Let's go."

If we were at home, I'd tease him about being grumpy, that it's been too long since he saw Serena even though he saw her yesterday. Instead, the pit of chaos grows into my chest as well, while I hurry to follow him out of the restaurant. Lukas hurries to his side and they lead me through the streets, Zade staying properly forward facing as a warlock should. Not Lukas though, he gives me many backward glances. I'd like to think it means something, that his concern has been proven as true as his connection to Zade. Yet, it's the type of unwarlock-like behavior that will bring the wrong sort of attention.

When Zade finally stops at a house, the mass of chaos is skittering frantically searching for something calm. Lukas pulls out a key, but as he unlocks the door, he mixes a spell with it. With his back blocking most of the view, I only catch a flash of bronze and no clear view of what he did.

He holds the door open and ushers us in. Zade casually looks around, though knowing him it's anything but casual. He then continues his storming on into the house. I hesitate a moment, remembering his temper, before crossing in. I only hope his temper isn't in too foul of a mood today.

Zade is already moving on to another room, which turns out to be a study, and flips on an electric light. When I follow, he grabs me by the shoulders before pulling me into a hug. A tight one that squishes the air from me.

"You're safe." His words are strangely shaky.

"Safe from everything but being squeezed to death," I gasp out.

He releases me. "Sorry. We've just been so worried. I've been so worried."

"But I'm fine."

"Yes, you are." His eyes narrow and he begins pacing the room. "Sit."

Yes, the temper is definitely struggling not to manifest now that he knows I'm not dead or worse. Oh, fabulous. As much as I want to argue with him, there's no sense making Zade's temper any worse. I really do need his help. I've bungled things badly this time. Not just badly, but horrifically. They thought they were sending me off to keep everyone safe, and instead, I've brought more danger to us all.

Lukas hovers in the doorway, watching Zade pace the room. He glances my way, gaze sympathetic, I try to hide all the turmoil roiling inside me.

"How did Edward come to free you?" Zade finally demands.

I ignore the stark feelings pounding through me and struggle with what to say. How do I answer? This is Zade. He freed Serena. He has given us all a reason to hope. He's put his life on the line for us. If I can't trust him, I might as well hex myself mute for the rest of my life.

Zade's jaw flexes, his temper probably struggling with me not responding. I glance at Lukas.

Zade looks pointedly at him. "Why don't you take a walk while I talk to Cynthia?"

Lukas glances at me, as if looking for my permission. Why he would want it is unfathomable. At least with Zade, I know where I stand. I know nothing about Lukas. I nod at him, letting him know I'm fine with Zade's request.

"I'll be back in a while if you need anything," he says to me and quickly leaves the room.

Once he's departed, I open my mouth, but Zade already knows what I want. He casts his salmon-colored, eavesdropping-preventative spell. It's pretty to look at, but now isn't the time to be staring at spells.

As soon as it surrounds us, I forge ahead. "I hexed Edward."

To Zade's credit, he doesn't look surprised. If anything he looks even more tired. And older. He slumps onto a nearby chair and rubs his forehead.

"Do you know what will happen if he tells the council?"

I swallow. "No."

"Every single person around you with the exception of me, though they hate me enough to add me to the list, will be spelled to forget you ever existed."

Never existed? His words bite, stinging into me as if they're a hex. No one will remember they care for me? Or that they hate me? I don't know what I was expecting, but this certainly wasn't it.

"After you're completely forgotten by everyone outside the council, in a secret meeting you'll be sacrificed to the Grand Chancellor."

Horror rips through me. The girl from the tournament, the only sacrifice I've ever seen, flashes in my mind. The blank expression on her face as she climbed onto the sacrificial stone. Her silent acceptance as the Grand Chancellor sliced her neck and spelled her blood into him. I realize I'm shaking. I clasp my hands together. "I didn't know."

"This is my fault. If I'd known you'd figured out how to tap into your powers, I would have said something."

He bolts to his feet and slams his fist into the wall. I clasp my hands tighter as he studies the dent he made. "I should have said something anyway. Serena's just so afraid of magic, and none of you seemed interested. Except when you were deciding who to marry, you asked about other countries. I should have known. I shouldn't have been so caught up in my own problems. And I shouldn't have hit the wall." He faces me, his shoulders slumped with defeat. "I'm sorry."

It's difficult to focus on his words; I'm too worried over what will happen to me if they find out. "It will be fine. Edward won't tell."

"You can't know that." His gaze cuts into me, exposing my uncertainty.

"He won't. He was frightened when I hexed him, even afterward when he was telling the servants he was freeing me, he seemed distressed. None of this will be heard of."

Zade collapses into a chair and places his head in both hands.

"Please don't worry," I say, putting more emphasis into it than I feel. "I'll be fine."

Still, he says nothing.

"He released me. Gave me my ownership like you did to Serena. He doesn't have any power over me."

"That's something at least." He leans back in his chair. "Yes, it's something. As long as he doesn't tell anyone why he released you, there may be a chance this doesn't end badly."

I hope Edward doesn't. I hope that my threat was enough to keep him from saying or doing anything. But how can I know for a surety? There's no guarantee those I love will remember me and that I will not be sacrificed.

CHAPTER 7

In the silence that follows I'm uncertain what to say or do. I've never been in a position like this before. How did Serena feel after she was freed? I wish I would have been there to see her, to see what freedom was like without the worry of the high cost that may accompany it. If I would have escaped to the ballroom just a little earlier, I could have. Yet missing something important, especially something for my sisters, won't happen again unless I choose it to. I can go where I want. I just don't have anywhere to go.

Or perhaps not entirely. The one place I want to be is the last place I should probably go right now. If I go home, I'll take the extra strain of my freedom with me. If I stay away, maybe I can at least minimize the impact.

"I don't think I should return with you. Serena has enough problems. My presence, especially now that I'm freed, is only going to complicate them. If I stay away, perhaps it won't be as bad."

"You're right." Some of the strain eases from his face. "But as soon as she finds out you're free, and not coming home, she's going to be upset."

I'm already upset enough for the both of us. "Will you at least send my love? And to Waverly and the girls? I miss them."

"I will."

"There's one other thing. I hate to ask, but do you know where I can stay until I determine what to do? I don't want to be a burden, but I'd prefer to not be outside in the rain again, one night was enough."

"I'll figure something out." He looks at me, really looks at me for the first time since he came to the restaurant. "No one should have to sleep in the rain. I have your clothes. Serena didn't know if Edward would buy you anything or not, or even if he'd accept them, but she sent them just in case. At least now we won't have to worry whether or not he'll allow them."

"One good thing at least."

"I should have grabbed your trunk first thing when I realized it was you in the restaurant and not some other girl, but the circumstance was distracting. Let me fetch it, and I'll think about what to do with you. Wait here."

He's out of the room before I can say anything. He'll think about what to do with me? I clench my teeth.

Yet my frustration seeps out of me as my limbs realize their heaviness. Exhaustion soaks through me. I just put all my problems on him. What else did I expect, if not help? If I'm truly free, I don't want to let others manage my problems. I must learn to take control of them. Except, it's not like I have any money, or any knowledge of what to do next. Perhaps I'll be stuck the rest of my life depending on Zade for support. That sobering thought swirls in my head as I lean back and close my eyes.

* * *

"Cynthia." Someone shakes me awake.

I blink at Zade's blurry face until he comes into focus. I must have drifted off. How long was I asleep? I rub my eyes and then sit up in a more dignified manner. Lukas is standing behind Zade. Whether his presence is good or bad, I can't decide.

"Your trunk is in the bedroom." Zade's words pull me out of my wonderings as he hands me a heavy bag. "This should last you a while. I've got to go now. I'm sorry I can't stay longer. There's a council meeting I must attend tomorrow, and if I don't leave now I'll never make it in time. I'll return when I can, and I'm sure Serena will send a message."

And I believe she will as well, except his tone says, unlike me, he's not happy. Not happy at all. It's too late to do anything about it. He's out the door before I have time to process any of what he said or thank him. That council meeting must be serious. Lukas looks just as wind-blown by Zade's departure as I feel, staring after him long after he can't be seen.

It's just us now. And I'm certain to look a mess—smeared face paint and my tangled hair. And the smell. Please don't let me smell foul. Not sure why I care, though. It's almost as if that girl I pretended to be for years, crazy about boys, is becoming a real part of me. Frightening. The need for sleep must be scrambling me more than I thought.

"I suppose I should show you to your things," he finally says.

"I suppose so."

I follow him through the house, hoping it doesn't take long so I can get cleaned up soon. The hall is tight, crowded in. There are no electric lights, only the light from the candle he's carrying. Though father's house had electric lights most of my life, many of the girls at school had never even seen it. Perks of father being on the council, perhaps? Yet Edward had it as well, and he's not on the council, though he did seem ridiculously wealthy.

"Whose house is this?"

He shrugs one shoulder. "It's for people like us who need a place to stay."

"Us?" Hot embarrassment rolls through me. He's not an owner

or a brother. He's, well I don't even know who he is. "I can't stay here with you."

"Don't worry. I'm going somewhere else. At least until the tournament starts and all the hotels are filled."

Relief fills me, but it's tainted with guilt at kicking him out of his house. As we reach a room where I see my trunk resting at the foot of the bed, I realize what he said. The tournament. It's six weeks away, and I have the status of a warlock.

I am a warlock.

CHAPTER 8

All thoughts of going to sleep flee. A warlock! An inkling of an idea so fantastic yet so wildly out of reach tempts me. How can I make it happen? "Are the cupboards stocked?"

"They are. You shouldn't have to worry about going hungry or venturing out for something."

"Thank you." Though I'm not grateful for losing my excuse to leave this place, him being here can still be used to some advantage. "Please let me make dinner as a small repayment for your kindness, especially when I was short with you."

"You weren't short."

I wave his response away. "Don't be so amiable. I was. It's been long enough since lunch that you must be hungry. The least I can do is make you a hot meal."

He shifts toward the door, shoulders slumping forward. "I don't know if I should."

"Please, let me. It would make me feel better." Except for the guilt from using him, but it can't be helped. "If you're worried over how long it will take, I can be quick."

After another moment of hesitation, he says, "Time isn't the issue. Don't you want to get cleaned up?"

I must smell after all. "If you don't mind waiting a bit, I can clean up fast and get something made even faster. I'm used to helping my sisters."

"I can wait. I have a few things I need to pack up to take with me anyway."

"Perfect. We'll eat shortly then."

I hurry to the room, which is now mine, to clean myself up and put on fresh clothes before he changes his mind and leaves, stashing the rolls I snuck earlier in a dresser. It's doubtful I'll have an opportunity such as this again. I dress, again grateful Katherine's clothing designs allow me to do this myself. Once I'm presentable, I scurry to the kitchen where, to my relief, he's sitting at the table working on some papers.

"Do you need help finding anything?" he asks.

"I can manage."

"Well, if there's something you can't find, don't hesitate to ask."

After opening the pantry and finding ingredients to make soda biscuits and smoked ham, I ask, "How long have you been in Chardonia?"

"Two weeks."

I measure my flour into a bowl. "How did you become acquainted with Zade? You aren't from the same country."

"No we aren't, but outside of Chardonia, many countries interact frequently."

Which isn't really an answer to my question. "So you two interacted previously?"

"Do you need help with anything?"

"I'm fine. Thank you." Why is he still deflecting? I haven't even started the hard questions yet. Besides, I can make biscuits in my sleep. "You and Zade?"

He twists the pen in his hand. "Let's just say we have similar interests."

What does that mean? "You want to be on the Chardonia council?"

"Are you kidding me? Those guys are crazy." He coughs. "I mean, that's not really my thing."

"What is your *thing?*" The phrase feels odd on my tongue.

"I'm not sure I've entirely figured that out yet."

Doubtful. He's obviously up to something, though the idea is familiar enough. There have been more times than not I've thought the same thing. Still, how much more can I get out of him? If I accost him enough on a subject he's reluctant to speak of, perhaps the questions I truly want answers to will be such a relief, he'd be happy to respond. "How well are you connected with Zade?"

He shrugs, but doesn't look me in the eye as he replies, "Well enough."

Must be well enough if Zade is comfortable not only leaving me with him but trusting Lukas to continue to stay in my presence. I clear my throat and roll out my dough with perhaps a little too much enthusiasm. "Are you planning on entering the tournament?"

"I am. That's what this paperwork is for."

So I'll need paperwork. I throw the biscuits in the oven and slice the ham "And that's why you're here. Have you been here long enough to know your way around town?"

"I have."

Perfect. I plate the ham and add some fruit. "Perhaps tomorrow you can show me the town."

"I don't know if that's a good idea." He shifts in his chair. "It's not a big deal, but Zade told me to keep an eye out for trouble, and this seems like it could lead to trouble. But I think..." He shakes his head. "Why do you want to go?"

After pulling the soda biscuits from the oven and plating several, I set his plate in front of him. "Just thought it'd be nice to have a better idea of where I am. Especially if trouble comes." Don't need to mention the fact that I'm going to go searching for it.

"I suppose it probably would be best to make sure you know your way around. Will tomorrow morning work?"

I suppress my real grin for fear it will give away how deeply I feel about this. "It will suffice."

* * *

THE NEXT MORNING, I discover a town very different from the one I encountered upon first arriving. At first, I'm still lost, but it doesn't take long for Lukas to orient me. While showing me how to get to the market, he also points out the quickest ways out of town and the hotel he's lodging in.

Once safety is covered, we wander around shops figuring out where to find food and clothes, though it's probably something I shouldn't do without Lukas. Even though I'm running toward trouble, I'm not entirely stupid.

He doesn't say anything, yet the way he hesitates with everything around the shopping area, constantly checking our surroundings, he doesn't appear comfortable either. I'll just try not to need anything. Right. There was plenty of food in the pantry and any clothing needs that come about I'll order through Katherine anyway.

"So," I say casually, trying to bring up what I want. "The tournament. Have you turned in your paperwork?"

"Not yet. I filled out paperwork to get in the country, so they know, but I haven't turned in the paperwork to enter the tournament yet."

"You turn in the paperwork here in town, correct?"

"Yes, it's just around the corner." His gaze shifts to the left but quickly flickers back.

"We could turn it in now since we happen to be close. Then you wouldn't have to return later."

Suddenly his full attention is on me with a strange, intense look. "Is there something you need there?"

"Certainly not." I laugh the cute way girls do. No more pushing for now. "What would I do there? I just thought it might save you some time."

His lips pinch together as if he doesn't believe what I'm saying. Which he shouldn't. "It's not much extra time. Besides, they probably wouldn't look kindly on having a woman brought in. And as much as I think you're capable of being outside on your own, this town makes life hard enough without worrying if a law officer, or someone worse, will stop by."

Though I dislike it, he's correct. Yet it's a problem I'll have to handle at some point. I need to do this. And I may not know which building is exactly the one I need, but I know the general area. This excursion has been a success.

As if to prove Lukas's point from a moment ago, a warlock bumps into him, almost shoving him to the ground.

I expect an apology spell, or at least a head nod or something. Warlocks are usually respectful toward each other, even if they aren't respectful to women. But not this warlock. He sneers at Lukas, whipping up a mix of anger and fear in me as he says, "Watch where you're going."

"My mistake." Lukas's response yanks my attention from the offending warlock. Why is he admitting fault when he clearly wasn't?

The warlock seems surprised as well. He pulls back a moment before growling and getting in Lukas's face. "Don't let it happen again. I don't like foreign scum touching me."

That explains the antagonism usually reserved for women. Lukas nods his head, and the man strides away, seemingly satisfied.

"Why did you let him treat you such?" Even being a foreigner, I'd expect him to demand better. He's a warlock. They don't ever get pushed around. Until now.

Lukas's shoulders slump. "It doesn't matter."

Except it does. I didn't know foreign warlocks, except the Envadi, had a difficult time of things.

"We should go," he says.

Together, we head back toward the house, and while I'm grateful we went, it feels as if I lost more than I gained.

CHAPTER 9

Warlocks have been coming and going from the medium-sized building all morning. Women never enter. Instead they're forced to wait outside with another male while their owner goes in. I'm the only woman alone, of course. Yet with so many people about no one appears to notice.

The area has an almost jovial air about it. Warlocks bantering and laughing as they go in. Even a few foreigners, tall like Zade, or darker-skinned like Lukas, come in and out of the building. This has to be it.

Except I can't bring myself to do anything about it. If I enter, there's no turning back. Conundrum. I can't bring myself to go in, yet I can't bring myself to leave either. This is the one chance to show everyone what a woman can do.

The idea has been growing in my mind like an uncast spell clambering to happen. The feeling only grows bigger and fiercer as time passes, restless to have me follow through. This is something I want. The women of Chardonia need to see that we can do magic. Not only just casting spells, but succeeding at them. Those blasted warlocks need to be shown they can't keep us in the dark any longer.

The problem is, Zade's words keep coming back to me, about them erasing part of everyone's memories and sacrificing me. If that's what they would do when I was owned, what would stop them from doing it now, even though I have the status of a warlock?

My footsteps slowly lead me away from the place I need to be. I want to make a difference, but people's memories being erased and becoming a sacrifice won't help anything. I want the impossible.

* * *

THE NEXT DAY is rather droll as I think on how to fix my fear of entering the tournament, though I do hear some strange noises in the morning. There's nothing out the window when I check, so I continue my hopeless musings until midday when there's a knock at the door. I open it to find Lukas carrying a bag sagging with food.

"Hey, I brought you some fresh fruit and vegetables in case you were running low."

"Oh." Not really running low. And I'm not sure if I want to spend time with a warlock I don't really know. Except, maybe, I can discover more from him about the tournament. Like when there's going to be the most amount of people at the tournament sign ups. That may be my best chance, to be around so many people that it would be too difficult to erase all their memories. Is that even possible? I don't know. I have to hope, and for a foreigner he seems to understand the process well. Or at least better than me.

"Thank you." I gesture for him to come in.

He carries the bag into the kitchen and sets it on the table. "Not a lot, just the produce plus some fresh bread, milk, and eggs. If there's something else you need, just let me know."

That is a lot of food. "No, this is more than generous of you.

You've shown me around. I could have obtained this myself. I hate to be a bother."

"It's no bother." Meaning it's easier to get things for me than to have to take me wherever I want to go with the constant threat of death hovering. I probably shouldn't mention that I checked to see if Serena had sent a letter while I mailed one to her and Katherine.

And I definitely won't mention all the staring at the tournament building that's been going on. Or how I had to hide when the Grand Chancellor came striding down the road with his son Nathaniel and entered the building. They probably were there to sign Nathaniel up for the tournament. Nathaniel may have helped my sister at the ball, but I still don't trust him. Especially not with his father around. Both men are deadly.

"Well," he says, breaking my thoughts.

"Well."

He scratches his cheek. "I suppose I should be going."

Not yet! I need more information. Or maybe just enough information to give me a boost in confidence. Besides, it's been so quiet here all week. I don't want to be alone, even if it means inviting him to tarry.

I clink my bracelets together. He seemed nice enough from the little interaction we've had. He seems to be a warlock more like Zade than father. "Why don't you stay? You brought more food than I need. I could cook you dinner again."

"This is too much food?"

I laugh. "I couldn't possibly eat this all myself before it goes bad."

"Oh." He looks sheepish a moment before joining in with my laughter. "I always did eat a lot."

Not that his trim frame shows it. "Then you'll stay?"

"Suppose it would only be fair, so I don't make you waste food." He grins at me, and something inside me melts like one of Waverly's chocolates.

79

My hands shake. I grab a bowl to distract myself from it and get to work. The strange feeling doesn't leave; instead, it persists in trying to get me to think on his smile. It's a very nice smile. Warm and personal. And in no way related to the information I need to find out from him. I need to focus on getting answers, not strange, melty, shaky-making feelings.

"Did you turn your paperwork in for the tournament?" I ask.

"Sure did."

Good thing he didn't do it when I was stalking the place. "Are there many others signed up yet?"

"More than last year at this time. Interest is picking up. I think many people from other countries are more curious since a Chardonian woman gained her freedom. Serena is becoming famous."

I wonder what she'd think of that. "Were you there last year? Did you see Zade win?"

His smile sobers into a line. "I did."

Was he sickened as I was by the whole turn of affairs? Not that it turned into a horrid event like we thought it would,. It was the best thing that could have happened. Yet, Serena being won first by Thomas and then Zade shouldn't have had the chance to happen. "What do you think of our ways?"

"What do you think of them?"

That they are wrong. "I don't know much about our ways. Women are kept in the dark as much as possible. I know little."

"Does that bother you? I can't tell how you feel about it. You're hard to read."

I slip him a smile. A real smile. That was the best compliment anyone has ever paid me. But then I let it fade. "Of course it bothers me. I can't believe it doesn't bother more women." As much as this is a good topic of conversation, it's breaking away from what I want to know. "So you signed up for the tournament last year as well?"

"No. Last year I was just spectating. My mentor, Arthur, signed up, and I followed him around a lot."

"Did he sign up a ways out from the tournament as you did?"

"No. It's too busy right now. The wait is really long, both to get in the country and to sign up. Everyone wants to declare themselves while it's early. There's much to be won if you kill, someone, many like to show off the fact they think they'll excel at it." He looks at me out of the corner of his eye. "Is there a reason you're so interested?"

I falter. "Just curious is all."

"Are you sure that's all? Because it seems like there's something more to it." When I don't respond, he continues. "Does it have anything to do with the same reason you were outside the tournament headquarters yesterday?"

He did see me. Blast. My hesitance at him discovering my intentions vanishes for distrust. "You've been following me?"

He shrugs, completely unashamed. "I thought you would know someone is keeping an eye on you. Zade said there would probably be attempts on your life and to keep someone close."

"Oh, he did, did he?" The one male I thought capable of giving women our space and freedom. Naturally, he'd turn out more like them. I hate this. I hate the way things are. That hate simmers in me, pulling at my magic, tugging at my will.

"Calm down. He's trying to help."

"By dictating my life? By having me followed? I'm sick of this life. And you—" I point the spoon at the door, splattering sauce everywhere. "—can leave now."

He stands, completely ignoring the fact I'm huffing like a crazy person, and keeps his voice soft. "I know this is hard, and not what you want. I'd be just as angry. If you really want me to go now, I will, but I'm not going to stop protecting you."

"Clearly, I'm fine on my own. There's no need for any of this." Why am I losing my temper with him? Why can't I hold myself together?

His voice is calm, too calm for how much I'm yelling. "You're not fine. We've already stopped two attempts on your life."

The words fizzle my anger into coals of fear. "Two? That can't be. I'd know if there had been attempts."

"You didn't know because they were stopped before they got to you. Because we've been doing exactly what you want us not to do. We're giving you as much freedom and privacy as we can, but we're not going to let it go just so you can feel better about yourself. You need us."

"There were strange noises outside this morning. Was that one of them?"

"Yes."

No. "You really stopped two attempts?"

"Well, I personally only stopped one, but Xyer stopped the other."

The unfamiliar name is something easier to grasp on than my life being threatened. "Who's Xyer?"

"A friend of Zade's." He waves his hand. "But that's not important right now. What's important is you know we are protecting you." He inches closer, his voice going soft. "I'm sorry for the intrusion this causes."

All day I've been so lonely, yet I've had people watching over me and I didn't even know it. Not only that, but they've risked their lives for me. Xyer, a man I don't even know, and Lukas, who I barely know. He turns and heads for the hall leading to the entry.

"Wait. Don't go." He stops, but doesn't turn around. "I—I'm sorry, I didn't know."

He finally looks at me, but doesn't say a word. His gaze is unnerving; his cocoa-colored eyes feel as if they can see through me, into me like no one's ever been able to before. I feel exposed. And stupid. Very stupid.

"It was wrong of me to get upset with you. I didn't understand the situation. I'm not usually so volatile, it's just…" Just something about you makes it hard to keep my feelings inside. "Please ignore what I said. You can stay. I won't fling anymore food about."

Finally, he chuckles. "It does add some nice color to the place."

I hurry to clean up the sauce. "I'm so embarrassed."

Once it's cleaned, I take the fruit, biscuits, and chicken to the table. Without any sauce. There's been enough of that. Suddenly, he's beside me. His hand reaches for a biscuit and puts it on the plate. I'm frozen, watching him serve himself. I've never seen anything like it. Not ever. The only males who serve are tarnished and lower class. Even Zade doesn't serve himself. Or maybe he does when I'm not around, or perhaps he wants to let his servants do it so they have work or something, I don't know. Whatever the case may be, I'm entranced by the idea of a man helping with women's work.

He finishes loading his plate before looking at me. "Are you all right?"

"Um…" My throat catches. I clear it, and then continue. "I'm well. Thank you for your help."

"It's my pleasure."

We stare at each other a moment. Awkwardly. I twirl away from him and hurry to finish eating my own plate of food, though my thoughts are too busy for me to be hungry.

"So," Lukas says, "you never answered my question. Is there more to your interest with the tournament or is it really just curiosity?"

"Just curiosity."

"Hmmm."

Hmmm? That's all? His tone implies he suspects more. And there is more. He's saved my life. With him being from a different country, he has to think differently than all the Chardonian warlocks. And Zade trusts him. More than that, I think I'm beginning to trust him. He doesn't act like any other warlock, not even Zade. As good as Zade is, Lukas may just be better.

"Fine. You win. There is more to it. I want to enter the

tournament."

His eyes widen. "You know how to do magic?"

If I'm going to do this, I might as well take it all the way. My magic is eager to answer, heating within me, hungry to show itself. I let it out in a spell that explodes with pink and purple dancing overhead. Harmless, nothing more than colored lights, a display of my pure magic, yet by his widening eyes, effective.

"Yes, then," he finally says. His eyes relax, his smile, so small, but bringing so much warmth to the room.

It takes a moment to process the fact that he's happy about this. I thought he'd be upset like Zade. Perhaps uncaring or irritated that I did it, but joy? Never that.

"Why just staring at the headquarters then?" he asks. "Why haven't you entered?"

I stop the spell, using it as an excuse to turn away so he won't see the flush of embarrassment racing through me. The words are painfully accurate. I should have entered by now. He said it was the busiest time. There was a plethora of warlocks coming in and out of the building. I should have risked that it would be enough.

"It's not that easy. I don't even know if my freedom has been made known yet. They'll be more likely to punish me than to let me enter." Excuses, but at least they're something. "Even if word has spread, what is there to make them believe I am the girl that was freed?"

He cocks an eyebrow at me. "Is this all that's bothering you?"

"No." How does he read me so well? Probably because I give too much away in his presence. Why do I continue doing that?

"What is it? Please let me try to help."

Here we go. I take a deep breath. "Do you know what they do to women in Chardonia who do magic?"

His face loses even the hint of joy. "It's part of why I'm here."

This conversation is bringing more and more surprises. I thought he was just here for the tournament. "What do you mean?"

"You don't know about Zade?"

"Zade? What does he have to do with any of this?"

"Everything. Well, not him specifically, I suppose, but well...I should let him tell his own secrets. Suffice it to say that some in Chryos don't like what's going on here. The new changes with the tarnished have made it more difficult for them to get out. We're still getting a few tarnished men who make it, but no women have made it for a long time. And the stories we're hearing..." He shakes his head as a disgusted scowl crosses his face. "We wanted to help before, when so many were coming to our country in need of aid. I must admit that when the flow lessened, many thought we shouldn't help anymore, but my own desire only grew."

"Which is why you're here helping me, because of these refugees you've seen in your country?"

"If it doesn't stop, I'm afraid of what could happen. We're trying to help fix things before they get worse."

"By having you come here and enter the tournament?"

He scoots his chair closer. My chest constricts, and I grip the handle of my fork tighter as he says, "It's getting harder and harder for foreigners to enter Chardonia other times of the year, except for trade, which is strictly regulated. The tournament is the one excuse we can use to get closer to our goal."

He moves his hand. Is he going to touch me? My breathing quickens. What is it going to feel like? Except instead of his hand moving closer, he adjusts his glasses. Disappointment arcs through me. What is going on?

He scoots back, and I can breathe again. I use the opportunity to focus on the topic and not on my confusing feelings. "Just an excuse? What are you planning to do while you're here then?"

"I'm going to help you safely register for the tournament, and then we're going to practice until you're ready to defeat them all."

For the first time since I decided to enter in the tournament, hope courses through me with the thought that it may actually happen.

CHAPTER 10

M y nerves bounce about like bits of magic bursting to get free as we near the tournament headquarters three days later, yet I don't let them show. I do slow, though. With Lukas at my side and a plan in place, there's no reason not to go through with this. I can do it. It will work. Except knowing so doesn't make it any easier to slog on.

"You do know that by participating in the tournament, you could die," Lukas says.

And there is that. "Thank you for being so encouraging."

"Sorry. It just occurred to me we never talked about the usual risks. The fact you're a woman trying to cross into a man's world and the council hunting you down seemed like enough."

Yes, all that. With everything against me, the usual risks seem minor in comparison. Warlocks did die last year though, some of them hexed painfully to bring about their end. My voice is small. "I know." And I keep walking.

He nods like he approves of my determination. Or perhaps he's just agreeing. The door to the building swings closed after a warlock enters.

"I'm right here," Lukas says.

The words are reassuring as he opens the door for me and guides me in with a hand on the small of my back. The light touch is comforting. I draw strength from it, but the moment the door closes behind us, it's gone. The loss is immediate and aching, especially with everyone in the room staring right at me. Not the type of staring one wants either but the type of stares that send girls crying into dark basements.

I've seen those looks before. Too many times. I've survived them. Serena may have done much to protect me, but I wasn't wholly kept from punishment. I've lived through hexes before; I can live through them again. Whatever comes, I'll take it and come out stronger. Or dead.

Wish that thought had not have come. It's harder to paste the smile on my face. Yet, I do it. I give a smile that's faker than a warlock being kind and march to the end of the long line.

The warlocks stare at me as if I've jewelry pouring out my ears. The desire to stare at the wood-slatted floor is unbearably strong, rife with years of acquiescing, yet I keep my gaze firmly locked on the white wall behind the warlocks at the counter. No longer will I look down for them.

The warlocks at the counter are having a hurried conversation while one of them sends a spelled message flying out the window. As they debate, the collar of my dress grows more choking, tighter and tighter as if someone has hexed it to render me unconscious. Yet, there is no hex plaguing me, only the stifling expectations of women's dress crowded by my fears.

Thankfully, I'm not forced to wait long with the imaginary hex. Unthankfully, one of the warlocks from behind the counter has stopped debating and is heading straight for me, meaning a real hex could be unleashed momentarily.

We have a plan. This will work.

"Get out. Women aren't welcome." A burgundy hex flickers at his fingertips, proving my fears valid, but he doesn't strike me. Yet.

"That may be. Except I'm not just any woman." I widen my smile in spite of it all. "I am Cynthia, Stephen's daughter, and I was given my freedom, which means I have the status of a warlock."

The man's face scrunches with anger and disbelief, but his eyes contain a hint of fear. "That can't be. Those are just rumors."

I want to cower. To slump my shoulders, lower my head, and play the dutiful role I'm accustomed to. But if I could play that role well enough to trick everyone, I can do the same with this one. I can and I will. "Not rumors. Truth. So I'd suggest you treat me with the proper respect."

"But—"

"No buts," Lukas interrupts. "It's as she says."

I chafe at him having to enter the conversation. When we discussed it, I knew it was likely needed, yet I wish I could have accomplished this on my own. Lukas hands the warlock several official letters. One of which certifies the fact of my freedom. Procured from Zade, rather unwillingly though still quickly, from Edward. The whole thing was official. It even had spelled on it Edward's confession so there can be no doubt about its authenticity.

The other letters are from high-ranking warlocks of influence, both in this country and others, who explain how anxious they are to see me perform in the tournament. Some are wondering if I can actually cast spells, or if I will be making a fool of myself for their enjoyment. No matter, though. They should give validity to me so I can at least sign up without payment of death. In this building anyway There's no telling what will happen once I leave. No telling if the officials will go along with the plan, either.

He's taking much longer to scan the letters than I expected, his face bunching together more and more as he reads until it looks like he bit into a bad lemon. Finally, he folds the papers and moves to put them in his coat. Lukas calmly holds his hand out.

"If I may," Lukas says, though from the tone of his voice it's clearly not a request. The man's nose flares, but he hands them back.

Lukas proceeds to read aloud, the words making everything more real. Almost too real. I can't believe I'm actually here doing this. Hearing about my freedom, read aloud to a room full of warlocks. Hostile warlocks. I force myself not to edge closer to Lukas as he finishes.

"And just so we are all clear," Lukas continues, "I have personally sent an official letter to all those of high rank both in Chardonia and its surrounding countries, declaring that Cynthia has the status of a warlock and is using that status to enter the tournament. I've already received replies. Her performance is highly anticipated."

And hopefully this is enough to keep them from murdering me and trying to erase everyone's memory. There's simply too many memories that would need to be erased, some not even in this country, in places where the council and Grand Chancellor have no control.

The warlock sputters, glares at me, then stomps back to his place behind the counter. He calls out a gruff, "Next."

They are truly going to let me sign up? The plan had merit, yet to see it actually work makes me want to dance across the floor letting spells of yellows, golds, and reds twist through the room in rhythm with my happiness.

But we agreed it'd be best to keep my magic contained, to make them wonder whether or not I'll actually perform any spells.

It takes a moment, but then the next warlock clear at the front of the line steps to his spot. Things begin again after that. The line moves slowly, but still moves. The stares are still hostile, but I do my best to ignore them. My collar is still choking, only not as strong of a panic-gripped, hex-like fear as before.

The movement of the line has no real pattern. Sometimes it quickly moves through warlocks. Other times it doesn't move at all. When the warlock before me is called to the counter, my collar suddenly tightens again, encircling my neck more roughly than ever. I struggle to keep my expression neutral and breathing calm. Forever seems to pass before a warlock calls out, "Next."

I stumble forward, ignoring my ungraceful gait, and hand the warlock my prefilled application, grateful Lukas had the forethought to help me fill it out. We went over it together an innumerable amount of times, making sure there was nothing they could find fault with.

The warlock scrutinizing it takes longer than on any of the other applications, longer than I stood in one spot while in line. His finger taps over every line, traces every word. Even with the extra time we spent preparing it, he's likely to find something amiss with this sort of scrutiny.

Suddenly, a warlock slams the door open, striding straight to us. The warlock looking over my paper says, "Ah, Chancellor Ryan, we're so glad you could make it to help us with this... dilemma."

The Chancellor? As in the second-highest warlock in the government besides the Grand Chancellor? The Chancellor position held by only two individuals—him and Zade. The Chancellor that Zade and Serena both loathe?

"Let me see the paperwork." Chancellor Ryan studies my paperwork with even greater interest.

Why did he have to come? I hold myself as still as possible, waiting for news. The world pricks with black spots as the breaths I take are too shallow. His hands can just as easily tear my application apart as they can give me what I desire.

The world tilts and sways. Ever so slightly, I lean forward, balancing my weight against the counter. I force myself to take deeper breaths, clearing not only the spots from my vision, but the possibility of fainting in front of a room full of warlocks who likely wish to see me dead.

Finally, the Chancellor thrusts the papers back at the warlock.

"Sorry. These are legitimate. Good news though. She'll probably be dead on the first day."

Fear scrambles my insides, yet I work to keep my face calm. The warlock scowls, but sets the papers aside, makes a note in his ledger, and thrusts another stack of papers at me.

"Next," he calls out.

I grab the stack, hurry past the Chancellor and out of the building as fast as I can, while still maintaining my dignity. Once we're a few blocks away, I finally slow and take a deep breath of fresh air. My head clears and thoughts come easier.

"The Chancellor came just to look over my papers."

"No one said it would be easy."

"At least this part is over." Though I already saw what the warlock wrote, I take a closer look. Lukas peeks over my shoulder.

"Looks great," he says

"Dueler number two hundred twenty-three." That's going to be me. That is me. I am officially entered into a tournament that has never had any woman do any kind of work at except serving the warlocks or being sacrificed. And most definitely never had a woman dueler.

"You know what this means, right?"

"That death will come from either the council trying to kill me or a warlock in the tournament."

"Nope. It means we need to practice."

The thrill of his words flares inside me. Being able to not only practice magic but doing it with another person dulls the fear. And then I realize it's not just another person I'm going to be practicing with but Lukas. The thrill intensifies. I wonder what new types of spells he knows that I've never even seen before.

CHAPTER 11

W hen he said we needed to practice, he meant it. As soon as we return to what I now think of as my house, even though it's not really, he leads me to the sitting room that Zade took me to the first time I arrived.

I don't even bother trying to hide how like an unstarched dress I feel. I plop down on the couch, letting it support all of me. That was an experience like none other and not in a good way. To think it's only the beginning of what's to come. Lukas sits across from me, elbows on his knees, hands clasped together in front of him, and eyes intent on me. Too intent. I sit up straighter.

"What do you know about fighting in a tournament?" Lukas asks, not giving me any time to think over how terrifying the experience of signing up was. Just as well, since it drudged through my thoughts unceasingly on our return.

"Not nearly enough, I'm certain."

He smiles at me, soft and comforting to my taut nerves. "Don't worry. That's why I'm here. Let's start with what you do know."

I let his reassurance build my lack of confidence. "It was difficult to learn much of anything at the tournament last year. No one wanted to tell me anything, and I was afraid of asking too many questions. I know there's some sort of a point system. And time limit. If you're killed, your stuff goes to the winner. Luckily, I don't have anything."

His gaze grows intense with something much stronger than talking about spells. "You have something more important than simple things."

I duck my head down so he won't see the flush flooding my cheeks.

He clears his throat and continues as if he never said anything, which is probably for the best, yet it leaves a tinge of disappointment. "You've figured out the basics. You have two minutes to attack your opponent as many times as you can. Attacks to the limbs are worth one point. Attacks to the head or torso are worth two points."

"So it's as if you attacked someone physically. Arms and legs won't be as effective as vital areas of the body."

"Exactly, but it must be with a spell. And any form of defending yourself from an attack is one point."

"No differentiating of points for defending? It seems like those spells could vary a lot."

"They do, and defending is important, but Chardonians don't think it's as meaningful as attacking an opponent where they could be critically injured."

I don't want to think on the critically injured part—neither giving nor receiving. "Chardonians don't think? What about other countries? Do you have a tournament like this in Chryos?"

"All the time. And other countries, too. Chardonia is the only country that doesn't participate in tournaments outside of its own. Most other countries are fairly friendly, but travel between countries is very difficult so it's not as easy to maintain as we'd like."

"Truly? Do women participate in other countries? In Chryos?"

He laughs. "You're insatiable." I twist my hands together under the table, wondering if that's good or bad, but before I can decide, he continues, "The tournaments in other countries vary a lot. Some are small, a lot are bigger, mostly because Chardonia makes it tougher and tougher for outsiders to come in."

"But you're here. And others come. Why not just go to another country's tournament?"

"Trust me, most do. But some, like me, are trying to get in to help. Or, in the case of this year, seeing if any changes are happening. Others want to show Chardonia up. I don't know why they still think that, when only a Chardonian council member has won for as long as anyone can remember."

"Someone from the council always wins?"

"Always. Well, except last year the Grand Chancellor's son won, but he might as well be on the council."

It's true. I remember, after Zade beat Thomas and won Serena, hearing the announcement while I was waiting for her to wake and fretting she might not. For many hours I feared father wouldn't allow her to. "Well, I suppose we'll have to see what we can do about that then, won't we?"

And it hits me that not only are we both competing in the same tournament, but that we may compete against one another. I don't want to fight him. Though with as many participants as there are, it's highly unlikely we'll have to fight against each other, unless we both make it far in the tournament. If that happens, well, I'll concern myself with it if it happens.

I change the subject to distract myself from that disturbing line of thought. "What about women? You didn't answer that question."

"Only because you ask so many questions it's hard to keep up." I start to apologize, but he smiles and says, "It's not a bad thing. I like it."

He does? That's certainly new, but something I could become accustomed to. "What about women then? Do they enter tournaments in other countries?"

"Many do. Some countries still have more men competing, but

Envado sometimes has more women than men. Probably another reason Chardonia doesn't participate in them. They could never stand losing to a woman."

Yet to me the thought has a nice flash of appeal. It also reminds me of Edward's cowering. "I can understand how that might bother them. But I'm willing to defeat them anyway."

"You will." He winks at me, and a trill of happiness bounds through me.

There are still so many questions I want answers to. So much I need to learn before the tournament. There's little time to think on his smiles and winks. I probably shouldn't inquire, yet I can't help it. There must be more to know about the man who's willing to help me. Willing to wink and smile at me. "Did you have someone you left behind? Property you signed away?"

He gives me one of his grins, though this one has a touch of something I don't understand. "No family. No property."

"Oh." I study the rings on my left hand. No probably about it. I shouldn't have pried. "I'm sorry."

"Don't worry about it. I've been an orphan for a long time. I'm used to it, but it left me with no money and very few things." He shrugs. "It happened so long ago, it's just part of who I am."

"Don't you get lonely?" Even though I should have already learned my lesson, I can't help but ask because I've been lonely for a long time, except for moments like now when he's here.

"Nah. There's a couple who took me in when I was a kid. They've taught me a lot. Sent me to school and made sure I had a lot of kids to play with. I was always the one that was sent to school with enough treats for everyone. Extra treats for someone having a bad day."

"I can see how you'd get along well with lots of people."

"You seem like you would, too."

The thought startles me. "What makes you say that?"

"Other than the whole trying to evade me in the beginning, you've been really nice to talk to."

The compliment warms me, stirring my magic. "I've never truly been given the chance to get along with very many people. I only ever had my sister and a few classmates. Class isn't the best place to build relationships. The ball was my best chance to get to know more people, and I ruined that."

"What ball? How did you ruin it?"

I rub my hand on the cushion next me. "Serena's ball, the one where she was given her freedom. Do you know of it?"

"I'm quite familiar with it. What happened there with you?"

I learned too much from my outspoken sister. Though it's good I did. If I hadn't, I don't think I'd have my freedom now. "I was being inane and taunting the freedom I'd gained under Zade's supervision in front of Father. Wearing what's considered tarnished clothes. Naturally, as soon as he saw me, he banished me from attending the ball and locked me in a room. I snuck out, but by then, all the fun was over and it was just fighting."

"You've never been to another ball or other big activity?"

"No. Serena went to one other ball when she turned sixteen before she ever met Zade, but hers was supposed to be my first. I've been around people at the tournament last year but didn't have many opportunities to get to know others. We're discouraged from mingling. Other than that, the only chance I got was at class, and the most girls they'd allow in a class was ten. The boys could come and go as they pleased, or probably as their parents pleased, so their numbers varied a lot. Some weeks there would be no boys. Other weeks we'd have twelve to fifteen."

"That sounds like a horrible idea."

"Oh, it was. It was supposed to be a good chance for us girls to learn what it would be like should our owners ever do something like take us to a restaurant, or ball, or some public event to show us off." Thank magic I escaped that fate. "Mostly, it was an excuse for the boys to get huffy because there weren't enough girls giving them attention. Some were nice, though. It was just better when they kept in smaller numbers."

"I bet."

His gaze becomes intense, like he's trying to see how much I hurt from the memories. To distract us both, I ask, "What about other Chardonian women? Why haven't they figured out how to do magic when I have?"

He leans back. "I don't know for certain. You have a phenomenal amount of power. That's probably the biggest thing. Having so much of it makes it harder to not have something happen with it."

"That makes sense. I remember the first time I cast a spell, it was like something was struggling to get out of me."

"What happened?"

It feels strange to tell someone, but also like my magic, the story is bursting from me, excited to be told after years of cowering. "I convinced Serena to throw mud at the councilman's horses after sneaking out during one of their meetings. When father found out, Serena took the blame and the worst of the punishment. I don't know what he did to her, but she never again joined in my antics. Just as well. Father sent me to the basement alone without any light for my part in it. I kept thinking about how scared I was and how I wished more than anything there was light. Something built and built inside me until it popped out, a bright flicker of hope among my dark guilt."

"And you never told anyone?"

"I wanted to. I usually tell my sisters everything, but I was seven. Even then, I knew well enough that women didn't do magic. I didn't know if I was broken or what, but I did know it was something I needed to keep to myself." It was then I started showing everyone only the side I wanted them to see."

"It's great that you figured it out yourself, but what's even more amazing is that you kept it to yourself all these years. That's quite the accomplishment." His words fill me with warmth. "It sounds like it was the fact that you have so much magic charged with an emotional experience that helped you discover it. There's a lot of things Chardonian men do to make it harder on woman. Not only do they punish you into submission, but they say women can't. And they put restrictions on you, like wearing gloves."

"Gloves change magic?"

"Many people find it difficult to cast through any sort of barrier. That's why most cast spells through their bare hands."

"But I've cast spells through my gloves many times."

"Harder, not impossible. And again, your level of magic would make it easier. Have you ever tried a spell with your gloves on and then the same spell without?"

"No."

"You should. It'll probably be different."

I smooth down my hair with my usual spell, same as always. Then I take off my glove and try again. Only this time, the spell rips out of me so powerful, my hair will probably be stuck to my head for a week. "Wow."

Lukas chuckles. "Gloveless for the tournament, I think."

"That would be wise." This will take some getting used to. "Why do you wear glasses if you could fix it with magic?"

"I don't know enough about eyes to fix it myself and can't afford someone who does."

I hook a finger around two of my bracelets. "Is that why they can't fix Zade's limp? I thought he had a lot of money."

"He does, at least from my understanding. His problem is that the warlock who first tried to heal it did so incorrectly, and he has yet to find someone that both knows how to properly fix it and has enough magic to do so."

The thought lingers with me, reminding me that even when I gain more knowledge about magic, some things are still impossible to fix. Poor Zade. "It's getting late. We didn't spend much time preparing for the tournament."

"This is all important, too. You can learn a lot from what's outside yourself." He leans a little closer. "If you don't mind, I'd like to come back tomorrow."

Mind? I wish it was already tomorrow. "If you have time, that would be nice."

He gives me his smile small and full of happiness. Something warm and wonderful rushes through me, like magic, but brighter. It's because I'm excited to finally be able to ask questions and actually get answers. That's all it is. Asking and answering.

"Tomorrow then," he says.

"Tomorrow."

As I watch him go, I keep reminding myself it's only about learning magic. But it feels like so much more.

CHAPTER 12

Lukas not only comes the next day but comes when I'd usually be asleep. He's much too chipper for the early hour. If my own anticipation of him coming and teaching more hadn't woke me extra early this morning, I'd think his sunny personality was wrong. Instead, it brightens me even more.

"You must be serious about helping if you're here this early."

"Course I am. I've had years of practice. You only have about six weeks."

My throat falls to the pit of my stomach. And here I was hoping for something a little more... There isn't anything to hope for except learning and surviving. "Thanks for the reminder."

"Wish I could say sorry, but I'm not. You may have power and strength, but you don't have the training, knowledge, and experience needed with it. Surviving long isn't likely unless we change that."

The thought of my death flashes through my mind. "When you put it like that..."

"We should practice. And no getting sidetracked today," he says, like we both need the reminder. "What spells do you already know?"

"Not many. Mostly things I saw father do, or things I suppose I wanted bad enough. My hair spell you saw yesterday." I shrug. "I don't really understand how most spells work and why I can do some things but not others."

"We'll start there then," he says. "The spells you can cast depend on your knowledge and power you have. Your spells have probably been working fairly well since you have a lot of power. But could be better since you don't have the knowledge that goes with them."

"When I hexed Edward, why was it so effective? I didn't know what I was doing. I was only more frightened than I've ever been. The spell was a reaction. Never used it before, yet it was entirely effective."

"You must have tapped into your power. Your emotions sent you into survival mode."

"Survival mode?"

"Instinct, if you will. Everyone has a natural sense of self-preservation. But it can only take you so far. Knowledge is key. And using barriers like we talked about, like women wearing gloves, play into that knowledge."

"So spells are affected not only by knowledge one has, but also by barriers?"

"Yes. Distance also weakens them."

"What about the colors of spells? Do they mean anything?" I ask.

"Yes and no."

"You're a very clear teacher."

He laughs. "Only because you didn't let me finish."

Good point.

"There isn't a straight answer," he says. "Colors mean various things to different people." He flicks out a spell of green tinted with yellow and swirled with blue. "This is nothing but a flash of magic colored by my emotions. What emotions do you think they are just from looking at it?"

Green, blue, and yellow, just like bruises. "Pain or sadness, yet that doesn't seem to reflect your mood."

"For me they mean happiness. Green grass, blue sky, yellow sun. A warm, sunny day spent with someone I care about." He clears his throat and releases the color. "But it illustrates my point. We're very different in our emotions, and how we perceive things. It changes what colors our magic is."

Much cheerier thought. Does that mean my magic will always be darker than his?

He continues. "But it can change over time. Since your feelings aren't always the same, you won't always produce the same-colored spells. And likewise, you may find two people can cast spells which look almost exactly alike if they have similar views and feelings."

"If the color of spells comes from feelings, it makes sense they would change." My own feelings have been ripped, yanked, and pulled into all sorts of new places lately. Perhaps they won't always be dark?

"Exactly. Also, since mood also affects it, the color can change or be tinted with another color even if the person's perspective of the spell itself hasn't changed."

"That's why father's spells were always tinted with red when he was angry."

"Red is a very common color to pop up with anger, but it can change from person to person and day to day. My anger might be black this morning, but red tonight. Though it usually changes more over a longer period of time. Or I knew a lady who would have yellow tints to her spells when she was angry, even though that color usually comes up when people are happy. There are more possibilities than there are spell casters. How about an example?"

"That'd be fantastic."

"Cast an image of whatever you like and I'll duplicate it."

The first thing that comes to mind is the necklace I'm wearing. It's simple enough, casting light to look similar to it, though the light is just a transparent replication of the real thing. Perhaps with more practice it would get better. Lukas smiles at the sight before stepping closer to get a better look at it. After a moment, he duplicates my spell, with some subtle changes.

"What do you notice?" he asks.

"Your spell has red tints, but you don't seem angry. Why are they there?"

His gaze is so intense; I want to look away but can't bring myself to break the connection.

"Do you really want to know?" His voice is husky. The red in his spell grows darker, deeper.

Oh my. "Perhaps I shouldn't delve into your personal feelings just yet." And I'm not sure I want to delve into mine either. This strange power coursing through me is unfamiliar, almost like magic, but the warmth carries something entirely different. And while it's not entirely unwelcome, it's not going to save my life during the tournament.

He gives one of his small, powerful smiles, and that power turns to hot water, making me want to melt onto the floor. "Not yet, then. Maybe you'd like to try casting a spell right now, and we can talk about the colors in it."

I keep my breathing steady, despite how difficult it is. "Perhaps later. I'm famished. Don't you think we should break for lunch? Otherwise, my spells will all be tainted with hungry emotions."

"Well then," he says, voice still husky, "we should eat and then continue practice. It'll be easier on a full stomach anyway."

Right now, it seems anything but easy. I nod, not trusting myself to speak. What is going on with me? Why am I reacting like this?

Without another word, I charge for the kitchen and quickly pull lunch together. We eat in silence. An awkward silence at first, but it shifts over time. He winks at me before tilting his head to the side and crossing his eyes. I laugh, and more of the strange tension dissipates. By the time we finish, I'm starting to feel more like myself again.

As we clean up, the strange tension tries to creep back in. I shove it away. I don't want whatever it is interfering with my learning. It's not the time for that old, fake Cynthia to come back. Though this feels much more real and intense than anything I ever tried to fake. All the same, it's not time for games. I've got to learn this.

The hours flow smoothly, just like the new spells coming from me. It's hard work that takes a lot of thought and concentration, but Lukas is a good teacher. He's patient and kind and always has a smile lingering nearby, even when I struggle to make a spell work the first several times. What would my sisters think of him?

Finally, he says, "It's late. Later than I thought. I should be going."

I wish it wasn't. His company has been too enjoyable for it to be time for him to leave. But it is late. The realization sends me yawning.

He laughs. "Yup. It's definitely past time for me to go."

Waking did come too early this morning. But… "Are we going to practice again tomorrow? At the same time?"

"I think we should."

It will be worth getting up early again. "Thank you for all your help today."

"I'm happy to. Be sure and rest up tonight. You need to replenish your magic."

"It goes down?"

"Just like you need to rest after running, you need to rest after using magic. It will regenerate itself, but time and rest helps."

"Will it grow more powerful over time then?"

"No. What you have is all you ever will have, unless…"

"Unless what?"

"Unless you take someone else's magic." I don't know if I like the sound of that. He asks, "Do you remember the sacrifice at the tournament?"

I remember that. And how Edward tried to steal blood. My magic. The memory is still ripe with fear. I give a wary nod.

"That's how you gain more. You take someone else's blood, their magic. The more you take, the more you gain. Their magic becomes a part of the person who took it, so their overall power increases."

Serena mentioned that it worked like this, but I only worried about it in terms of owners. I almost hate to ask, "Does the Grand Chancellor usually do sacrifices at the tournament?

"Not usually." The reply eases the tugging at the back of my mind until he adds, "Always. And he is always the one to do a sacrifice at their council meetings, too."

The thought makes me want to smack the Grand Chancellor with a hex. "How can Zade sit through that?"

"I don't know."

A creak sounds somewhere close. Strange house noises. I don't know how long it will take me to get used to them.

"Did you hear that?" Lukas says.

A chill runs through me. "I did, but I thought it was just the house. I'm not accustomed to it."

He stands there, head cocked to the side. I keep quiet as he listens, and I listen, too. I strain for any sound that would explain the chill in me. But there's nothing. Perhaps it was just the house. It takes a few moments longer, but he seems to come to the same conclusion I do. His face relaxes.

He says, "I really shoul—"

The window shatters, an amber light breaking through it. Glass flies through the room, slicing my body. I spin away from the onslaught. Lukas grabs my arm and hurtles me down the hall in front of him. Without further prompting, I run for the front door. What is happening? Who is attacking us? I rush out the door, Lukas close behind. Flashes of amber, violet, and magenta chase after us, lighting the dark of night.

CHAPTER 13

I'm running, pushing myself as fast as I can to get away until suddenly I realize Lukas isn't behind me. I stop and see him waiting just outside the house. I skitter back to him. "What are you doing?"

"Go," he calls out, a vivid jade light flashing from his hand toward the house.

"And leave you here alone? We're staying together."

"But they could—"

"I'm not leaving you."

He growls, but the corners of his mouth are slightly turned upward seeming to indicate that as much as he's miffed with me, he's grateful I'm loyal. "Come on."

After shooting another jade spell, this one leaving a faint wall in the street, he leads me to a nearby house. We hunker behind it, hiding from direct sight of the still-open door. "I'm going to try to find out who's attacking. As soon as I do, or if they discover where we are before that, we run that way." He points down another dark alley. "Got it?"

I nod. Running is easy; it's when you're caught that's difficult.

"Better. They're coming at us hard."

He peeks around the corner. I stare at him, jealous of his being able to see everything taking place. Except, there's no reason I can't as well. He never said I couldn't. I brush close to him, just so we can stay in the shadows, his warmth seeping into me, and peek around the corner. I dig my feet into the pebble-covered ground with a crunch, ready to run.

A moment later, fuchsia lights soar from the house. They follow our path straight down the porch and front lane until they hit the street, smashing into Lukas's spell with a splat. The attacking spell slams against the green shield a few times, whittling away a little more pink each time until it's gone.

Though they won't know exactly where we're located, the tension coiled in my muscles keeps me ready to run or react at any moment.

A warlock exits the house, hooded and cloaked in black, just like those who attacked Zade at the ball. Blast! Why one of them? Another warlock follows him out, hooded as well, but something about the shape of his build is familiar. I grip Lukas's arm.

After the two warlocks converse, the first casts a few spells, greens and blues and pinks, but nothing moves toward us. I bend my knees slightly, ready to run the moment that changes. But it doesn't. Instead, he returns inside, the spells flashing after him.

"What's he doing? Why didn't he look for us?"

Lukas scoffs. "Magic makes things too easy. Why hunt for something when you can make a spell do it for you?"

"But your spell stopped him. He couldn't find us."

"Maybe." He's watching the lights flashing inside the house, eyes tight. "Maybe not. We're not going to find out any more than we already have. Let's go."

I glance back at the house. "That would be—" An orange-red spell zips out of the house, hurling straight for us.

CHAPTER 14

Lukas shoves me to the ground. My hands catch my fall, jagged pain screaming up my wrists, scraping my palms against the dirt and rocks. I bite my lip to keep from calling out and turn just in time to see Lukas cast another jade spell, stopping the light. Stopping it only paces from us. But the orange spell hovers right outside his wall, not bounding itself to pieces like the others, the glowing light a beacon to us.

"Run," he says.

As I stand, I tell him, "Not without you."

"Tracking spell. It's hunting you down."

"If it's tracking me, running away won't do any good."

He grunts.

"Tell me how to help." Behind the jade and orange spells, someone exits the house. "Now."

His eyes close, face tightening as the orange spell presses closer to his. "Disguise yourself. Focus your magic. Picture someone else you know well, anyone else. Wrap that person around yourself with your magic."

Do it now is implied so forcefully, I jolt into action. I close my eyes and picture the first person that comes to mind. Bethany. I concentrate until her image appears as full and real as I can. Lukas grunts. The warlock has to be getting closer. I wrap the image of Bethany around me and let my magic flow to it.

"Perfect," Lukas says, his voice no longer strained.

I open my eyes. The orange red spell is shifting aimlessly through the area wandering away from us. Though I fear it, at least it's not right next to us still. And Lukas is different somehow. Taller.

"We've got to run quietly." His voice is low.

The warlock who attacked is nowhere to be seen but must be close by. Did he spot us when the spells were flying around only moments ago? He must have. I run in the direction Lukas pointed to, putting my feet down as carefully as I can while still moving fast, trying not to make more noise. He hurries after me, but is it enough? A warlock, especially one armed with a spell, may catch up to us if he discovers which way we went.

I put a hand on my side, pressing into the pain. I push myself to run faster, but Bethany's thin legs don't respond the way I'm accustomed.

"I'm cloaking us, but if he has backup, it won't be enough." He gently touches my shoulder as we both jog on. A flash of orange flares close by. They're catching up to us. "Can you keep going?"

If I have to. I don't waste breath on a response, just push myself harder. Lukas leads us through the streets, weaving around buildings. At one point we see another warlock who gives us a strange look, but doesn't bother us. That's when Lukas stops us. I gasp for breath.

"We're drawing more attention to ourselves by running now. I think we've lost them." He rubs the palm of his hand across his forehead. "I told you people were trying to attack you. You shouldn't have waited for me."

That doesn't dignify a response. Things turned out well enough. "What do we do now? Is the house unsafe?"

"I don't know. Probably. We should find somewhere to stay for the night."

"We?"

"I'm not leaving you alone after that."

I want to protest that I'm perfectly capable of handling myself, except if he hadn't been there, I wouldn't have escaped. Even if I could have run away, it never would have crossed my mind to use magic to hide myself like this. What if he had left a few minutes sooner? A chill bounds through me. "Where will we go?"

He runs a finger across the side of his glasses. "I don't know. We could go to where I'm staying, but they may know about it already."

It's not something I want to suggest, but what other options do we have? "I stayed in an alley behind garbage the first night in town. Would that be safe enough?"

"I don't like the idea of staying outside."

"How is it any different from staying inside?"

"It's cold for one thing. And we'll be vulnerable out in the open. We could stay at a different hotel."

"Unless they come around asking for you. You look distinctly different than others around here," I counter. "Of course you could change your appearance, too."

"Which would work well until I need that energy for defending us against an attack. We'll stay away from people."

"Which is another reason to go to the alley. No one found me, or bothered me there, unlike what just happened while we were *inside the house*. It's not like we have anywhere else to go, and I think we're close by."

He takes off his glasses and rubs his eyes before putting them back on. "I suppose we don't have any other options."

"One question. Do I have to stay disguised as my sister?"

"That's who you are? One of your sisters? She doesn't look much like you."

"She looks the most different out of all my sisters."

"Ah. Well, you should stay disguised as her. Now that you're wearing it, it shouldn't take much more magic to keep it in place, and we don't know how long they're going to be looking for you using that tracking spell, hoping you let your guard down."

"Being Bethany isn't so bad, I suppose. For now." Though I think I'd be happier if it included not only looking like her, but getting to be back in a warm cozy house and with my sisters.

I lead him to the alley. Nothing looks different from when I left it, except there's less trash in the tin. Thankfully. We hunker behind it, trying not to touch anything. Once there, we sit side by side, huddled together for warmth. The night air is chill. At least it isn't raining.

"Can I heal that for you?"

I'd almost forgotten the pain in my hands until he said something. The damage is easily seen though, and with the stinging that radiates up my arm, I don't know how I could have forgotten. Trying not to wince, I say, "Yes, please."

He gently places his hands beneath my own, both of our palms up. The warmth is immediate, the faint, dark blue light encompassing my palms taking not just the sting away, but also bringing heat that feels nothing like healing. When they're completely restored, he pulls his hands from mine.

"Thank you."

After a quick nod at me, he turns toward the street, peeking over the tins.

"Do you think they'll find us?" I ask.

"If I did, I wouldn't have come."

That's mostly reassuring. "Who do you think they are? The warlocks wore cloaks like the others who attacked Zade at the ball."

"A group devoted to keeping things the way they are."

Meaning warlocks who want me dead. Though I know that actually living through it, in a place I thought I was safe no less, makes me shake with more than just the cold.

Drips splatter on me, slow at first, but quickly increasing.

"Fantastic," I say. "Perhaps this spot is cursed to rain whenever someone uses it."

Lukas gives a hint of a smile. "Do you mind if I do something to block the rain?"

"Why haven't you already?"

"Didn't think of it until you said something. My thoughts are stuck elsewhere..."

I glance over his soaked clothing. "It must have been somewhere pretty heavy."

"Indeed."

It's a wonder I'm not drowning in heavy thoughts too after the night we've had. "My sister takes more after Serena than I do when it comes to body fat. I'm freezing. I'll feel more sympathy for her next time she asks me to find more blankets or start a fire. Now would be a good time to keep us from the rain." And I'm most curious to see how he's going to keep us dry.

He peeks over the tins. "We'll have to hunker down more. We don't want the spell to be spotted."

This does not seem like a good plan. I glance around at the dirt and rocks. At least there isn't any refuse on the ground. I flip over and lay on my belly. At least if I get something on me, I'll be able to see it.

Lukas follows suit. A dark silver light flashes from him and becomes shaped like an umbrella over our heads. It hovers above us just as a real umbrella would, only no one has to hold it, and I see through it to the rain splattering down. I twist around and watch as the drips splat against the faint light.

"You like it," Lukas says.

"Who wouldn't like it?" Serena wouldn't. Oh, she'd be grateful for the opportunity to be dry, but she'd prefer a real umbrella. How many other women in Chardonia are like her? If most of them are, will my doing magic in front of them make them more or less likely to embrace what we can do? What warlocks have taken away from us? "Will they see it from the street?"

"They shouldn't. It's down low enough and it's pretty dark," he says. "Sorry I don't have a coat to give you this time. I don't want to cast too many spells and wear myself out in case we're found. Otherwise I would do that."

"It's all right." My voice is taking on the mumble that comes with nearing sleep. No longer caring about my clothes, I roll over to get more comfortable, and I relax my head against my hands. "This is nice. Or rather, as nice as it can be when one is chased out of their house by warlocks who want to kill you."

"Which brings us to the point that I'm not seeing the nice part."

My eyes give a heavy blink, unconcerned with my trying to keep them open as I watch the rain splatter on the softly glowing light above us. "I've never been around someone who does magic so openly like this. Father mostly did hexes. Zade's better, but he tends not to cast spells often. I think he's worried about Serena because the few times I've been with him away from my sister, he seems much more liberal with his magic use. But still, it's not like this." I gesture at the steely light above us, faint silver shinning through it. "This is peaceful and calm. Something I want to be a part of. I like it."

His voice sounds distant as I close my eyes. "I guess we'll have to spend a lot more time together."

That sounds very nice.

CHAPTER 15

As cold and wet as the night started, it only gets worse, even with Lukas's spell. After initially drifting off, the temperature dropped further, making it difficult to stay asleep. It's almost as difficult as the first night I was here. Only this time, Lukas helps keep me warm and dry with his spell and company. Still not a place I want to ever spend the night again. I thought I missed home before, but it's nothing compared to how much I miss it now. At last, morning finally arrives.

"Do you think it's safe to return?" Please say yes.

"I don't know. You should probably stay here while I check it out."

"I'm not remaining here while you face danger meant for me. It's my fault. I need to go along to see what's happened because of me."

He huffs, and I know he wants to argue. His eyes stare me down like he's trying to use all of his will power to make me change my mind. It doesn't work. There's no reason I should stay here while he faces whatever has been left behind on his own. If something happens to him, it will be on me. Besides, how would I know what happened to him? I wouldn't. And then I would eventually go looking for him, and the same would happen to me. At least this way, we'll be together.

To my relief, he says, "If you're going to come, might as well get rid of your disguise. We'll see if they're still looking for you before we do anything else."

It would be nice to be myself again, though I'm already missing the small link I have to Bethany.

"Be ready to change back and run if you see a spell coming toward you," he adds.

With that note of encouragement, I start to follow his words. Until I realize, I don't really know how to do that.

"Um…" This is so embarrassing. I was willing to sign up for the tournament, but I can't even do simple spells. What was I thinking?

"Did you change your mind?"

"It's not that. I—I don't know how to change back to myself."

Instead of laughing, he says, "That should have been my first thought. If I wasn't here to help you, what would you try?"

I shrug. "Perhaps try what I did to cast the spell, but the opposite? This time, picturing myself?"

He beams. "Exactly. See, you don't even need my help. And if it went long enough, your magic would wear itself out, returning you to your original form. Yours just takes longer to wear out because you're so powerful."

It feels good that I got it right and that his confidence supports me, but I should have figured it out on my own. I've got to think through spells more. Not only is it finally acceptable for me to do them, but if I want to stay alive at the tournament, I have to.

It only takes a moment to repeat the process of changing my appearance, this time picturing myself. I keep my eyes open and watch the multicolored spell surround me. One moment I'm looking slightly up at Lukas. The next we're at eye level.

"You're a quick learner."

His words fill me as we hover at the edge of the street, ready to run, hoping it's not needed. When no spells threaten, he motions me to follow him. "We're going to Xyer first, to see if he's heard anything."

This is a good chance to get to know who else is protecting my life. I keep my steps evenly matched behind him. It's much easier now that we're not being chased.

Even though a tracking spell didn't manifest when I changed back, tension plagues my muscles. Worry and strain exude from each of Lukas's quick steps. My own stride tightens to match his. It doesn't take us long to find Xyer at a hotel and inform him of what is going on. Even less time for him to be ready to join us.

Though I've seen him briefly before, this is the first time I've really gotten a good look at him. He's tall of course, like all Envadi, but thinner than Zade with brown eyes and brown hair that leave him rather average looking. He could blend in easily just about anywhere if it weren't for his height.

The walk back to the house is long, both in terms of time and the route we take, weaving through streets making sure no one is following.

I don't know what good I can do, but I grab hold of the magic in my core, ready for anything. The thought makes me feel as if I'm being silly. If I can't figure out how to change back to myself, how am I going to handle stopping a hex, or my life being threatened repeatedly at the tournament? Perhaps I've made the worst decision yet. And I probably should have stayed in the alley. But there's no turning back now. At the very least, father was a good example of how to hit and make it hurt.

The thought makes me ill.

I pull my magic back some, but keep it close enough to still do… something if needed. Once we're behind the house across the street, we carefully peek around the corner. Last time, this led to spells fighting in a way I'd never seen before. Despite how fascinating it was, this time I'm hoping things are calmer.

No one is outside and nothing looks any different. But who knows if they're lying in wait or not.? Or if they've left some nasty surprise behind? Lukas and Xyer watch it longer than I have patience for. I eventually give up to look around the house we're crouching behind. Hopefully, whoever lives here doesn't mind my snooping. They shouldn't because there's nothing back here but rocks and dirt.

Finally, Xyer starts forward. Lukas motions for me to follow. We slink across the street to the front of the house and stop at the boardwalk. I stand close to them but just a little behind. As much as I want to be here and helping, I'm not ready to fully throw myself into the fray.

Lukas casts a spell that flies into the house and keeps his hand up in the air. And then we wait. And wait some more. I want to ask what Lukas is doing, but his eyes are focused and his forehead is wrinkled as if whatever he's doing is intense, so I keep quiet. The light continues to flow from him into the house. I wish I knew what was going on in there.

What is his spell doing and finding? If there was someone waiting for us, wouldn't they have come out and attacked us? Something would have happened, as eager as they were to attack last night. All this waiting and spell casting seems unnecessary. His arm must be growing weary, staying in the air like that. Another minute goes by. What is taking so long? Why doesn't Xyer seem fazed by the wait like I am?

I roll my shoulders and glance around the neighborhood. There's no one about, but that has been typical with this neighborhood. At least from the little I've been here, it seems that way. Perhaps I've scared them all off with my snooping. Or perhaps all the spells from last night convinced them to hide.

Suddenly, there's a loud crash from inside the house. Lukas is holding steady, Xyer focused on the house. I'm riveted to the spot, ready to attack anything that comes out. Not that I know exactly what I'd attack them with, but something. Maybe smoothing down their hair will be random enough to startle them, at least slow them down?

There's not another sound, but my magic is still jumping about inside me, itching to be released. I'm ready to give up and ask what is going on when the spell comes crashing back to his hand and disappears as he lowers it.

"It's safe." The dark circles under his eyes are bigger than before the spell, and guilt pricks at me that I've been standing here thinking this is all for naught.

"Your spell told you that?"

"Yes. It checks not only for people, but for hexes that may have been left behind."

"What was the crash? It didn't sound safe."

He winces. "A hex that was left. I disabled it."

Xyer and Lukas start for the house, and I trail after them.

"Disabled it? What do you mean? And what type of hex was it? And how can someone leave a hex behind?"

Xyer cuts away from us, going around to the back while I follow Lukas to the door. He pushes the door all the way open but doesn't go inside. "You sure ask a lot of questions for a Chardonian girl."

I bristle. "I'm not just a Chardonian girl. I'm a warlock now."

"Hey, I didn't mean that as a bad thing. It's a good thing. A real good thing." The intensity of his gaze not only holds truth, but something warming.

"Sorry, it's been a tense twenty-four hours, and I'm tired, hungry, and not in the mood to have people trying to attack me."

"No, I'm sorry. Let's not be tired, hungry and attacked again."

"Agreed."

Together, we head into the house. It's just as he says. No one comes out and attacks us, and no spells go off. There is a big mess in the sitting room. Couches are turned over, stuffing pulled out, chairs broken, and windows shattered.

Xyer meets us in the hall. "Looks clear for now. I'm going to secure outside and stand watch there while I send a note to Zade."

Before he goes, I say, "Thank you."

"Just doing my duty."

Once he's gone, we move back to the sitting room, and Lukas says, "This should be fun to clean. With the risks going on, I can't waste my energy on spelling it."

"Let's save it for later. I'm too tired and hungry to clean now." I yawn, emphasizing my point, too tired to even note his sarcasm. "Is there someone we can report this to?"

He gives me a look.

The look has a point, except it feels like there should be something done. A course of action that would fit the situation. "What do warlocks usually do if their house is broken into? You can't tell me nothing would be done."

"Sure, if it was a regular warlock, they'd call in a law officer, but for you? It's the worst thing we could do. They'd be more likely to blame you for it. Disqualify you from the tournament at best. At worst, well, being tarnished would be the least of your worries."

"The least? What more could they do?"

"Imprison or kill you."

Nothing ever turns out the way I think it should. "So even though I'm a warlock, I still have no rights."

He gives a little frown. "I thought you understood that already."

"I do. Really I do. It's just—" I growl. "This is ridiculous. I simply want to be like a warlock in more than just name alone."

"It's ugly," he says, pulling a chair up off the floor. "But we'll get there. It's just not going to be easy or fast."

I collapse on the chair. "I know."

He kneels in front of me and takes my hand. "After what I saw last night, you're the bravest woman I know. You can do this. You competing in the tournament is going to cause trouble, but you'll also be able to open the eyes of many Chardonians as to what a woman can really do. It will be a start."

His touch is reassuring. And makes me feel a little guilty for complaining in the first place. "I'm sorry. It's just harder than I expected it to be."

"It's all right."

For a moment, it's silent. I should say something, but I don't know what. Perhaps I should at least take my hand away from his, but I don't want to. Except I really am hungry and tired.

"Perhaps we should eat and rest."

"Wise plan." He stands, our hands dangling apart. "And we have to figure out a way to protect you in the meantime."

"I thought you already were protecting me."

"They're upping the threat. We have to up your protections."

Does that mean I'm going to see more of him? More than just for a little training? I like that idea. I don't like the idea of being under a warlock's protection all the time, though. It's what I just escaped from. If I was strong enough to protect myself, this wouldn't be a problem.

"Is this house safe to stay in, or should I relocate?"

He shrugs. "Maybe. I'll talk to Zade. We'll keep a closer watch on things for now. I'm worried. No matter if we stay here or move, they'll still attack. For now, I think we'd better stay here where we have defensive spells in place and increase them. Xyer's probably already started on some of it."

"If you teach me, I'll help with them."

"Deal."

"First, I'm going to make something to eat," I say.

"Need help?"

"I can manage. Thank you."

"I'll talk to Xyer, see what he thinks we should do, then. Holler when it's ready?" His tone is sincere and nice. Not at all demanding.

"Certainly."

As I sleepwalk to the kitchen, it's difficult not to think on how close the attempt was to succeeding, and how close things will likely continue to be. Close enough it may never matter what spells I learn for the tournament.

CHAPTER 16

It's only been two days, but naturally, Zade is already here, responding to the message Xyer sent about the current situation. The way he's been silently storming about for the last few minutes proves nothing good is about to come. Even though I'm the one keeping my distance from my sisters, I still wish Serena had joined him. I miss them. And they would have helped to buffer his temper.

"I don't know why I helped with this insane plan. Why did you have to sign up?" Zade says, his words as hard as the look on his face.

It's difficult to remember any rational reason I had when he's bearing down on me like this. I shrug.

"That's it? You don't even know more than enough to shrug at me?" Zade says. "Are you insane? Do you know how many people are going to try to kill you now? That already have?" He turns on Lukas. "And you! Why did you have to insist on me helping? Why did you help her with this nonsense? You want her dead?"

"This isn't his fault," I say, anger rising to match his.

"It's fine," Lukas says to me, much calmer than either Zade or I. To Zade, he says, "You know I don't want her dead, but she's doesn't belong to anyone. She has the power to choose. We both agreed on that when you helped secure the letters for her. I won't even attempt to take that away."

"At the expense of her life?" Zade rubs the back of his neck. "Serena is going to kill me."

"That's what this is really about?" I say. "Serena being upset? I love my sister, but she is no longer my owner."

"It's not like that," Zade says.

That he's practically my brother-in-law and was the one to give Serena her freedom, but is still treating me this way, burns a white-hot rage deep inside. I don't hide it. I let its flames crackle my words. "Clearly it is."

Zade's jaw tightens.

"She's right," Lukas says. "If this were any other woman whose sister you weren't courting, you'd do everything you could to help, not hinder. It's why you helped before. Why you know this is right. It's what you're here for."

"I don't want to be here," Zade yells. "I want to take Serena and her family out of this stupid country. I want the woman I love protected. I want her family, and mine, safe. Instead I'm stuck here with people who make everything worse."

He stomps out of the house, slamming the door behind him.

His anger, more righteous and founded than mine, is like splashing icy water on my own. And now I feel worse, guilt mangling my insides. I can't take back my entry into the tournament. Not that I want to, yet it feels like I'm ruining the good Zade has done. Made things so much worse.

"He really loves her. He's worried about her and your entire family," Lukas says.

Thinking on Zade's words before he stormed off, I say, "Perhaps more than I originally suspected."

Lukas takes off his glasses and rubs the bridge of his nose. If I wore glasses, I think I might do the same.

The silence that follows leaves me time to think more on not just what Zade said, but the implications. "Even if Zade is supposed to be here to help, I don't think it's going well. For anyone. Look at him now. He's been here fighting longer, almost a year. He knows how hard and futile it all is. How can we beat a system so overwhelming that even the best get pulled under by its weight?"

He reaches up and lightly brushes my cheek. "We share the weight."

My breath catches.

The front door creaks open. Lukas and I jump apart as it closes. His glasses skitter onto the floor with the movement. Zade walks in as Lukas crouches to the floor, hand fumbling for his spectacles.

"What are you doing?" Zade says.

"Dropped my glasses." Lukas's expression is so calm and innocent, like his glasses really just accidentally fell, leaving me wondering whether or not he felt anything that I just felt. Perhaps he only wants to help, and I'm conjuring the other feelings all on my own. I sink onto the couch as Lukas finally finds his glasses, and Zade slumps into the chair across from me.

"I'm sorry," Zade says. "I shouldn't take my temper out on you both. I just had to keep everything so tightly hidden when I got here, and now you both know just about everything going on. It was hard to keep it in place like I should."

"It's fine," I say. "I shouldn't have become so angry either."

"No, it's not. Mom would tan my hide if she knew I treated you both like that."

"I like your mom already," Lukas says.

Zade smiles, but there's no real warmth, and it quickly fades. "Cynthia, are you sure you want to risk your life, not only by being in the tournament itself, but dealing with more incidents like the one two nights ago?"

It's almost tempting to step down. "I know it puts pressure on you and my sisters. I know that's exactly what I was trying to avoid. I don't want to make things worse. But, Zade, I can't with-draw. I need to be there. People need to see what I can do. Women need this. I need this."

His shoulders sag. "I know you do. I know. It's just…"

"It's a lot of pressure."

"For us all."

The silence that follows is heavy, fraught with hexes and threats to come.

Lukas finally breaks the silence, his words loud and strong. "I'll be here. I already told her I'll teach her whatever will help keep her alive. And I'll do whatever I can to protect her."

His words light through me, both warm and cold. A flame of emotions I don't know what to do with.

"I'm grateful for your help. Xyer has pledged his help as well," Zade says. "But as we've already seen, we'll need more protection. We should move into Thomas's house."

Fantastic. Just fantastic. That place holds only memories of me trying to convince Serena she was doing the right thing when she should have been running from it all. At least things changed after Thomas died. "How soon?"

"Today, if possible. I'm sending a few more men there as soon as they can come over from Envado. Lukas, if you have anyone from Chryos you trust that could help, I'd recommend getting them, too. We have seven warlocks protecting Serena's house, and it's kept them safe. The girls don't even know there have been threats on their lives yet. I'd suggest trying to do something similar here."

"Is it really necessary to have so many lives devoted to keeping me safe?" Both look at me like I've gone crazy. "It's not that I don't appreciate it, it's just that it feels silly, and honestly, I'm guilty. Seven warlocks watching over just little old me. I don't want to be a problem."

"We're trying to keep you safe so you can be the solution to the problem," Lukas says.

Can I really be a solution to the problem? The thought stuns me silent.

"More warlocks are arriving from Chryos soon," Lukas continues. "Some won't be any use, but a few I trust to help keep her safe. I just don't know how much I trust some with getting close to the situation."

"More hands would help. We'll have to keep them busy and paired with those we trust more."

"I think we can manage that."

And I'll have to manage doing nothing while they all protect my life. The thought leaves a bitter taste in my mouth.

CHAPTER 17

True to his word, Zade helps me move to Thomas's old house. It's big, cold, and empty. I take the same room as before because I know where it is, and want to spend less time bothering them while I try to find something else, but I hope nothing haunts me while here.

Lukas and several other guards set up rooms in various other places spread through the house. Zade also sets up a temporary room but warns us that he doesn't know how much he'll be around, quickly proving his point by leaving immediately after. Other warlocks should be coming soon, filling the house a little more. It's difficult to think this was all because of me.

Part way through bringing supplies in from the wagon, a rider pulls up. After he swings down from his horse, Lukas greets him with a firm handshake. "Conrad, you made it."

"The border guards gave me some guff, but otherwise, it was just all the hours in the saddle that took so long."

I want to tell him to come in and recover from his journey, but I haven't been introduced. And I don't really know who he is except that since his skin is a few shades darker than Lukas's. I assume he's likely from Chryos. He doesn't have glasses, though, and is slightly shorter and built thicker. His eyes are a piercing hazel that seem to see right through me.

"Glad you didn't have more problems. How are Arthur and Emma? They always claim everything is fine."

"Just like them," Conrad says. "Emma is bossing around everyone who comes anywhere near her and stuffing them full of her good cooking to make up for it, as usual. Arthur, though, I think he misses having you around."

Lukas's lips turn downward slightly. "He still plans on coming?"

"Doubt the crazed Grand Chancellor himself could keep him away."

No matter what's expected of me, there's no keeping silent after that. "We should take this discussion inside."

"Sorry, miss. I forget what things are like here." His tone is so sincere, it makes me wonder what it'd be like to live in the world he does.

As we walk toward the front doors carrying the last of the supplies with us, Lukas says, "Cynthia, this is a friend from Chryos, Conrad Wilkins. He's going to be helping us through the tournament."

"That's right. I was just coming to watch, but when Lukas told me what you needed, I was happy to do something more useful."

"I appreciate it."

The men continue chatting as I let them continue on ahead. One more person whose safety is in question because of me. Yet, it also means one more person who believes in what I'm trying to do enough to protect me with their life. I hope I can live up to the challenge.

* * *

A FEW HOURS after Zade leaves, a knock sounds on the door. Despite the protections on the house, the fact that Lukas is outside with several other warlocks, including Lukas's friend from Chryos, Conrad, and my own growing knowledge of magic, my hands go icy. It's difficult to pretend the uncertainty of who's there doesn't bother me like an unwanted spell. At least years of practice pretending have been good for something.

When I get to the door, I do the spell Lukas taught me yesterday. I focus on being able to see beyond the door and release the spell. The transparent white light squirms its way to the door and washes over it, making the door transparent for me, but not for whoever's on the other side, showing them through a shine of white. Perfect spell for watching for trouble, but this time it's not trouble. Waverly!

I release the spell and throw the door open with a squeal. "What are you doing here?"

Her smile lights up the lonely places my sisters haven't been able to fill for the last week. "I'm here to help, of course. You didn't think Serena would leave you all alone to deal with this, did you? And even if she hadn't sent me, I would have come anyway."

I squeal again. "I've never been so glad to see someone. Come in, come in!"

It's then I realize she has a trunk on the ground beside her.

She says, "I hope you don't mind if I stay with you a while."

"Are you teasing me? There's no one but overly serious warlocks in this place. I need you here."

We take her things inside and quickly get chatting about how things are back home. Oh, how I miss playing with my girls! I wish I could sneak away to see them, but the need to protect them is stronger than my desire.

"I heard you've entered the tournament." Waverly says.

I keep my expression neutral and keep a close eye on hers. "Zade tell you?"

"I wrestled it out of him." She winks. "Finally made sense why he's been so uptight lately."

"Did he tell Serena?"

"No, and he made me promise not to tell either, but I'm not holding that same promise to you. You need to let her know what's going on."

Do I ever. It's just the last thing I want to do. "I can't write her something like that. She still doesn't have a clue that women can even do magic. Will she even believe me if I tell her? I have to talk to her in person."

"There are no plans for her to come here. She's keeping away at your request, and Zade's insistence. Any thoughts on going to see her?"

I want to. Oh, how I want to. "I can't put them at risk like that."

"Then you have to write her."

I shake my head as I lead her to a room close to mine. "She'll never believe me."

"Maybe, maybe not. Did you use magic for anything while you lived at home?"

"All the time."

"What for?" She unpacks her trunk, sorting her clothes into the wardrobe.

"My hair for one thing. It's frizzy and crazy if I don't smooth it out with a spell."

"No! You have amazing curls that are always well behaved."

"It's true. My locks are insanity."

She eyes my hair as if trying to find a hint of their natural state. "Perfect. When you write Serena, tell her about it. It will make more sense to her if you explain things like that. She'll understand it," Waverly says.

"She hasn't seen my real hair in years. I'm not sure she'd believe it."

"Please just try. I really think it will be best to tell her, and this will help her understand."

"I suppose." And if she doesn't believe me, well, at least I won't have to see her distaste for my magic every day. Not like what Zade has to deal with.

"Zade will probably come by sometime after he learns I've come to stay. If you can have it ready by then, he can take it directly to her. Then we won't have to worry about it getting in the wrong hands."

I nod, though still uncertain what to write. "Waverly?"

"Yes?"

"How many women in Envado do magic?"

She puts away the last of her things before turning to me, and her expression grows solemn. "Most of us. Some to a lesser degree. Some to a greater degree. But it's widely accepted."

Most? I'm not as alone as I always thought. Now that I know, I wonder how I could have gone so long without figuring out others could do it as well. And then I realize what she said.

"Us? You do magic?"

Her grin turns sly. "You don't really think Zade did everything for the ball all by himself, did you?"

What? "I—I thought he did, but now that you mention it, there were a lot of spells. Plus, he didn't do much with the planning. I just assumed someone told him what needed to be done. Serena or you."

"I can't tell you how enjoyable it was helping come up with ideas that I got to implement. That was one of the most fun things I've ever done."

"Wow. I'm feeling very…" Shocked. Surprised. "…amazed. It was one of the most fantastic things I've ever seen."

"I thought your dad locked you up so you couldn't go?"

I shrug, pretending to be nonchalant when inside I'm dying to tell her. "He did. Not just with a key, but spelled the door closed as well. It wasn't anything a little magic couldn't work around. Though I didn't get to wear the dress Katherine made me. I've been waiting for an excuse to wear it ever since."

"I wonder if we can find somewhere for you to wear it…" She looks deep in thought until her expression brightens. "Wait—were you the one who cast the spell to catch Serena?"

My bracelets suddenly seem to hold a very entertaining clink when bumped together.

"You were," she exclaims. "If it wasn't for you, she would have broken a bone or two and everything would have turned out differently."

I feel myself start to blush, so I look at the floor and shrug.

"You could have been caught. Did anyone see you use your magic then?"

"I don't think so. Everyone was riveted by the men attacking Zade and then Serena's stunt," I say. "Are they still threatening Zade?"

She shakes her head. "Zade is always under some threat or another, but the group that attacked him has stayed away. Maybe the Grand Chancellor's words did some good."

"Or the fact that he locked up my father." He never did anything good, but I can't help but wonder where he's at now.

"Perhaps." Her lips tighten.

"You don't think any of it actually helped?"

"I wish you weren't so good at reading people sometimes." She sighs. "I think there's something deeper going on. I just don't know what it is."

The thought is worrisome, especially since she's most likely correct. Whatever is going on, will it affect me? Whether or not it does, things are still going to be hard. I need to learn more.

* * *

ONCE WAVERLY IS SETTLED, we gather in my room. It's the most secluded room I can think of and my nerves are all a flutter to finally speak to another female about magic.

"What's your favorite spell?" The question pops out of my mouth like an eager surge of magic.

Her grin spreads. "There are too many favorites to count. And I'm so excited to finally have someone here I can talk to about them. It's been too long since I've been home, and no one here who knows about magic ever wants to discuss it. Zade will probably kill me when he finds I'm going crazy talking about it, but it can't be helped. I don't know how you Chardonian women stand being treated like this all the time. No offense."

"No offense here, only agreement. I can't do much to change things, but I will still try." Will it even make a difference? Who knows. "So what's one of your favorite spells?"

"This one." She holds out one hand in front of her, then waves her other across it. Purple and teal fly to her fingernails. Once the spell stops, she wiggles her newly colored nails at me. Purple with mini-sparkles at the bottoms with bigger teal sparkles fanning out across the tips.

"Incredible. And nothing like I expected." I giggle.

"Sadly, there's not much need for frivolous things here."

"True, but there should be. Can you teach it to me?"

"Love to! What color do you want? It will be influenced by your feelings, but we can adjust for that some."

Over the next few hours, she teaches me how to pick colors and focus them on my nails until they become that color. At first it's harder than I expect. Even though I see her do it, I've rarely seen colored nails and it's difficult to think about colors melding onto them. Finally, I get a variant color of blue firmly in mind, close my eyes, and push it onto my thumbnail. The result is not exactly like what Waverly showed me, but I love it. The blue, ranging from a deep midnight to a soft sky color, swirls lazily onto my nail, leaving parts of my nail still visible.

"That's great. The swirl means you need more practice getting it on there fully, but you've got the basics."

I grin. "Guess I should get the rest of them done."

Without waiting for her reply, I close my eyes and I repeat it to each of them. It grows easier to imagine pushing out the color with each one. Upon inspection, perhaps I did too well, as the nails are fully midnight blue.

Waverly laughs. "You've definitely figured it out."

"So it seems, but I think I like the swirling pattern best."

It takes another hour for me to figure out how to pull some of the color off my nails so that only varying swirled patterns remain. I don't think I'll ever go without colored nails again.

"This is fantastic. Thank you!"

"You're welcome," she replies. "You said something earlier about smoothing your hair down. How do you do that?"

The spell flows out of me with familiar ease.

Waverly oohs over it. "How did you figure that out?"

"Before I started casting it, Serena would always get in trouble for not keeping my hair properly pulled back into a bun."

"This explains why your hair was always so easy to do when I've helped with it," she says. "Your hair's natural state isn't something you should be punished for. It's not yours or Serena's fault."

Maybe she's right, but there's no way to change how father reacted to it. "In any case, the spell helped a lot with not having so many punishments."

We continue trading ideas and working together on spells. It's hard, but easier than when I was trying to do things all on my own.

"Any other secret spells you've been keeping from me?" Waverly asks.

"There is one bigger thing left. I always spelled my needle to do a good job sewing for me."

She laughs. "You actually aren't the best seamstress in your household?"

I snort. "Not hardly. I can't sew a stitch without it going crooked or making knots. Once I discovered how to spell my needle to make perfect stitches, even when I didn't know how, things got easier. I was left alone a lot more. Sometimes literally alone, by myself, but usually with the others. They were around but wouldn't really pay attention to me because they knew I was working. It was a good trick."

"I wish I would have thought of something so clever."

"Weren't you just attempting to convince me to be nicer to myself? It's the same for you. Things are different here. You get good at learning things when beatings and hexes are doled out if there's nothing done to circumvent them. Besides, you are clever. You helped with Serena's ball."

"But those are things that are taught in Envado. I didn't learn any of them on my own," she says. "In fact, how did you manage to learn to do magic on your own? Most are trained from when we're small. Occasionally, someone with magic will come along that doesn't use it. They don't figure it out on their own and need training. How did you?"

I explain the same thing I told Lukas, but my thoughts aren't on the telling. They're stuck on how two different magic users have been surprised by my teaching myself magic. It's always seemed to me that it was a product of my circumstances, except then Serena would have learned, too. She would have done even better than me, even if they say I have more magic in my blood than her. Yet, she didn't. As far as I know, there's not been another girl I know that has. What gave me the strength and curiosity to learn?

CHAPTER 18

A knock on the front door echoes down the hall, followed by the creak of it opening and Lukas calling out, "May we come in?"

We?

"We're in the sitting room," I call back.

There's the sound of two footsteps, one nimble and one heavier as I set down my plate, which is sadly bare of cookies. Lukas appears with a warlock behind him. A very tall warlock, who looks familiar. Where have I seen him?

Waverly suddenly busies herself arranging our now-empty plates on the tray.

"Waverly," the man says.

Her hand hovers over the tray, and I wonder who this man is to make her withdraw. She turns to him, a very controlled, neutral expression on her face. "Chadwick." That's who he is! Zade's manservant. "Have you been sent to force me back to Zade's?"

He looks almost… sad? "I've been sent to help with keeping you both safe."

Sent? That doesn't sound very reassuring. The way he waits, his gaze lingering on her, I keep expecting her to reply. But there's nothing from her so I do. "That's kind of you. Thank you so much. I wish I wasn't causing such a burden for everyone," so incredibly much, "but unfortunately I am, and more help would be fantastic."

"You will never be a burden."

And though his reply seems directed at me, and I believe he will protect me, I know he means Waverly. The deep, down-trodden cast to his gaze as he tries, and fails, not to stare at her twists in my chest. It would be wonderful to have someone look at me with that much emotion, though maybe in a more positive light and not such a depressed one. How I wish I knew what Waverly is thinking right now.

AFTER WAVERLY and I fed those helping watch over us, which they insisted on doing in shifts so there was always someone outside, we take up residence in my room. Feeding them was a quiet affair, not like the ruckus that usually comes with a room full of warlocks.

Waverly was most helpful getting them meals, but it was hard to miss how blatantly she walked the long way around the room instead of going the short route by him. She seemed to not notice when he needed something, though she was extra attentive to the other warlocks. They probably didn't know what, exactly, is going on with Waverly and Chadwick; I don't even know what is happening between them, yet the men still seemed to sense the tension.

Except Chadwick and Lukas. They never came in for dinner. Conrad said they weren't hungry, but it's the first time Lukas has turned down food of any kind. Presumably, he's helping Chadwick with something. And I want to help Waverly; only I'm not sure exactly how to go about it.

Waverly asks, "Can I brush your hair?"

It's not a direct way to help her but should be a good opening for conversation. "If you like."

She picks up the brush and runs it though my hair. The strokes yank in a way that stings my eyes instead of her usual gentle care. "Is something wrong?"

"Everything's fine."

The brush catches on a particularity big knot, and she tugs hard enough that I bite my lower lip to keep from calling out.

Once I've recovered enough to speak without giving away how much it hurts, I say, "Are you sure there's nothing you want to talk about? You haven't been yourself since Chadwick arrived."

She throws the brush on the nightstand and flops down on my bed. Thank my earrings.

"It is Chadwick then."

I silently wait for her to speak. It's a tactic Serena uses. Even if it seems to get results for her, it's difficult to stay silent for long. Questions leap to my mind with such persistence, it's almost impossible to not say something, anything. Just when I'm about to explode, she says, "We knew each other in Envado."

Huh. Serena's tactic did work. Though sharing thoughts about how I remember Chadwick from living at Zade's would have been much easier. "I gathered something along those lines. Did something happen?"

"Nothing happened. That's the problem."

That's as clear as my hair is straight. "What exactly didn't happen?"

She puts her hand over both her eyes. "We grew up together. He was always hanging around and I often didn't have a girlfriend to spend time with, so I would follow him around. When we grew older, everyone assumed we would marry, but then he came here with Zade and didn't come back when the tournament ended. It was strange for a while, but by the time I decided to join them, I hadn't thought much about it. Once here, things were, well, I don't know, things were just... stiff. Weird. So I've done the sensible thing. Avoided him."

"You've been avoiding Chadwick for over a year?"

"It seemed like the best option."

"But do you even like him?"

She sighs. "That's the worst part. I don't know." She looks forlorn, hands twisting together, eyes cast downward. Nothing like the Waverly I've known. "He's wonderful, but there's just nothing igniting between us. I don't know what love is supposed to feel like, but it seems like there should be more... something. But still, everyone expects it of us."

She does have expectations then, only different from the ones here. Not punishable with beatings or hexes, but not meeting expectations is clearly still difficult for her.

"It's hard when people expect something from you, and you don't know if it's what you want or not." It's my whole life. Until now. I'm finally doing what I want, and it feels so right. "I think you should keep following your feelings and not what others expect."

"Maybe you're right."

"And maybe we can talk about it again the next time it bothers you without having you torment my hair."

She laughs. "No brushing when I'm upset."

"What if I brush your hair out for the night, and you can talk about what you want, whether it's about Chadwick or something unrelated?"

"That sounds nice."

So we reverse roles, and as I run the brush through her blond hair, it's surprising how much it feels like I'm with one of my sisters.

CHAPTER 19

Lukas is across from me, a thumb hooked in his right trouser pocket as we get ready to practice. My heart feels bright and melty, like a golden spell that's gone all soft and gooey. What's wrong with me? I can't allow myself to let my feelings for him cloud my learning.

He motions to the room, one I've never been in until now. "This should be a good place to practice."

I ignore the gooey feeling inside, look around the tiny room, and focus on the task before us. "There's a lot of stuff that could be hit or broken."

"Don't worry. Nothing in here matters. Thomas didn't have any other family left to care about it and Zade said he didn't need any of it."

That makes more sense. It's tight, crammed with all sorts of items—books, medals, trophies, bags, blankets, pillows, and many other seemingly random things. There are a few pieces of jewelry scattered about, but none worth more than a passing glance.

"Still, I'd hate to have to clean up if I accidentally break something."

"It'd give you a good reason to practice a cleaning spell."

I stick my tongue out at him. The gesture is even easier and more natural than it looked when he previously did the same.

He chuckles. "I knew you were a quick learner."

"At least a clean-up spell would have practical use."

"All too true," he admits. "Let's see if you can make this a little easier for us. Focus on the room. The air in it, the space contained in it. The things it holds."

I scoff. "We just got done talking about how much stuff is in here. How am I supposed to focus on all of it?"

"Not focusing on all of it individually. All of it as a whole. How it fits in the room."

"It doesn't fit."

He shakes his head, but those lips of his turn up in a smile. "That's not the point. The point is the space."

"The space that isn't big enough to work in. We've established that."

"But we're going to change that."

"What?" His statement finally pulls my focus away from his mouth. "Change it? How can we do that?"

"Focus on the room, like I said. The air, the space, the things."

Sounds strange to me, especially with all this stuff. Still not sure I understand the concept, but I suppose I can try. I get a feel for how it is, not a cursory glance like before, but a deeper, searching gaze. Finding the pictures hanging on the walls, the thick layer of dust coating everything but the floor, the air heavy with dust. "I think I've got it."

"Good. Now take your magic and push it through the space, telling it to get wider and higher."

I pull my magic together and attempt to shove it out, but nothing happens. "This spell doesn't seem to be working."

"You're trying too hard," he says. "How did you learn spells before, without help?"

Tried everything I could think of, many of which feel too silly to try in front of him. "When possible, I'd watch warlocks casting spells. Once I had managed a few rare moments alone, I'd play with it. It usually takes at least a few months for me to get anything, unless it's really simplistic."

"Months? Why didn't you give up?"

"It was one of the few good things in my life. A rare thing I actually wanted."

"You really are amazing." Before I can stammer an appropriate response, he asks, "What's the easiest spell for you to do?"

"Smoothing out my hair so it's not a tangled, flyaway mess."

His gaze darts to my hair. "It's not a mess at all, it's always slicked back in Chardonian fashion. You must be really good at it. Or maybe it's not as bad as you think?"

I splash my magic out across my hair, pulling the slicked back spell off my locks. To further my point, I pull the pins from my hair and let it tumble down my back, past my waist. Even without a mirror, I can see some of the curly locks are scattering everywhere. Despite this he smiles.

"So it isn't well suited to Chardonian ways." He leans closer. "I like it."

Warmth shines through me. He likes it? No one ever liked it when I was young. But then, maybe it doesn't always have to be to our society's standards. Serena's hair looks good even when it's done in Envadi-style, better than the usual Chardonian style even. Perhaps the comments about my frizz had more to do with punishments than what it actually looks like?

"You are really good at it too. Perfect."

I blush. "Thank you, but how does that help right now?"

"We can use it to discover how you learn spells when not stressed. Think about what it feels like to cast it. You don't have to tell me, but I want you to remember and feel it. What did you do when you first figured it out? What do you do to cast it now?"

That first time I finally figured how to cast the spell was amazing. It always is. I think on it, how I closed my eyes and felt the air become thicker and used it to keep my hair in place. The feel of the magic streaming from me, responding to my desire. Once I figured it out, it was so simple. No other spells have ever come so easily.

"Got it."

"Good. Now take that same feeling, that push of magic, and apply it to this spell. Feel the room around you, the things in it, and then expand everything."

Somehow, the repetition is easier to do when I am alone. When there's no one around to see me fail. I try again anyway. It feels as if something starts to give, like my magic is pushing on the air outside me, but then I lose it. "I don't know. It doesn't seem to be working."

"Maybe close your eyes. Visualize it in your mind."

"I'll try." And I do but feel a little foolish, considering the circumstances. Like I'm playing a game with one of my youngest sisters instead of learning magic from a warlock. But he's not only a good warlock but nice to look at. Really nice. So I try anyway. Besides, I must figure this out, whether or not I feel silly in the process. Too much is depending on it.

Picturing the room, the things in it, and the space and walls expanding around them. The air stretching is the easy part. Getting it to actually change, much harder. I grab hold of my magic, taking it straight from my core, and attempt to let it fill the expanding space. There have been no results with that so far, so I go further by shoving it with everything I can muster.

A yelp echoes through the room.

My eyes snap open. Lukas is hovering in the air high above my head, near a ceiling that is far, far above me. I gasp, snuffing my magic. He gives another yelp as he starts to fall to the floor. A gasp escapes me with a squeak. How do I save him? This wasn't part of the lesson. He's going to crash!

I jump forward hoping I can at least break his fall, and brace myself for pain. Before he smashes into the ground, a blue spell zips from his hand and quickly surrounds him. His rapid decedent halts with a jerk.

With a giant exhale, I slouch. If he hadn't stopped himself, that would have really hurt. Slowly, he floats to the ground, and the blue light disappears back into his hands.

"Did you forget to picture me in the room?" he asks.

For once, I don't look away as a blush heats my cheeks. He could have been seriously injured; the least I can do is look him in the eyes. But I'm not admitting why I neglected such an important detail. Picturing him in the room was too distracting. "Sorry."

He laughs. "It's fine, just surprising. You really pack a lot of magic."

Seeing him at ease makes me laugh, too. "Maybe you should have placed more emphasis on how important it was to picture you in the room as well."

He puts both hands on his chest. "You've got me there. In my defense, I didn't expect you to cast the spell so forcefully. Especially when you started off having trouble with it. Most warlocks I know can't go from not being able to do a spell at all, to surpassing expectations with it.

"This is a great sign," he continues. "You're a natural. It should be easier to prepare you for the tournament."

This time I do turn away as I blush, which allows me to explore what I accomplished. The room is ten times the size it was before. Everything in it, the pictures, trophies, jewels, all the items are the same size as they were previously and about the same place as before, only more space stretches between them now. The ceiling soars overhead, making it almost feel as if we're standing outside.

"It would be wonderful if that were really the case. I can't believe I actually did this. Is it bigger on the outside as well?" I ask.

"No. You could do that by picturing the outside as well, but for our purposes we don't want to draw extra attention to ourselves."

I nod. Any indication of something going on in this house that would be an excuse for law officers to investigate would be bad. I'm sure they'd find an excuse to get me out of the tournament, anything to do away with me.

"Where does all of the extra space come from, then?"

"From what you did to it. You took what was already there, and expanded it, made it bigger."

I frown. "Then why isn't it bigger on the outside as well? Shouldn't it expand everywhere?"

"Only where you tell it to. Magic is a powerful thing. It can create and destroy much."

If that's really the case, then... "Can it make something from nothing? Like food? I've never been able to make food on my own."

"Yes, but it's harder. When there's something present to work with, it's much easier to stretch it out. Make sense?"

"I think so."

"Good. Shall we start your lesson then?" Lukas asks.

"I thought we had already started."

"That was just a warm up."

He moves closer to me but stops when he's about ten paces away and I find myself wishing he was closer. I'm sure I'll be able to see what he does well enough from here. "This is about how far you'll be from your opponent in the duels."

Suddenly the distance seems too close. Much too close.

He casts a bright green spell that leaves a circle on the floor around us. I could lie down and stretch out in it comfortably without hitting the light. "This is the size of the ring. Most warlocks don't move far from their original spot, but you are allowed anywhere inside the ring. If you step out or get knocked out of it, you lose."

"Simple enough."

"Until someone slams a wind spell at you."

Why am I getting myself into this? "Point taken."

"Any thoughts or questions so far?" Lukas asks.

"Why don't most warlocks move from the original spot?"

"Chardonians are a strange bunch. The way they do everything isn't based off how effective it will be, but how it appears to others. They think by using only their magic, and no physical movement, they look stronger."

"Does that mean I can touch the other duelers?"

"Sort of. If you somehow managed to accidentally bump into your opponent, it's fine. But using anything other than magic to defeat your opponent is against the rules. So even though you can touch them, they'd probably call foul and say you were trying to defeat them without magic."

"No touching them. Understood."

"Right. But it'd be good to move around. Do it a lot, since they won't be used to it. They won't be expecting it. Just don't go near them. They are going to do whatever it takes to kick you out of the tournament."

"Naturally, move but don't move too much. Why didn't I think of that before?" I roll my eyes before growing serious. "Do you think I can survive this?"

He takes my hand. "I've never met anyone that has as much raw power as you. The only thing you're missing is knowledge. We'll teach you everything we can. You'll not only live through this, but you will make history."

I don't know what warms me more, his words or his hand on mine.

The door opens, and we jump apart. Waverly whistles as she strides in.

"This is nice work."

At first, I think she's talking about Lukas holding my hand, but then I realize she's examining the room. It's good she didn't notice. Even if she's talked about how she feels about Chadwick, how I feel about Lukas is so tumbled, I wouldn't know what to say.

"It was all Cynthia," Lukas says.

I rub my hands together, still thinking of how it felt a moment ago encased in his.

"Nice work," Waverly says again. "To think you've been hiding this much power all along."

"Thank you." I glance at the floor as I blush.

"What else have you been working on?"

Something you interrupted. I banish the thought. This is silly. She didn't interrupt anything but Lukas helping me feel more confident about doing well in the tournament.

"Going over rules mostly," Lukas responds. See? Nothing here to worry about interrupting. Except it makes me wonder if he feels what I just felt. If there's something between us, or if he's just being nice. Maybe in Chryos, taking a girl by the hand and offering words of encouragement and support are a common practice.

She nods. "I'm going to get dinner going while you two work. Is there anything you'd like?"

"Whatever you make is fine. Thank you," I say.

"I'm not picky," Lukas replies.

"Pickled pig's feet it is."

Gross. Can that possibly even be a thing? I manage to hold back a groan, but Lukas doesn't.

"What?" she says. "Don't you like pig's feet? You should have made a request when I asked."

He forces a smile, taut and wholly false, but trying. "I'm sure it'll be great."

She laughs. "Don't lie to spare my feelings. I was only teasing."

Her laughter echoes through the now cavernous room as she leaves. I'm ready to get back to where we were before she interrupted, but it doesn't come. Instead of the current flowing between us being filled with something new and exciting, there's only awkwardness.

He scuffs the toe of his shoe on the floor. "Guess we should keep working."

Picking up his words, I say, "Guess we should."

Once we return to practicing, the awkwardness lessens, though doesn't fully leave. It's easier to absorb his lesson now that we both understand how I learn. Much easier than when I used to attempt to teach myself spells. But still hard. I hope it will be enough.

CHAPTER 20

Waverly and Lukas alternate helping me train, sometimes working together. Each has such a unique perspective that I can't decide who is better to train with. Lukas teaches attack and defensive spells, while Waverly shows me fun spells similar to the nail changing, in addition to coloring my hair, as a way to better understand my magic, how it works, and to practice using it regularly.

My knowledge and skills grow, though still feel small compared to theirs, and nothing to what they should be to compete in the tournament. I keep pushing through, hoping it's enough, but fearing it's not even close.

I rarely catch a glimpse of my protectors. Unless I count Lukas and Waverly, who I see every day. Lukas always drops in, and Waverly's presence has been good. Though she was right about Zade being livid. He didn't stop by, just sent her a scathing letter. Strangely enough, Waverly read it out loud to me, laughing at inappropriate times. At least she seems happy, and I'm glad to have someone else in the house. It's not as cold with her here. Except right now she's gone with Chadwick to get some groceries. I'm alone. Well, as alone as I can be. I'm sure there are at least a few warlocks watching over the house to keep me safe.

I'm supposed to be practicing a blocking spell, but instead I'm playing with moving the air in the room. Sweeping it back and forth, sometimes lightly in a powder blue and sometimes with large blue-violet gusts. When it's strong enough to make an item fall, I rush the air as quickly as I can to catch the item and put it back. It's like a game, but it would be more fun if someone else was here to push the air back and forth with me.

A knock sounds at the door. I can't imagine who it would be, but if it was someone dangerous, the guards would have stopped them. Even if the guards couldn't, I'm certain the attacker wouldn't be knocking. I pull my magic back into myself and head for the door. I almost open it, but then decide even if it seems safe, I should still be cautious. I do the one-sided, invisible-door spell I'm getting quite good at. Once I see who it is, I squeal, yank open the door, and try to wrap Serena and Bethany in a hug at the same time.

Once I'm done squeezing them, or at least finished hugging them on the porch where anyone can see us, I beckon them into the house.

"What are you doing here? I thought it wasn't safe."

"I'm done being safe. I'm here to find out what's going on with you because something clearly is," Serena says.

"And I made her bring me," Bethany says.

"But I'm not staying in the same room as before," Serena adds.

"Wouldn't dream of putting you through that again." It must be hard enough, just coming back here and reliving the memories. I hug them again. "I'm so glad you're here. Thank you, thank you." Tears prick my eyes, so I hurry to change the topic. "How long are you staying?"

"Just the night, unfortunately," Serena says. "We want to stay longer, but they need us at home."

"Who is tending the girls?"

"They have mother. She claimed she's feeling well enough for the task," Bethany says.

Serena adds, "I also think she's becoming more accustomed to the idea of father not being around."

"I think so as well," Bethany says. "Besides, the older girls are helping."

"They're not as young as they used to be. None of us were ever really young for long." The thought makes me ache for all of us. I wish we would have known things could be different sooner. Or that we lived in a different country. Or, even better, that someone had already given a woman her freedom before Serena came along, and that another woman showed us all girls can do magic as well. Things could have been so different. But the only way it will change now is if I keep pushing forward.

"I'm thrilled you're here. Really I am. But isn't this going to put more pressure on our family? There's already negativity and worry surrounding us. Won't you being here make it worse?"

"It's a little late to be worrying about that. The rumors of your freedom are spreading."

"I'm sorry about all of this." My voice sounds as tiny as I feel. "I didn't mean to make everything worse. I wanted to make things better."

"Don't be sorry," Serena says, her voice fierce. "It may be harder on us, on our family, but what you're doing—" She blinks away the wetness in her eyes. "Zade freed me. You freed yourself. I wish I was brave enough to be as strong as you are."

My chin quivers. "That's not all. I've done something that could be deadly."

They both look at me with patient disbelief in their eyes, like they believe I have done something but not something deadly. They did grow up with me after all and know most of my antics are usually easy to hide. Part of me wishes that was the case this time while the other part finally feels like I'm doing what I should.

"What is it?" Serena's voice betrays only a hint of her agitation at being presented with another of my problems.

I take a shaky breath, but it does nothing to calm me. "I'm dueling in the tournament."

Bethany's eyes crinkle before lighting. I can almost see her putting thoughts together, all the little pieces from us growing up starting to make sense. Serena's a different story. Her forehead bunches as she grips her skirt.

"Don't be silly, Cynthia. You may have the status of a warlock, but the only way you could compete with them is by using a gun. I doubt they'll let your status remain if you try that."

"Why don't you sit down?" I say.

Serena eyes the sitting room, a place we never entered when staying previously with Thomas. "I'm fine. We just need to clear this matter."

"Cynthia's right," Bethany adds. "It's probably best if we sit."

Serena takes a step back. "There's no reason to sit. We just need to talk this over rationally. There's no need for you to duel. You don't cast spells."

Guilt pricks my chest. "Serena…"

She backs up until she hits the wall. "No. I'd know. We'd know. Women don't do magic. We can only carry it. We don't do it."

"It's true."

"No. You can't. Women can't."

"What was my hair like when we were little?"

She shakes her head, staying silent, but Bethany says, "It was everywhere. Your curls were hard to manage. You, mother, and Serena were often punished over it. Until your hair suddenly became more manageable…"

She eyes my locks. Serena does as well, her fist gripping her skirt even tighter.

"They became more manageable when I learned how to keep them spelled in place."

Bethany bites her lower lip, but nods like it all makes sense.

Serena, though, her eyes tighten. "Edward must have done something to you. Spells leave light. You know that. We'd see it."

Now doesn't feel like the time to tell her it wasn't Edward that did something to me, but rather that I did something to him. "They do leave color, but some are more noticeable than others. Father's silencing spell?"

Serena clamps her mouth closed.

"It's clear," Bethany replies.

"And so is this one, mostly anyway. It does tend to take on the color of my hair, but no one's ever noticed."

"This explains the burned blanket I found at the bottom of your trunk," Bethany says.

My face heats.

When there's still no reply from Serena, Bethany says, "Please show us. Just nothing that will burn another blanket. Something nice."

Immediately, magic stirs within me. It's been aching to show itself to my sisters for years, and now it has the chance. Only, I don't know how well Serena's going to take it. Pushing aside my misgivings, I close my eyes and let the magic flow from me. There's a gasp, but I don't look yet. The spell meshes with the spell already on my hair. I picture the spell returning to me, leaving my hair in its natural state of disarray. Once complete, I finally chance opening my eyes.

Serena's hand presses against her mouth, eyes riveted on my hands.

"That was amazing," Bethany says. "I can't believe you've been hiding it all these years. What made it finally come out?"

"Edward tried to take my blood. My magic. I couldn't let him. The spells just flew out of me."

"You hexed a warlock?" Serena is pale, eyes wide.

"I did," I say and hastily add, "But don't tell anyone. If they find out, I'm sure not only my ownership would be under question, but my life and your memory of me, as well."

154

"Our memory?" Bethany asks.

It's something I wish I never had to admit. The position I've put us all in. "Zade said whenever a woman in Chardonia does magic, the council kills her and erases everyone's memory of her."

Bethany emits a small gasp.

After too long a moment, Serena says, "It will take some time for me to get used to this idea, but I promise to keep it secret."

Relief courses through me, though not nearly enough of it. "Until the tournament at least. I'm certain the council knows, or at least suspects, I can do magic, but since the only people I've shown are keeping it to themselves, there's no proof as of yet. That, backed with those in high rank and from other countries who are expecting to see me in the tournament, to see if I really can do magic or am just faking it, is enough to keep the danger away for now."

"Just for now?"

"We're trying to figure out a way to show so many people I can do magic at once that the council has no choice but to leave me be. It's more danger for our family, though."

Bethany wraps her arms around me, her soft voice full of surety. "Chardonia needs to see this, even if it means putting our family in jeopardy."

Emotion burns my eyes at her words.

"We'll be here for you." Serena takes a deep breath, her voice quivering. "I'll be here for you, supporting you as much as I can so you can do this."

The tears come harder but with them a new resolve. "I'll do my best."

CHAPTER 21

E ver since Serena and Bethany's all-too-short visit, I miss the
girls more than ever. The days are long, full of practicing
and longing to be with them. Waverly picks up on my mood,
though, and spends extra time with me. Most of it is spent practicing magic.

Today we're in the ballroom. Not as big and grand as the one
at Zade's house, but more than ample space to practice. All we
really need is a circle of space that's much too confined.

"Let's try again," Waverly says.

"I just don't want to hurt you." I'm currently working on
mastering spell that Lukas taught me which isn't lethal but leaves
a painful sting.

She huffs, probably upset that we've had this conversation
too many times today. And the rest of the week. "You are
competing in a tournament which requires you to throw hexes
at others. If you can't do that, you're not going to come out
alive."

"I know. I know." A sudden urge to stamp my foot like Sally
does overtakes me. No point in me acting like one of my younger
sisters, though, no matter how much I want to. "You're not a

warlock. It'd be so much easier to hex them." Though that thought still leaves me feeling guilty.

"You know that's not true."

I give her a look.

"Oh, don't give me that. You can't hex Lukas any better than you can hex me."

I scuff the teal-spelled line making up the circle with the toe of my boot. It flashes bronze every time I touch it. "That's different."

"It's not, Cynthia. You have to change your frame of mind. What if you two end up competing against each other? You'd have to cast a spell against him or lose."

My stomach tightens like a chain has been wrapped around it. "There's so many people entering. I doubt we'll be paired against each other."

"True, but what if you are?" When I don't respond, she continues, "Or what if you're paired with someone who turns out to be as nice as Lukas? Chardonians aren't the only ones competing, you know."

"I'll channel my father."

"Then channel him now."

Raising my hand, I call my magic together picturing a horde of bees stinging her, but as soon as I see her face, I drop my hands. "I just don't want to become him."

Waverly puffs out a breath and crashes though the spelled circle, flashing it bronze for a moment before leaving me alone inside its teal bounds. "You're not like your father."

"How can you know that? You weren't there. You didn't see what I did to Edward. You didn't see how I relished it. Part of me still relishes it. There has to be a way I can win without becoming like them."

She comes back over to me, wiping the spelled ring away with a flick of her wrist as she does so. The sharp, frustrated lines of her face have smoothed into worried frown creases. "You aren't like them, Cynthia. You're nothing like them."

"Maybe. But I feel like I'm drifting closer to being like them than I should. One day, I'm afraid I'll realize I've become just like them, and worse, I won't even care."

"That's the difference between you and them. You do care. You don't want to become like them and you're staying aware of it. As long as you keep doing that, you'll be fine."

"What happens when I get to the tournament and I start hexing all of them? What if it feels good to get back at them after so many years bowing to them?" Even now, I'm wishing that Chancellor Ryan was participating instead of helping the judges. That's one warlock I'd love to throw a hex at, and that thought only proves how all too right my concerns are. "The tournament is going to change things. It's going to change me."

"I can't deny that you'll change," Waverly says. "But that doesn't mean you have to become a worse person for it. Zade competed last year. Do you count him in the same group as the other warlocks?"

"Well, no. But he's not from here. He's grown up learning different things than I have. What if it all wears off on me?"

"Councilman Daniel is from here and is very kind. And what about Jacob? The man who Thomas defeated grew up in Chardonia, but he worked hard for women's rights and finding kindness and balance while he was a Chancellor, part of the council."

She has a point. "I'm just scared."

"I know you are. It's perfectly fine for you to be. In fact, I'd be more worried if you weren't." She wraps her arms around me. "You're going to be just fine."

She may be right, but chancing it worries me. I don't want to lose myself while trying to find myself.

CHAPTER 22

averly left this morning saying she was bringing back a surprise. I'm not sure what it is, but it had her awake early. When I finally hear the front door open, I don't wait for her, but rush to greet her. When I get to the hall and see who's standing in the entry behind her, I run faster.

"Katherine!" We hug, and I laugh. "I didn't think the surprise was going to be a person."

"I figured it was about time I visited this part of Chardonia. Make sure there are no new fashions for the tournament I'm missing out on."

I can't stop smiling as I look at her, even though it's still difficult to get used to her altered appearance. Her tattoos glow fuchsia today, portraying the color the warlock in charge of the tarnished has decided it needs to be, I suppose. But her eyes are bright with something that she always seems to carry with her.

"You'll be staying through the tournament then?"

"Just staying for the night. Business calls me away, but I will return for the tournament."

"I'll set up a room for you, Katherine," Waverly says. "You two chat. Come find me when you're finished."

"I can help," Katherine says.

Waverly waves her away. "I want to do it. You two catch up."

She hurries from the room. I ask, "What are you doing here? I can't believe it's just fashion. You seem to keep up with it well enough without traveling."

"I've come to help."

"Ummm…" The fact that she wants to help is fantastic, except she's a seamstress. What could she know about magic? "Do you know what I'm doing?"

"Entering the tournament. I assume you can cast spells somehow?"

"It's supposed to be kept a secret how much I actually can do, but yes, I can cast spells. And not just me, but any woman with magic can."

"I didn't think it possible."

"Apparently, the council has been working to keep it a secret, but I'm attempting to change that. Waverly and Lukas have been helping me hone my abilities. Did you know Waverly cast most of the spells for Serena's ball?"

"Lukas, huh?" She wiggles her eyebrows at me. "Not 'Lukas of Chryos', or 'Lukas, the most handsome warlock I've ever met in my life, who saved me from living on the streets'?"

I swat her shoulder.

"Fine. Don't give me details," she says.

"It sounds like you already have them."

"You're the one that wrote them to me."

The urge to stick my tongue at her is strong, but since I learned that from Lukas, it feels too much like proving her point. "Fair enough. Though I might not have been as liberal with the descriptions if I knew it would turn to teasing."

She laughs. "I don't think you would have been able to help yourself. I'm looking forward to seeing these… how did you put it? 'Charming good looks' for myself."

I turn away from her as I feel the blush coming on. "You didn't answer my question."

"You didn't answer mine."

I sigh, a big, dramatic one.

"If you must be that way," she says, "I'll pry the details of this Lukas out of you sooner or later. Or I suppose I could just ask him anything I want to know."

Mortified by the thought, but just a little curious to see what she would ask and how he would respond, but mostly mortified, I change the topic back to more neutral territory. "You're here to help? Can you do magic as well?"

"No, I don't cast spells. If I did, things may have turned out differently for me."

"You'd be erased and sacrificed instead of tarnished."

She presses her lips together like she's trying to keep her words from spilling out.

"Sorry, I didn't mean to be insensitive."

"It's not that. I—Well, I—" She sighs and shakes her head. "I'm not here to help with the magic. I'm here to provide any attire you'd like for the tournament. I didn't know if your current wardrobe would be suitable or not."

"Oh." The thought hadn't even occurred to me. "What does one wear to duel in a tournament when one is a girl?"

"We can start with the basics and build on them. What do the warlocks wear?"

"You don't know? I thought you knew everything there is to know about clothes."

She shrugs. "I've never been to a tournament before, and when I asked Serena about it, she was trying so hard not to get upset over your situation that nothing she said was of any use. I figured I might as well come here and speak with you myself."

"I'm glad you did." Beyond glad. Though I don't know how far I can stretch my coins to pay her. She's probably going to insist on doing it for free, but I'll make sure she gets compensated for it. It's a wonder how she manages a thriving business when she's always offering to do so much for free.

"Do you remember the warlocks' attire?"

"The warlocks all wore breeches and shirts in black. Each participant had a band around their arm, the color depicting which country they're from."

"Sounds like a uniform." She taps her lip with a finger. "I wonder how mandatory they are."

"The paperwork says more on it. The kitchen is just through there." I point down a side hall. "Why don't you go have a seat, and I'll grab them for you to look over while I make us a snack."

"Sounds wonderful after the journey here."

She hurries in the direction I indicated while I fetch the paperwork out of my room and follow after her to the kitchen. Only when I get there, she's not sitting down; she's busily making something in the kitchen. "I didn't mean you needed to cook."

"Oh, posh. I like to. Besides, I was sitting in that carriage for much too long. I'm done sitting for a while, I think. It will only take me another minute. I'm not doing anything fancy. Though there will be enough for Waverly, if you'd like to see if she wants to join us."

Waverly is eager to join, adding cookies and milk to Katherine's sandwiches. A few minutes later, when everything is ready, we sit at the table with the paperwork spread out before us.

"The colors are strict." I point out the part about each country's colors. "But I don't see anything beyond that. I don't remember specifics from last year as to what the men wore. I was concentrating on other things." Like magic, even when everyone else thought it was the warlocks themselves.

"I bet you were."

I thread my fingers through my necklace, pretending I didn't hear. "It was hard not to get caught up in it all. I've never seen so many spells in one place before. I just wanted to devour them all, take the knowledge back to father's, and try them. Though I didn't go to father's for a long time after that. Which was a very good thing. There were more opportunities to practice at Zade's than I had ever found at father's."

"Sounds like Zade became a good thing for more than just Serena."

"He's great at talking to us or giving us space when we need it. Plus he's just nice. Usually. He's not very happy with me right now."

"Oh no. He lost his temper again, didn't he?"

"Not without my help pushing him there." I give a sheepish grin. "Look at all of this. I was trying to trade my ownership to another warlock so it would help take pressure off of Serena. Show everyone she was like the rest of them. Instead, I went marching past all of the rules and am bringing more attention than ever."

"It's fine. Serena never was like the rest of them anyway."

She most definitely is not. But now things are so much worse. I hold back tears. "He's afraid I'm putting them at risk. And he's right, I am. I let my ownership get transferred thinking it would be easier for them, but when Edward took me away and came after me like a mad man, I couldn't take it. And I feel like I've failed them in the process. There's even more weight on my family. Two misfit girls with the status of a warlock. That can't help anyone."

Waverly says, "It can help more people than you realize."

"It's true," Katherine adds. "Did you know more women are coming to me to design and make their clothing? And sometimes, when they come, they want to speak about more than just clothes."

"Really?" I try not to get my hopes up that this has anything to do with me, but it's the only time I've heard about anything good coming from what's happened to Serena and me outside my own family. "What do they want to talk about? Do many people know about my freedom? Do they know I'm participating in the tournament?"

"Many do. Since you entered the tournament, word has spread about both your freedom and your entry. And they know you're Serena's sister, my best customer, so it leads to all sorts of gossip. Which is great for business." She winks at me.

I'm starting to wonder what business, exactly, she's in. It sounds like more than just dresses. "And yet you're here instead of there taking care of them all."

"Posh. I have workers for things like that." She waves me away.

She's always so open. I have to ask. "Are your workers all tarnished as well?"

"They are."

I lower my voice, not for fear of someone overhearing, but out of respect for her. "How are you doing with the new laws?"

She braces herself against the counter, lowering her head. "Not well. The council has gone mad. Taking our small amount of earnings wherever they can, making the monthly check-ins mandatory, keeping track of our every move. Things can't last like this."

I hurry around the counter to put an arm around her. "I'm so sorry."

After a large sigh, she straightens. "So am I. But we'll keep doing our best to work around them until something better happens, or we break."

"I won't let you break," Waverly says, voice as rigid as Katherine's posture.

"And I will do everything I can to help." Though it seems like there's so little that can be done. At least I'm already on the council's bad side.

"Thank you both." She changes topic as if it's too much to

think on right now, and I can't blame her, though I do wish there was more we could do. "What if we went with some breeches?"

"You know I love breeches." In fact, they are all I ever want to wear now, but I still don't dare wear them in public. I have enough problems on my hands without adding that to my list of crimes. "But I don't know. Wearing them in front of warlocks just seems wrong."

Her voice is soft, but firm. "You are one of them now."

Only not nearly enough of one of them for it to truly matter. "Maybe. Except it feels like I don't fit in under expectations for either warlocks or women. The tournament isn't made for someone like me."

She puts her hand on mine. "I know. We'll figure something out, though."

"Knowing you," Waverly addresses Katherine, "it won't only be figured out but will far exceed anyone's expectations, and you'll have to hire even more workers to accommodate the new requests you'll have from whatever new style you come up with."

She blushes. "I'm sure it won't be that remarkable."

But of course it will. She has a way with clothes like I have magic in my blood.

She hurries on. "I'll make a couple different options, and you can decide which would be best. All of them will allow for maneuverability. I assume you'll need to move around a lot?"

"I don't actually know. I suppose some of them moved around a lot last year, but many of them just sort of stood there. Lukas thinks I should practice moving around, but I don't know how it's going to go over."

"Hmmm." She's quiet a moment, then says, "I'll make it so you can move easily anyway. Will you need a spot to carry a gun?"

"No. I don't carry one."

Waverly raises an eyebrow at me.

"I don't need one. I can cast spells. That's good enough for me."

"You know that Zade carries one even though he can do magic."

"Well, yes, but he's an Envadi."

She tsks. "And what, you're a Chardonian so you don't need one? It's up to you, but I think it's irresponsible to go around without as many forms of protection as you can. Even if you can't use it during the tournament, you don't know what will happen before and after."

I grumble, pulling at my necklaces, but she's probably right. "Fine. You might as well make a place for them, Katherine, but I'm not going to guarantee that I'll use it."

"That's fair," she replies. "It shouldn't take long to get them made. I'll have them delivered, but I am hoping to come back for the tournament. I've never seen one before. It's about time I do."

"You are fantastic! Thank you."

"I'm happy to help. Not only happy to, but I love the challenge and new opportunities it presents."

Waverly shivers. "A storm must be moving in. It's growing cold again. I should start a fire."

"Can I?" It's nice to finally have a chance to show others what I can do.

Waverly smiles as if she knows what I have in mind. "It's only fitting."

As my magic pulses through me, I think on warm things, sisters, fireplaces, and hot chocolate. And Lukas. The spell crackles from my hands in red and oranges, instantly heating the air everywhere it touches. When it's danced across the room, I pull my magic back to me, releasing the spell.

"It's definitely warmer." Waverly smiles.

"I may have overdone it just a little." Because it's sweltering. There's sweat dripping from me as if it were a hot summer day. "Or a lot."

Katherine's smile grows. "You are going to do wonderfully at the tournament."

And I hope she's right, but the tournament is more challenging than warming a room. There's performing in front of others, including Chancellor Ryan and the Grand Chancellor, and hexing others while maintaining a character of compassion and kindness. My power and growing knowledge may be useless against what I must face.

CHAPTER 23

Katherine doesn't stay nearly long enough. I miss her the moment she leaves. First my sisters, now Katherine. At least Waverly is here. Though I miss them all so much. Luckily, the feeling is tempered by how busy I am. The hours flood into days and the days into weeks. There's much to do and not nearly enough time to do it in.

I'm sitting on the floor focusing on the power inside me. By knowing it better and really understanding how it moves and feels, I have more control over it.

Lukas enters the room. "I found something that needs your attention." His grin, combined with his words, pull at my curiosity.

Serena and Bethany stroll in the room. I jump to my feet and pull them into a hug. "What are you two doing back here? You have responsibilities, and it's too dangerous."

"It is dangerous," Serena says. "But I'll not leave my sister without support when she needs it most. Someone from our family should be there when you compete."

"And you know I'm going to force her to take me with her so I can see you win," Bethany adds.

Not that I will. If the past holds true, Nathaniel will win. But at least they'll be there and I'll be trying.

Lukas quietly slips from the room, giving us time to talk I'm sure, but I almost wish he would have stayed. This feels like such a big step for them. It'd be nice if he could see the development. His absence doesn't distract me long, though. I take each of them by the hand. "Thank you."

With the support of them behind me, especially Serena's when she's been so hesitant in the past, makes me feel as if maybe I can do this. Maybe I can really show all of Chardonia what women can do.

THE SUN'S rays are just turning to the dark-gold hue of a finished day. We're cleaning up from dinner when a loud bang sounds from the front of the house.

"Leave it," I say, grateful we've been eating in the kitchen which has a quick getaway should the need arise.

Waverly helps usher Serena and Bethany to the back door. Bethany steps out but before the rest of us can escape, a warlock storms in.

I sag in relief as Waverly marches around the small servant's table to Zade in the other doorway and slaps his arm. "What are you doing barging in here like that? We thought someone was attacking."

"At least you have some sense." His words are cutting, sharpened by the jagged, angry lines over his flashing eyes. Eyes that are directed at Serena.

Bethany says, "Hello, Zade."

The soft greeting pulls some of the edge from his expression but not nearly enough. "What are you both doing here?"

"I think it's clear what I'm doing here." Serena's back is rigid, not a hint of her playing with her skirt.

"Cynthia," Waverly says, "why don't we go show Bethany how you can color your nails in my room?"

"No." Serena crosses her arms. "Whatever Zade needs to say, he can say in front of everyone."

For a brief moment, his expression softens but quickly returns to the hard look of a man who's about to give a sound thrashing. "I warned against you coming back. Don't you understand what could happen?"

"I'm well aware we could die, Zade. But Cynthia needs our support."

The pressure that's always with me, tearing at my choices, now lightens, but he doesn't share my sentiments. His hands ball into fists, and his mouth tightens. When he finally speaks, his words are choked with emotion. "I know. But you could die, Serena. Die. That can't happen. I need you."

Not the emotion I was expecting. Instantly, Serena is next to him, and he gathers her in his arms where she looks so tiny but seems to be a world of strength for him. As they embrace, we quickly sneak out the back door. I doubt that's what she had in mind when she said it was fine to talk in front of everyone. They'll work through this as they always do. And, by the way they were clinging to each other, they'll probably be stronger for it.

"How about that nail practicing?" Waverly says, deterring us from the raw emotional display we just witnessed. Though it doesn't do much to distract me from the constant guilt of bringing us all here.

"I really would love to see it," Bethany says.

Pushing past the emotions that leave me feeling like ice, I chuckle. "Only if we sneak in through the front."

"We can agree on that," Waverly adds. "As much as I love seeing them together, the last thing they need is us hovering."

"Is it normal for relationships in Envado to be like that?" I ask.

"Zade has always been bossier than most, and Serena's still

learning how to communicate with him, but all relationships have ups and downs like theirs."

It's strange to think about. Relationships I've seen consist of men ordering women around, not struggling to work together. "That was something."

Waverly snorts. "My brother never did learn to control his temper. Especially around those he loves."

I stop walking. "He's your brother?"

She puts a hand to her mouth. "Great. One more thing for Zade to be angry over when he finds out."

"Why should he be angry over us knowing?" I ask.

"With him on the council, and just being an Envadi, there's a lot of threats and stress directed at him. He's afraid if word gets around that I'm his sister, it will make things even more dangerous for me. So even though I trust you both with my life, I wasn't supposed to share."

Bethany smiles. "Don't worry, I already knew."

"What do you mean, you knew?" I say.

She shrugs. "They've always been familiar with each other but never had the same draw between them that he and Serena have. I figured it must be something else, and what else is there that close except siblings?"

Waverly smirks. "Yup. I'm related to the hot-tempered oaf. But please don't tell anyone. He worries about my safety as it is. If word gets out about our relation, he'll probably send me home."

"We definitely don't you want to leave," Bethany says.

"I said he would send me, not that I would go."

I laugh. "Still, we won't say anything."

"We all know Cynthia's good at keeping secrets," Bethany says with a smile.

"You know I would have told you if I wasn't worried about endangering you."

"You did what you thought was best. And maybe it was the

best thing. Only I have to wonder what things would be like if I had known women can do magic when we were younger."

The fluttering in my chest is a fantastic mix of happiness and fear. "You want to learn?"

"I think it may be a good idea," Bethany says.

Her words send a rush of happiness through me brighter than when I gained my freedom.

Waverly says, "Maybe we can try teaching you the nail spell then, instead of just showing you."

Bethany's expression lights up the night with its intensity, and I return it, feeling just as bright.

"What are you ladies doing out at this hour of the night?" Lukas's stern voice makes me start.

Once my initial shock wears off, a little happiness flares in my chest. Except we shouldn't be discussing magic outside, but at least it was just Lukas who witnessed my mishap. Thinking his name makes the flare brighter. "We were just giving Zade and Serena some privacy. They were, uh, blocking the hall from the kitchen so we're sneaking around."

His expression doesn't ease. "Let's get back inside. Quickly."

He motions toward the front of the house. We hurry along. Silence replaces the previously joy-filled moment with its heaviness. The night air feels more dangerous now somehow. The threats that always linger close.

A tall shadow comes into view, stopping us. My heart pounds. Do we need to run? Fight? Scream for help?

Before I decide, Waverly says, "Chadwick, is everything all right?"

"Get in the house. Now. Something's coming."

Fear sprints through me. I grab Bethany's arm, and we take off with Waverly. The night air is cold as it rushes past. Behind us, Lukas is close with his hands up, ready to cast a spell at a moment's notice. I want to follow suit, but how powerful my magic is supposed to be under wraps still. What if whoever or whatever is coming heard us talking about magic?

"Where are the other guards?" As much as I dislike having them all around, I desperately want them now.

"Spread out across the grounds. None of them are close." Lukas's words are quick and full of regret.

Suddenly, Chadwick stops and throws an orange shield spell in front of us, which protects the entire group. As we turn toward the back entrance, Waverly grips both my wrist and Bethany's, who is on the other side, closest to the house.

Lukas jumps in front of us, hands up with palms out. "Wait."

"We're surrounded," Chadwick whispers. "Who is it?"

"I don't know." But Lukas isn't taking chances. He zaps a shield spell as well, bright green with shades of blue.

Nothing. The darkness around us seems to deepen, filling the air with dread, but still no sound or movement. Perhaps all our fears are forcing us to think things are worse than they really are. Yet… there is something out there that makes goose bumps skitter across my skin.

"The back door is closer," Lukas says. "Let's stay together as a group and make our way there."

He takes a step forward, but as we all follow suit, Bethany lets out a squeak. My gaze follows hers. The shadows are moving toward us, very much in the shape of men wearing dark cloaks.

Lukas curses. "Chadwick!"

"Two more on my side as well," he calls back.

After a second bout of cursing, Lukas says in a rush of faint words, "Let us fight, Cynthia. Don't show your power unless there's no choice."

The shadows move closer, and a yellow bolt darts for us, slamming against Lukas's spell with a sizzle.

"Zade, help!" Waverly screams.

Movement out of the corner of my eyes makes me turn toward my exposed side. "Another one on our right."

Both Lukas and Chadwick's spells dart to cover the unprotected flank, but before they can meet in the middle, a pulse of silver snakes through and swirls itself around my ankles. The shields meet just as my ankles burn with icy pain. My magic itches to free itself, to attack the spelled chains that are causing pain to creep up my legs, but Lukas's warning stops me.

Waverly helps me move closer to the house, further from the threat as the pain shoots up my legs. The attackers are thrusting spells at us while Chadwick and Lukas throw spells back. The zip of lights and the rainbow of colors are smashing together in a cacophony so wild I can't follow them.

As the spell around my ankles tightens to blade-like pain, I realize even if I could show my magic, it wouldn't make a difference. How can I know what to throw at whom and how to shield when it is all lost among the reds, greens, and yellows hurtling across my vision?

The pain grows so intense, links so tight, that my feet become numb. I sway. Suddenly, Bethany is at my other side, helping Waverly to keep me up. I pinch my eyes shut against the blinding array of colors.

"Hold on, just hold on." Bethany's voice is distant.

We're losing. I'm losing. My entire weight slumps onto tiny Bethany. Her grunt at the suddenness of it is far off. The lights continue flashing, but with my eyes closed, there's no telling what colors they are, or if any of them are doing good or ill.

"I've got her," Waverly's voice hovers above me as my weight is shifted.

Something touches my face.

"Stay awake." Bethany's command is quiet and firm, yet I can hear the fear she's trying to hide.

The numbness crawls up my legs, almost blissful as it replaces the aching chill. I lean back, letting my weight shift on whatever's behind me. I force my eyes open. Bethany's face hovers in front of mine, eyes tight with worry. Behind her, the sky is alight with the rapidly-flashing spells.

I lull my head to the side. Lukas. There are fewer attackers now, but they're still flaying at the shield. This feels like one of those no other choice times I'm allowed to use my magic. There must be something I can do to help. What?

A fiery orange and red, puckered with teal, hurtles toward Lukas's shield in a giant ball.

I cry out, but too late. It slams into the shield with obliterating force. The ball flying toward Lukas is smaller but still strong. He throws up a second shield, a small olive-green covering only the area in front of his chest.

The light splats into it, demolishing the shield and most of the spell. A few remaining sparks spit onto Lukas. From behind, it's impossible to discern how much damage has been done. I reach my hand toward him while calling my magic together in a burning ball, imagining it forming a shield. If nothing else, I can help protect them.

An arm darts from behind me and slaps my hand down.

"Look," Waverly says, and I realize it was her that slapped me away.

I want to ignore her, to cast the spell that will give Lukas the aid he so desperately needs, but movement catches my eye. Zade, running toward the attackers with bright yellow and green flares shooting from him.

The attackers don't even try to defend themselves. They run, their dark robes quickly becoming one with the night around them.

I swing my gaze to the other side where Chadwick is still holding up his shield, but there are no attackers left on his side, either. There are, however, several guards running who must have come from the other side of the estate when they heard the commotion.

Lukas is at my side before I realized he was even moving

toward me. He kneels down, and in a few moments, a black spell streaked with crimson and hints of green breaks the chain spell around my ankles and dissipates into the air.

The feeling returns with sharp pricks, but it's not nearly as painful as what caused them to go numb.

"Anyone injured?" Zade asks as he jogs to us.

"Only Cynthia," Lukas replies.

"I'm fine." At least now I am, or will be after rest. My legs ache, head is a bit spinny.

Conrad stands guard close by like he's unwilling to leave my side after such an ordeal, but the others spread out, forming a wide arc around us.

"I'm going after them," Chadwick says.

"You can't," Waverly replies. "Not alone.

"It's too late anyway. They're long gone." Lukas says.

Waverly's still holding most of my weight. I try to push off her, to bear myself up, but I fall toward the ground. Lukas catches me, lifting me up into his arms. As my head rests against his shoulder, I start to drift off. His warmth is comforting after the aching chill.

"Don't worry," he whispers. "I have you."

CHAPTER 24

T he next morning, I wake feeling wholly like myself. It seems as if a spell that chilled me to my bones like that should have some lasting pain. But the only thing I feel is worry over endangering lives yet again and frustration that I couldn't keep track of all the spells flying around last night. And worse, I froze up, unable to think of how to help.

I quickly dress and am putting up my hair in its bun when there's a knock on my door.

"Come in."

Serena enters, looking as if there weren't enough spells flying around last night to keep her from sleeping.

"How are you?" Because I know, regardless of how she looks, that all that magic had to take her back to memories and thoughts she doesn't want to relive.

"The question should be how are you? I've been worrying about you all night. Any lingering effects of the hex?"

Of course, the only hint she'll give me about her own feelings is her worry over me. If she'd been with us when we were attacked, she probably would have jumped in front of me to take the hex herself, despite her hatred of magic. But it does stir up foggy memories of being in Lukas's arms. The thought leaves me warm and buzzing, much more than I should after yesterday.

"None. I feel the same as always."

Her shoulders lower slightly, the only hint of the stress escaping her.

"What about you?" I ask. "Are things well between you and Zade? Did you come to an agreement before the attack?"

Her lips twitch with a suppressed smile. "The only thing I'm saying is that while our lips did a lot of moving, we didn't speak much."

"Serena!" I giggle.

"Well, we didn't expect he'd be running off so quickly. Otherwise we would have had time to turn the lip moving into talking as well."

This makes me laugh harder. Whoever thought we'd be together in Thomas's house discussing her kissing the man she's engaged to with happiness instead of duty and fear?

"He's waiting with Lukas in the kitchen to speak with us."

"Let's go then."

It doesn't take me long to finish up. Zade and Lukas are waiting for us in the kitchen.

"Morning," I say to them and quickly move to get something cooking. I tell myself it's because I'm hungry and not because I want to avoid discussing my failure to comprehend a single spell last night. As we work, I grab some eggs while Serena starts putting together some biscuits.

"We need to bring your entire family to live here," Zade says.

"After last night?" I demand. "What if they would have been here? Something could've happened to them. We have to keep them safe."

"They were attacked last night, too."

His quiet response makes me drop an egg. Lukas hurries to help me clean it.

"Is anyone hurt?" Serena's voice shakes.

"Everyone is fine. Cynthia got the worst of it."

"Oh, thank goodness." If any of them would have been hurt…

"If your family comes," Zade says, "we can pool our resources together. Have all the guards in one place, not stretched across an area we can't protect. I think it will be safer for everyone."

"I didn't know it was getting so bad," Serena says. "Perhaps it was a mistake to come here."

"No, it wasn't. You were right. And I was wrong to be angry at you for it. You need to be here, and even if you didn't, it'd still be safer for everyone to be together. Chadwick went to help see them here safely."

I'll get to see my sisters and mother soon. I can't wait to see them, though I do wish the circumstances were different. How are they all? Have any of them grown since I've been away? I'm sure the baby has, at least. They change every day. And with mother so far along with this pregnancy? I hope they stay safe while traveling here.

With Lukas's help, we finish cleaning the last of the egg mess. "Thank you."

"Do you need help with anything else?"

"No. Unless Zade has any more shocking news, I should be able to manage."

"There may be some," Zade says.

"Bad enough to make me drop more eggs?"

"Maybe." Zade's words make me hold still, afraid to touch anything else until I know how bad it is. "The council is growing stricter with their rules. The Grand Chancellor seems to be gearing up for something."

I didn't think they could grow any stricter, and I'm not sure I'm ready to know what he could be getting ready for. "What are they changing?"

"No matter that they've been relying on other countries for much of their income for years, they're making it harder for foreigners to enter the country. Those of us already here have surpassed the changes being made, but for the rest, there's a lot more paperwork, all of which has to be approved by the Grand Chancellor or Chancellor Ryan."

Serena scowls. "They won't let you approve it?"

"Not unless I suddenly change into one of them. Even then, I doubt they'd accept me."

"They're getting even stricter," Lukas says.

Somehow it is, even though I keep thinking they can't get any worse. With this news weighing things down, breakfast is a somber affair.

* * *

AFTER ZADE and Lukas go outside to check on the guards on duty, Serena pulls me into the hallway.

"You really are excited for the tournament, aren't you?" she says.

"I am. Though I'd prefer if it didn't come with the worry for my life and the lives of those I love, but I've always enjoyed casting spells. Being able to do it in front of so many people is something I never thought could happen." It still might not.

"Would you explain it to me?" Her hand fists into her skirt. "Those hexes we always dealt with… I never wanted anything to do with magic. It's hard to understand why you're not only fine being around magic, but that you actually want to cast spells."

"Being hexed was ghastly. But when I realized there was a power inside me, something that let me cast spells as well, I wanted to use it. I wanted to explore it and eventually to do what I could to help. Like Bethany. Remember when she came to Zade's house hurt?"

She puts a hand to her chest. "How could I forget?"

No one could. "When you went to find Zade, I did what I could to ease her pain. It wasn't enough, or even much, but it was better than not doing anything, better than letting this power inside me go to waste."

Her eyes lose focus as she thinks about this. "I can see wanting to help, but I don't know. They say I have magic in my blood, but I don't feel anything. I don't think I can actually cast spells or do anything to help. I'll have to stick with this." She pats the pocket of her skirt where I know she keeps her gun.

I hope it's enough, but more than that, I wish I knew how to show her more of what's hiding inside her. If I can't show my own sister, make her understand, how am I going to make other women understand it's not just me that can do magic?

CHAPTER 25

Mother and the girls arrive in a flurry of guards, their faces etched with worry. I hurry to mother's side, putting an arm around her, and helping her in. "We shouldn't have moved you."

"It's no matter. There's no point in special treatment for bearing yet another daughter."

Her words slice into me even if they're true. It shouldn't be that way. Casting spells in front of everyone at the tournament doesn't seem like a way to fix it. The girls have all gone ahead of us, hurried in by Serena, Zade, and Waverly, but Bethany hovers close by us, waiting to help should mother need more assistance no doubt.

"How was the journey? Everyone looks tired and a little rattled."

"Rattled? Is that all?" She snorts, the most undignified thing I've ever heard her do. "We were attacked on the way over. I don't know what happened for certain, being in that dark carriage and all, but it was awfully noisy."

As we reach the sitting room, the closest place for her to rest, I help her onto a sofa while exchanging a worried glance with

Bethany. "Well, I'm glad you made it here safely."

Mother is already dozing. The journey must have been even worse than she said. I gently pull her feet onto the couch while Bethany grabs a pillow and blanket for her. Once she's settled, we leave the room with many backward glances.

"Is it going to be worse or better having us all in one place? There may be more guards to protect us, but we're now all in one convenient spot to attack."

Bethany bites her lower lip before saying, "At least they made it here safely."

Yes, at least there's that.

We spend the next few hours getting all the girls settled in their rooms and setting up mother's room for when she wakes. She continues to sleep on, though, and knowing the stress of the day, I can't help but ask Serena, "Should we send for a doctor?"

The line of her mouth is grim. "I don't know if there are any left we can trust. I'll check on her, though."

There's a shriek somewhere close followed by the high-pitched sound of girls fighting. I sigh. "And I'll see about entertaining the girls so they don't bother her."

She nudges me. "Don't look so grim about it. We all know you've been dying to spend time with them ever since you left."

I grin at her before hurrying off. It's all too true. I've missed my girls so much. And by the way they quickly respond to my herding them into the ballroom, they've missed me too.

"Now, this is where you can come to be as noisy as you'd like, but there's no fighting in here." I look them each in the eye, and they all look eager enough to comply for now but much too quiet in a way that will likely last much too long. The time with father has scarred them all, especially the older ones. "Go on now."

The girls run around the ballroom, filling the air with their echoing squeals of delight. Nothing like this ever happened when father owned us. I want to take it one step further. I should probably talk to Serena first, and maybe mother, but this is something

I want to give the girls. Something I want them to see and know without any chance of outside interference.

I gather my magic, pulling it close together while picturing small, transparent balls. The color doesn't matter really, so rather than worrying over what my emotions are like, I just release small waves of my magic.

The first spelled bubble is about the size of an orange and colored like one as well. None of the girls have noticed yet, so I release several more, the size growing bigger and the orange brighter each time. When I've released about a dozen, the room slowly goes quiet.

The girls are eying the spelled bubbles with caution. Sally glances at me, and I give her a smile. She takes the hand of the girl closest to her, Molly, and together they inch closer. Mindful of their approach, I work on cooling my emotions, finding peace and serenity in the moment. The next bubble I cast, I release slower but bigger than the others, about the size of a carriage wheel.

The girls gasp, but with a magical, happy sound mixed in and not with the fear I worried about. Working on remembering different things to bring about different emotions, I let the bubbles fly as quickly as the emotions are coming, letting out all sizes and colors. One of the girls giggles.

Sally and Molly have reached a bubble, a pink one with hints of purple. Molly reaches up to touch it, but Sally pulls her hand away.

"She's fine," I say, eyes riveted on the scene before me.

Without questioning me further, as I'm certain Serena would do, Sally picks up Molly and holds her closer to the glowing pink bubble. I lean forward as her finger draws closer. Without hesitation, she pokes the bubble. It pops just like a real bubble would, except it releases sparks of pink and purple that dissipate in the air. Molly's shriek of delight sings through the air as she wiggles down from Sally's arms and runs for another one to pop.

Soon all the girls have joined in on the fun, and I hurry to make as many bubbles as I can. Even though the girls make quick work of popping them, the bubbles soon crowd the air, filling the ballroom with their rainbow of happiness. The littlest girls run from bubble to bubble or dance in circles with their arms in the air, while bubbles sway across them all, bursting in an array of lights and colors. Even the older girls aren't holding back their enthusiasm.

"Wow."

I turn around to see Lukas behind me. "You like it?"

"I do, but more than that, they seem happier."

"Mostly, anyway." Presha is hanging back from the others, Grace and Ada wavering between joining her and exploring the bubbles.

"It's nice. Do you mind if I watch?"

Warmth blooms through me. "Please."

At some point Bethany joins us, though I don't know how long she's been here. Her eyes are as bright as the youngest as she plays with the girls among the bubbles and pops her own. The spell is easy enough to keep producing, though to my surprise, Lukas never joins in.

I continue for over an hour, making as many different types as I can and taking many requests from the girls. It's so good to see them laugh, knowing I'm the one making that come about, only it's also hard remembering I never had anything like this and that they only gained this recently. And while their joy has been gained, they've lost even more safety. It shouldn't have to be this way.

The back of my neck gets a prickling sensation of being watched. I glance around to find Serena leaning against the doorway, a faint smile gracing her lips but worry lines creasing the corners of her eyes. Next to her, mother enters. A faint smile graces her face as she watches the children. Suddenly she hunches over.

I hurry toward her. "Mother?"

"Just over tired from the day, I think. It's early yet. The baby won't be joining us." She rubs her belly.

"I'll be excited to meet my newest sister when the time comes."

"You sound different. Your speech sounds more like that drawling Chryon than what I'm accustomed to."

Her words make me blush and glance at Lukas, who's now chasing the girls with both himself and his own spelled bubbles.

"He's different than your father." Mother's words are sad, tainted with a longing I don't understand. "This is a good thing you've done for the girls."

Did she truly just say that? How I talk may be changing, but changing how she thinks is an even bigger accomplishment. Maybe there's more hope than I thought—if someone doesn't manage to kill us before that hope can become a reality.

CHAPTER 26

After failing to manage a sword-like stabbing spell too many times to count, Lukas says, "You're not focusing tonight. What's going on?"

I drop my hands and forget about the failed spell. "My sisters are more distracting than I thought they would be. Having them here is fabulous, but it reminds me of how things always were before Zade killed Thomas. And knowing they're in even more danger, I wish there was something that could be done. Some of the girls are eager. They loved the bubble spells I did for them, but they also take cues from Serena. If I can't get her to understand, how will I ever get anyone else to? Her fears seem to have eased some, but she's scared and I don't know how to work past that."

"You want to teach her magic?"

"If I can. Bethany too, though she actually wants to learn, and Waverly's already taught her a few things. If I'm alive after all of this, I want to teach all of my sisters. If they'll let me." Wonder what mother will think of that.

"I might be able help."

My gaze locks onto his. "How?"

"Come here." He takes a hold of my hand, helping me stand.

As he guides me to the center of the ballroom, I think on how our palms fit and press together. Then he lets go. Disappointment fills me but stays buried where it can't be seen. I shouldn't be disappointed; he's going to show me a way to help Serena, which is what I wanted. Yet, the feeling tugs at me anyway.

He stands across from me, close enough that if I stretched out my arm I could touch him but not close enough to feel the heat of his presence.

"Usually children are taught from when they're kids, just like we teach them to read and write. But occasionally there's a child who is having a hard time grasping casting spells for whatever reason. It could be a number of things."

"How do you help them?"

"We let our magic touch theirs."

A person's magic can touch another's? "Sounds dangerous."

"Not at all. It increases the magic a person feels, which makes it easier to recognize. Nothing harmful."

The idea is perfect for showing Serena what she carries within her. I rock forward, bouncing the balls of my feet. "How is it done?"

"I'd like to show you, if you'll let me." He watches me from the corner of his eyes. "Like I said, it's not dangerous, but it's something that requires closeness and trust. Like holding hands or sharing a hug."

Air whooshes from me. I've daydreamed about what it'd be like to have his arms around me but didn't think it would happen. And it's not. This is silly. He's just helping me learn how to teach Serena. But my reply still comes out like I'm having a hard time getting enough air to breathe. "That'd be fine."

"Ready?"

I'm not sure. "Yes."

He gives me one of his smiles and stands with his hands at his sides. Instead of a spell moving out his hands, something strange happens. A white light, bright and pure, swirls from his chest. It continues to build and moves toward me in a smooth, flowing line.

As it nears me, Lukas says, "Are you okay?"

It's not often a spell comes at me and even rarer that it's not a hex. It's too difficult to speak, so I nod instead.

"Here it comes then. It won't hurt."

That's easy to believe. There's nothing but raw magic contained in the spell. Lukas's raw magic. The palms of my hands grow sweaty. The light slows as it nears, but doesn't stop. My breathing increases even though I try to slow it. The moment the light enters my chest, the warmth of my core, the part of me that's magic, heats. Flares my magic with his magic.

The spell glows between us, brightening his chocolaty eyes. The warmth that fills me expands, feeling just like my own, but stronger and more powerful. Red blazes within the light. I want to step closer. To move toward him, but I don't know if it will affect the spell.

Maybe my expression says what I want because he steps closer, the light between us shrinking with the lessening distance, but the power and warmth inside me continues growing. I mimic his movements, and both of us quickly close the space between us. The light is only a tiny flash between us. Tiny, but a blazing, powerful red.

Even so, I wish we were closer.

"Feel that?" Lukas whispers.

How can I not? That flame between us, warm and bright, is like nothing I've ever felt before. Though the magic feels big and shiny and new, it's nothing compared to how I feel around him. How he makes me feel. How I want it to last.

Instead of answering, I lean the last few inches that separate us and press my lips to his. His response is immediate, warm and responsive. I've never felt more at home than I do at this moment. He tastes spicy and good, welcoming. He wraps his arms around me, pulling us closer together. Even through my closed eyes, the light of his spell is brilliant, smashed between us. Inside, my magic intertwines with his, curling around his with smoldering intensity, as if thrilled to meet a friend the same as it.

I don't know if it's been a minute or an hour before our lips finally part, but we're both breathless. Yet he doesn't let me, or the spell, go. We stare at each other, the glow of his face like he's just won a prize. Like he's won not just some prize, but the entire tournament. And I feel as if my face is glowing the same way. This feels better than gaining a whole new wardrobe with matching jewelry. Better than casting a spell eager to be released. Somehow, even better than when Serena took father's place as our owner.

Finally, the spell between us wanes. Its presence softens within me, and the light recedes until it's gone.

"Wow," I say.

His smile comes soft but intense. He opens his mouth, but before he can speak, Zade, with a sharp edge to his voice, says, "Yeah. Wow."

The mocking words make me take a step away from Lukas, but he takes a hold of my hand, and pulls me back as Zade storms in the room.

"So this is what you two have been doing. I thought you were training for the tournament, but instead you're standing around smacking lips together like a couple of guppy youth."

The heat is still inside me, but now it's burning with anger. "It's not like that."

"We've been working," Lukas adds.

"I saw that," Zade retorts. "Cynthia, can I talk to Lukas alone please?"

"No." His eyebrows lift in response to my denial. "I'm as much a part of this as he is. In fact, maybe you should leave so we can talk about what happened."

Lukas's thumb makes circles on the back of my hand, soothing some of my anger.

"Sorry." Zade paces across the width of the room a few times before stopping in front of us. "Have you two truly been working on magic, or has there been a lot of... cuddling happening?"

"We've been practicing," Lukas says. "That was the first, and only, time we've kissed. I don't think either of us meant for it to happen. And really, what business is it of yours?"

Zade squeezes his eyes tight a moment before collapsing into a nearby chair. "I'm sorry. I'm being an idiot again. Everything is so hard right now I—" He grunts. "Sorry."

"You've said that." Even if his apologies are softening me toward him, I'm not ready to easily let him get away with ruining my first kiss.

"It's true, even if it's not enough. I've no right. It's just that, so many lives are in danger. I wanted to see if you needed any help training, and when I found you two were kissing, I thought it was all being wasted for a secret courtship."

I step away from both of them so they won't see the heat warming my face.

"We really have been working," Lukas says.

"Actually, today we weren't," I say.

Zade gives me a look. "That was obvious."

"No, before what you saw." I clear my throat. "Lukas was teaching me a way that may help Serena sense her magic. If I can help her sense it, maybe she can learn a few spells like Bethany. Maybe she'll not only be able to see and understand more of the good magic can do, but have another way to protect herself and our sisters."

"That's what you two were doing?"

"It was."

He groans. "I really am an idiot." He puts his head in his hand a moment. "It would be good if you could manage this. Thank you for helping. Serena's trying to come to terms with magic. If you could get her to open up enough that she'd accept being taught, well, it wouldn't be enough, but it'd help. It'd probably help you grow stronger as well."

He walks over to us. "Why don't you show me what you were trying? Maybe I can add to it."

I glance at Lukas. His eyes are on my lips. At least we're both distracted by the same thing.

"Or maybe you two should talk first. I'll come back in ten." He heads for the door, but says before he leaves, "I don't want to be any more of an idiot, but there's one thing. I want you both to be happy. You both deserve someone who will care about you. But you need to remember how many lives are being risked for this chance.

"If your relationship becomes a complication, it won't help anyone. Cynthia, you could die in the tournament if we don't do everything we can to help you. Developing feelings for another is intense and interferes with clear thinking. I know from experience. The more I grow to care about Serena, the more I worry over her life here. I want to give up everything I'm trying to fight for, all those I'm trying to help, just to keep her safe. But I can't do that. I have to fight for the Chardonians who need me while trying not to make things worse for her. I wouldn't change my feelings for her, but it's left me torn and jagged.

"This isn't meant to discourage a relationship between you two, but maybe you could hold off getting any more serious? Either way, I won't say anything further, no matter what you decide."

With that, he leaves the room. We both stand there a moment, staring at the closed door. The silence is prickled with awkwardness. I know Zade cares for Serena, that their relationship is developing into something I've never seen before. Clearly I don't understand it or the intensity building with it.

Is that what waits for Lukas and me if we proceed? Our fingers are still entwined. If our lives become more entwined, will I be tearing him between me and his duty? Will I be tearing myself between what I want and what I need to do?

Finally, I take a step back from Lukas, letting our hands drift apart. He reaches his hand up like he's going to take mine again but lets it fall back without even a brief contact.

"He's right, isn't he?" The question feels more like a statement.

Lukas suddenly grabs both of my hands in his and holds them tight against his chest. "Did that kiss mean something to you?"

I start to glance away as a blush creeps up my cheeks but he gently takes a hold of my chin, and turns my face toward him. The blush leaves, but is replaced by something else. Something still warm, but stronger. My pulse flutters as I feel his soft touch and remember what it felt like when his lips were on mine.

"Did it mean something?" he asks again.

"It did." I can barely hear my own words, but by the light in his eyes, he heard.

"It meant something to me, too."

My breath catches.

"What are we going to do about it?" I finally ask.

His hand cups my cheek. "We're going to get you ready for the tournament. You're going to compete and impress everyone with your skills. And then." He leans so close I can feel the heat of him reaching up to meet me. "And then we are going to kiss again."

"I'd like that." More than like it.

His hand slowly leaves, fingers trailing down my face as he goes.

And I so much want to kiss him again now, not later, but instead we both step back. I take a big, gasping breath of the cooler air and give myself a moment to gather my thoughts before saying, "Why don't you teach me how to do that spell so I can show Serena?"

In moments, he's teaching while I'm trying to ignore the

undercurrent between us so I can learn all I need to. A while later, Zade rejoins us. Without a word about the kiss, or what we decided to do about it, he helps Lukas. His insight is valuable, leaving me grateful he's here. Yet, as much as I know this is the right thing to be doing, I can't help but wonder what would have happened if he hadn't walked in on my first kiss.

CHAPTER 27

It's been, well, not awkward, but not comfortable between us ever since our one and only kiss. I want to be with Lukas, but it feels like we're stretching ourselves in strange ways, trying not to get too close. Mostly, we haven't spent much time together. Zade and Chadwick have done almost all my training since the kiss. The wondrous, wish-it-could-happen-again-soon kiss. And I've missed being with him.

"Why don't we go for a walk?" Lukas says, as if he can read my thoughts. Besides, the house that seemed big not so long ago, now presses in on me, choking me.

"A walk sounds nice. Where are we going?"

"We'll ride to the tournament grounds, and I'll show you around."

Not very romantic, but since we're not trying to be romantic anyway, it's a good idea. "Do we have to take a guard, or do you think we're safe enough by ourselves?"

"We should take some guards just in case, but I think we'll be fine. They won't be expecting it since you haven't left since we got here. It'll be good for you to see the tournament fields before everything starts."

That's a relief, and it will be good to see everything before it's time to compete, though I wish a guard still wasn't necessary. "Great. Let's go."

The morning air is still crisp, nipping into my skin as we find Conrad and Chadwick who both agree to join us. We hurry through familiar streets, not quickly enough to be noticeable, but not lingering either. All those years wishing we could ride in a way that makes it so we can see outside, and now that I'm finally doing it, I feel exposed. The small window Chadwick helped Lukas install in the carriage has been spelled so that while I can see out of it, others can't see in. It still feels like they can, though. At least we didn't go with riding a horse like I wanted. Then the feeling would have been multiplied. Lukas points out landmarks through the open carriage window as we go.

"You shouldn't need to know the way, but just in case something happens, it's nice to know what to expect," Lukas says, raising his voice just enough that I can hear him.

"It will be." I'm already shaking, and it's not even a tournament day. Even with all the practice I've had over a lifetime, I don't know how I'm going to hide this fear when it's time to participate.

As the carriage pulls to a stop, the area becomes familiar again, bringing with it memories of last year. A time when I had such mixed emotions. Excitement over being at a new place. Worry over losing my sister. And a lot of fascination over seeing more spells in one day than I'd seen in a lifetime. And here I am, a year later, getting ready to join in the fray.

I exit the carriage, Chadwick and Conrad moving some distance away to keep an eye on things while Lukas shows me around. We're the only ones here.

"Duelers meet there." Lukas points toward an open field with a stone stands, taller and wider than me in the middle of it, polished smooth. "The list of who you're fighting is posted on that stone. Check it first thing. It never changes once posted. If you miss a duel because you didn't, and don't know where you're supposed to be, it's not an excuse. You'll be disqualified. "

It's a lot to take in all at once. Not only all the new spells I've learned, and harnessing my magic, but all these new circumstances. Things have never changed so quickly before, and this next week is going to be worse. "I think I can manage being on time, at least."

"Hey." His hand reaches toward me, but then pulls back. "I'll be with you as much as I can. Chadwick and Conrad will always be around, not just protecting you but supporting you. No matter what happens, things are going to be fine. You can do this."

I hate feeling like I have to hold back when I don't know what the next week is going to bring. "I understand we're waiting until after things have settled down to see where we are, but can I have a hug?"

The words are barely out of my mouth when I'm wrapped in his arms. He doesn't say anything, just holds me. The tension building in me over the last few weeks doesn't leave, but it sags under his soothing touch. My troubles may not be gone, but somehow being in his arms makes them feel smaller.

When I pull away, instead of feeling like I need to lean back into him like I expect, I feel better. Stronger. Like maybe I can do this, even during the times I have to do it on my own. I've had help and support, not just from him, but so many others. No matter how things go during the tournament, I will at least succeed at showing everyone what women can do.

"Thank you."

He shifts his weight. "There's something I'd like you to have, if you want it."

What else could he possibly give me? He's already given so much. "Oh?"

He reaches into his shirt, pulling out a chain which he lifts over his head and places in his palm. Strung on it is a silver ring, black stripe wound around the middle with flecks of the silver showing through. There's something inscribed on the inside, but I can't make out what.

"Arthur gave this to me. He said it was to remind me of what good I can do." He slips the ring off the chain and hands it to me. "I'd like you to have it."

The ring is light on my palm, but weighty in my chest. It's a comforting weight, like being wrapped in a pile of blankets on a cold day. I turn it so I can read the inscription.

Strength in yourself is strength for others.

"Thank you." I slip it on my thumb, a perfect fit.

He reaches for my hand and rubs his own thumb over the newly-placed ring before letting his hand drop. As much as I wish our hands would stay intertwined, the ring is a comforting reminder of both him and what I'm trying to do.

We should probably go, but neither of us move from our spots. After a few moments, Lukas says, "Would you like to try a mental duel with me, like we Chryons do?"

"I'd really like that."

He casts a ring for a dueling area the same size I'm accustomed to, but when I move to enter, he says, "Duelers don't enter the ring in Chryos, only their spells do and spells must stay contained inside the ring. Stand just outside it, and you'll cast everything into it."

I step up to the ring, the toes of my boots almost touching the white-with-hints-of-green line. "What type of things do I cast into it?"

"That's where the mental challenge comes from." He winks at me. "Instead of attacking each other, our spells do the actual fighting. So if I cast this…" A fiery spell darts from him into the circle, the magical flames dancing across the dirt but remaining inside the ring. "How would you counter it?"

"This." I zap a water spell in, its fluid-like light snuffing his flames.

"Exactly."

Not much different than the duels I've been training for then, just less risk to me. It's a shame Chardonia doesn't duel like this. I smile at him, until I realize there's something moving off in the distance behind him. Something dark, and it's getting closer. Lukas turns toward where I'm looking. Immediately, he throws up a vibrant blue shield tinted with green and yellow before grabbing me.

"Run!"

CHAPTER 28

I run, but only because he's coming with me. Conrad is hurrying toward us, though, toward our attackers. Can't have him and Chadwick fighting alone just because of me. Both of their lives are worth more than this.

"Leave them," I call.

"Just shielding your backs," he calls back as he darts behind us to join Chadwick in facing down our foes.

Ignoring my wavering, Lukas pulls me forward, putting me in front of him. At this point, it feels like running is the only thing I should be doing, but with each step, guilt jolts through me. Crimson and gray spells flash around us, proving running is the right thing to do, but also meaning I'm leaving others to face what's meant for me.

Lukas puts a hand to my back, pushing me on.

"Wait. I have to help. I can." I lift my hand and start to turn, but he grabs my wrist and ushers me on.

"They're following."

I glance over my shoulder to see that Chadwick and Conrad are retreating, but the attackers are following with a flurry of reds, yellows, and bright greens. We're going to die.

"Get in." Lukas shoves me in the carriage before I've had a chance to realize we've come to it, the door slamming closed behind me. Moments later, we're off, my heart frantic to beat out of my chest. Now that we've got horses on our side, I'm sure we can outrun them, but Chadwick and Conrad? Are they going to make it?

An amber spell smashes against the one-sided window with a pop. Suddenly the door is on fire. Someone screams. When I realize that someone is me, I snap my mouth shut, cover my hand with my sleeve, and kick at the bottom of the door that hasn't caught on fire yet.

It thuds and cracks against my attack but doesn't give way. The carriage has stopped, the air filling with smoke. I sit on the floor, bracing myself against the sidewall and kick as hard as I can. The smoke seems to be sucking my energy out along with my air. It's hot. Choking hot.

Is Lukas trying to help from the outside, or has some other spell attacked him? The thought makes me kick harder even as the flames lick closer to me. The bottom of my skirt catches fire, pain searing my lower legs. Can't give in.

I kick again, thrusting both feet out as hard as I can. The door crumbles open, the flames roaring higher with the new air, stealing it all. I jump from the inferno and run. Everything hurts like I'm still next to the flames. Then I realize I'm on fire.

Suddenly someone pushes me to the ground, smothering me, smacking at the flames still flickering across me. Pain racks through me, my vision going dark. Then the weight lifts from me, my body slowly cooling, taking the aching with it.

Opening my eyes, I find I'm encompassed by a blue spell cast by Lukas who's hovering over me. Another moment, and I'm feeling almost, but not quite, like myself, and the spell stops.

"Than—" Before I finish, he slumps to the ground. "Lukas!"

"Fine." His voice is faint. "Tired."

Chadwick is there, lifting Lukas as Conrad pulls me to my feet, his hand firm on mine. "We have to go. We've cut them off, but it won't last."

With Chadwick carrying Lukas, there's nothing left to stop me from running.

* * *

"I HOPE there are no further plans of me going out before the tournament," I say.

"Definitely not." Lukas says as he reclines on a couch, eyelids drooping.

"It is a good thing there are still two more days, or you wouldn't have enough time to regain your strength." I lightly brush my hand against his. "Thank you. For saving me and healing me."

He clasps a hold of my hand with a grip that's firm and reassuring, I wouldn't know he was so exhausted if he wasn't lying before me half awake. "I shouldn't have taken you in the first place."

"No, you were right to take me. I don't feel as anxious about going to the tournament now, and no one was hurt. If anything, we know they are still out there, keeping too close an eye on us. I just wish I knew who attacked. Do you think they are watching the house?"

"We've searched a lot, both physically and with spells, but haven't found anything. Seems likely, though." He closes his eyes, and I drop his hand, even though he tries to take it back.

"I should let you rest."

"Probably, but one more thing, and don't be upset about it. Just learn from it." Lukas takes a deep breath before continuing. "That would have been a good time to cast a spell."

"Blast it all! I will never learn."

"Don't be so hard on yourself. Everything up until the last few weeks has been to hide magic. You'll learn how to let it out."

Maybe, but with the tournament so close, there isn't time. The next opportunity I have to go to the tournament grounds will be to show everyone what I can do. And possibly die for it. Seeing how I almost died today, that possibility has grown all too likely.

CHAPTER 29

"Councilman Daniel, good to see you." Zade's words draw me to the entrance to find not only the councilman, but his wife, Annabelle, and Katherine.

"Katherine! Annabelle!" I wrap them both in hugs. My loud exclamations bring the girls from all around the house down as well.

Soon the entrance is alive with chatter and excitement. Finally, mother sneaks in long enough to say, "I'm certain our guests don't wish to make their entire visit in the hall."

The girls immediately quiet and line themselves along the hall wall. The thought sends a pinch through me from all of the times we were trained to calm ourselves before father scolded us. Or worse, being caught doing something that required scolding.

The thought quickly passes as Waverly ushers the youngest girls back toward the playroom, and Serena leads our guests to the receiving room.

Before I follow the others in, Katherine stops me by putting a large bundle in my hands. "Your clothes for the tournament. A good variety for you to pick from. We can size them before I go, but I'm sure they'll all fit."

I squeeze the bundle closer to me. "They'll be perfect."

"You haven't even seen them yet."

"But you always come through."

"One of these days, I may disappoint you."

"Unlikely," I counter. "But if you did, I'm sure you'd find a brilliant fix for it in no time at all."

She laughs. "You're too nice. Sadly, though, I can't stay for the beginning of the tournament. Hopefully, I can return to watch it sometime toward the end."

The purple glow of her tattoos suddenly looks sinister. Blast the council. "I understand and will be happy to see you when you make it," I say. "I'll be in as soon as I put these away."

"See you soon."

I take my things and head to my room, wondering what marvels she's tucked in this package for me. It's been hard being here and not seeing her as much. I miss her.

"That girl sure is sweet." Mother's voice makes me stop. She's standing just inside the last door I passed, the door to her room.

"She is."

I linger, wondering if there's something more, but not knowing what to say. Suddenly, mother says, "Your baby sister is kicking. I think she's the most active yet. Would you like to feel it?"

The package in my hands seems like a very good excuse not to. Although she always seems to be pregnant, I've never felt one of the babies move before. I've never done anything with them until they were old enough to be weaned. Bethany and mother always took care of them before that.

"Do you miss father?" The words blurt out before I realized my thoughts were traveling there. Why would I ask her such a thing? Why do I even care? Our lives are so much better without him around.

She looks at some point far past me. "I don't know if miss is the right word for it."

I move closer to her, leaning against the doorframe. "What do you mean?"

"Almost my entire adult life, he's been around. That's the way it was supposed to be. Me obeying his every whim. When your sister gained her freedom and first became our owner, I was so lost. I didn't know what to do. Not having your father around to punish anyone was a blessing."

"Very much so."

"Yet, you must admit it was odd."

A deep, grating sort of exhaustion pulls through me. "It is still odd without him sometimes. But I wouldn't want him here."

"No, none of us want that." But her voice sounds as heavy as I feel. "Sometimes I just wonder where he is, what he's doing. I still find myself thinking on what chores I need to complete for him. Things I'd still be doing if Serena wasn't our owner."

I rub my ring. "Are you upset she's your owner?"

"Not upset. Just worried." Her hand presses tightly on her belly.

"And what I'm doing, does that worry you?"

"Of course it does. Everyone seems to think it will be all right, though. Zade has us well protected." The fondness in her voice when she says his name is unmistakable. His presence probably has done more for changing mother's attitude than having father gone.

"You know, I could teach you a spell or two."

Her face goes pale, but she recovers quickly. "And you could feel your baby sister kicking."

I'd rather go practice more even though it feels as if I've done nothing but practice. I never deal with the babies when she carries them. Still, if she needs to see me be brave to do the same in return...

I reach my hand out. A jab pops out of her belly before I even reach it, making my hand dart back. "Uh. I don't think she's ready to say hello yet."

Mother laughs. "She's probably just so excited to hear your voice she can't contain herself."

Can she hear my voice? Has she heard what I'm trying to do for women? For her? Not that she would understand it, but when mother's belly shifts again, it doesn't make me want to run down the hall like before. After placing my package on the floor, I slowly reach forward and hover my hand over mother's belly. She reaches up and presses it firmly against her stomach, just in time for a swift kick to my palm.

I laugh, but let my hand fall back to my side. "She really is eager for something."

"Most active of you girls yet, that's for certain."

I pick up my package and step back into the hall. "So when can I teach you a spell?"

She simply smiles and retreats into her room. Guess I shouldn't expect too much progress in one conversation. Still, it's something. I understand her a little better now. And my sister. That push against my hand wasn't like I expected it to be. The thrill was almost exciting rather than scary.

That sister, she's going to be the first born under Serena's ownership. If everything goes well, the first to know, from birth, that women can do magic. What will become of a female who knows their worth and what they are capable of?

CHAPTER 30

It's still dark when I leave the house. Lukas left earlier this morning to make certain things are going well. And they are, a little too well. We'll not be able to take the carriage all the way to the grounds because of how busy it already is. My skirts are full, swishing around my legs as I get in the carriage. A new one with no spelled window for me to see out. No matter. I suppose I could fix it, but the dark is familiar. No sense rattling my already withered nerves.

The carriage moves, the sound of horses clopping filling the air. While many of the guards are staying to protect the girls, and others are going with Bethany and Serena, several are accompanying me. I grip my skirt the entire way, too much like Serena, but this is it. This is the day.

My stomach feels like revolting, also like Serena. I'm glad I left before she or the others could see me off. Things are frayed enough without having to hide more emotions from them as well. Each bump or dip of the carriage is another step closer to my doom or salvation, yet all I want to do is stay in this carriage. Never leave its dark confines.

All too soon the carriage stops. There's chatter outside but not close by. A few moments later, the carriage door opens. My hands grip my seat as if that's enough to keep me here, but of course my own will power and desires propel me, even if I'm having a hard time remembering what desires those are. Chadwick, Xyer, and Conrad are in a semi-circle around me.

"Where's Lukas? I thought he was to meet us here."

Chadwick glances around as if simply looking for him will make him appear.

"I'm certain he'll be along shortly," Xyer says.

"Right." I guess it's time, then.

I pry my hands from the seat and step from the carriage. My black skirt swishes around me, loose enough I can move easily, but full enough to hide a gun if I choose to carry one. It feels so useless today though. The blouse I'm wearing is also black to conform with tournament dress code. Despite the dark color, it's light and smooth against my skin. It's tucked into my skirt and draping down my arms to allow for full control of my arms without getting tangled. The only part of my outfit uncomfortable is the orange band I must wear denoting my country. Katherine has done wonderfully as usual. Still, I'd rather be wearing breeches.

They follow as I head toward the grounds, Conrad close by, while Xyer and Chadwick spread out. Others are about, but not as close as I thought, and are quickly leaving us behind. No sense tainting themselves by arriving when I do.

Perhaps I should have waited for Lukas before starting my walk of doom. He should have been here. If something happened to him—no, I won't think such thoughts. He's probably just running behind on one of the most important days of our lives. At least I can find out not only when my duels are, but his as well, in case whatever is keeping him continues until it's almost time to start. I'm sure it's nothing.

The air around me swirls, brushing against my skin with a chilly bite that feels menacing. Almost like something is there besides just air. Like someone is watching me. Waiting for me to stop, or slow down, or take the wrong turn so they can make it so I don't show up for the tournament. Even with my guards here, it doesn't feel like enough. I increase my pace until I'm running. The air whips past my skin, chilling my already cold skin further.

"Is everything all right?" Chadwick says in between breaths as he runs up beside me.

"I don't know."

He glances around and asks Conrad, "What do you think?"

"I'll check the area. You three go ahead, and move fast."

He stops running and spells fly from him, zipping off in all directions. Chadwick and I turn back toward the grounds and run again. Where is everyone? Did they run off because of me, or do they know something we don't?

Chills want to cripple me, to keep me from moving forward, but I force myself on. My lungs burn as my feet crunch against the road. We dip into an alley, a shortcut, but the houses press in on me from both sides. If anyone should come, there's only one way out. If more people come, blocking both sides, we're trapped.

I push myself harder. We're almost there. Just a little farther and we'll make it. There are people in the distance, wandering on the field where we'll join the tournament. Not much farther. I bound out of the alley into a clearing. The panicked fear gripping me on the run is immediately replaced with something much more certain. I've arrived. I'll sign in, check the list of competitors, and will soon be competing. As much as my nerves are tumbling around my insides, churning things about, I force my outward appearance to be cool and calm, as if this is commonplace and accepted.

Several groups of people, mostly men but a few women, are scattered throughout, though none close to us. They're all staring at me. I pretend like my running turned to a stroll was all part of the plan. What plan, I have no idea, but people who duel in tournaments must have a plan, yes? Like warming up or something, not that I got scared on the way over. What a way for me to introduce myself to everyone, to show even more how I don't belong.

As we drift through the clearing, the attention leaves us. It's hard not to think, and worry, about Lukas. Any moment he should be joining us, but there's no sign of him. I glance to where a few duelers are already signing in. The gate in the fence dividing the duelers from the spectators is guarded by a fierce warlock, dark, stringy hair down to his shoulders, with a nose so hooked I can see it from here as he scowls at the warlock currently trying to check in.

The worry in my chest suddenly feels tighter, strangling my ability to breathe. But this is what I came for. What I've trained for. I need to do this. To be strong and show everyone my magic.

We head toward the gate but then stop. Chadwick and Xyer have been nothing but helpful. They've saved my life. I want them to come. To support me. But having warlocks around while trying to sign in feels like it goes against what I'm trying to accomplish. I need to do this on my own. Dread flashes through me. I hate when the right thing to do is also the hardest thing to do.

"I'm going to go sign in. Would you mind letting me do it on my own?"

"No problem," Chadwick says. "I'll be back here but still making sure your safe."

Some of the dread eases from me, just not nearly enough of it. "Thank you. And if you see Lukas, will you let him know where I am?"

"Will do."

After thanking him again, I stride toward the admitting gate, pretending like I'm not covered in fear. Thankfully there's not a line, the warlock who was signing in a moment ago is walking through the gate now. Maybe it's worse. It means I'll have to face him now without having more time to think on what to say. Once there, a stringy-haired law officer stops me, a gap between his front teeth visible now that I'm closer.

"Where are you going? Where's your owner? Why are you dressed in black with an arm band?" he snaps.

The rapid questions mixed with his presence leaning toward me, hand up, ready to cast a spell makes me want to run all the way back to the house.

I straighten and in my most commanding voice, learned from father, I say, "I'm participating in the tournament. See this?" I point to the orange band on my arm. "You know it means I am a participant."

He shrugs. "You could have stolen it."

Even though I expected this to be difficult, I hoped it wouldn't be. But hopes are almost always in vain. "You had to have heard a woman, with the status of a warlock, would be participating this year."

His eye twitches. "I'll have to look into it." He waves another law officer over, this one with a fluff of blond hair. "This *girl* claims she's participating in the tournament. Would you look her information up?"

The warlock laughs. "Not worth my time."

Rage flares inside me, which is better than fear at least. Good thing my paperwork is in my boot. I pull it out. "Proof that I didn't steal anything." I give the gap-toothed warlock a pointed glare. "Let me through."

The guard grabs for my papers, but it's doubtful he'd return them. I clutch them to my chest, though it probably won't stop him for long.

"If you're not going to show them to us then they must be fake. Quit wasting our time before we find your owner and fine him for your nuisance."

The crowd that had been scattered across the field is taking notice of our disagreement, looming closer. Some are clearly from other countries, tall or darker skinned, but only a few sprinkled throughout the crowd. Toward the fringes of the multitude there are even a few women.

Chadwick and Xyer are nowhere in sight. They said they'd keep me safe. What could have happened to them? My fingers tremble, giving away my trepidation. First Lukas, now Chadwick? But there's nothing that can be done until I fix this situation.

I scan the crowd again. Is it big enough for me to let loose my power? If I cast a spell now and am sacrificed for it, will enough people be here that they can't cast a memory loss spell for what I'm about to do? This wasn't the plan, but forget the plan. If this isn't the time to make a statement, I don't know what is. But it has to be big. Really big. Something that will be hard to erase from so many memories.

The threatening warlocks are distracted by fighting over what to do with me. Perfect. This is it, the test to see what's going to happen to me once everyone knows what it is exactly I can do.

My hands shake. but Lukas's ring is steady on my thumb. I take a deep breath, gather my magic, and force it to fan across the clearing in a wide array of colors. All perfectly harmless, but bright and flashy, some even flaring as they dance through the crowd. They gasp as the light bounces in and around them.

I flash it not just around them, but high into the sky. High enough that questions will have to be answered even if everyone here loses their memory. Though the answers may not be about me if they can erase all these memories, but it's something. If only it's enough of something. It has to be enough of something. Whether or not it is, I'm lighter than I've ever felt before, and my hands have stopped shaking. My chest is a torrent of emotion with use of my magic in front of so many. Finally, *finally*, I'm showing everyone my true self.

Once I'm certain I have their attention, that everyone knows it came from me, I wrap a floating spell around the papers that proves I'm free along with my tournament entry and make them float in the air before the stunned law officers.

The look on their faces transform from shocked to fierce and angry. Fluffy hair reaches out again to snatch the papers, but I push the air in the spell back away from him, keeping them just out of reach.

I hold back a laugh as he jumps for it as it taunts him. "You can look, but don't touch. I'd hate to lose such important papers."

He growls. "Take your paperwork and find your place."

I raise my voice, "So you accept that I have the status of a warlock and am allowed in the tournament?"

"I said find your place."

I want nothing more, except maybe to know if Lukas and the others are all right. "Once everyone here is assured that I'm supposed to be here, I will."

He's turning a brilliant red, nose flaring. "You're a dueler in the tournament. Now get out of my face."

Slowly, I drift the papers back down, letting the spell flash a few times for effect before rolling them up. "I'm only too happy to oblige you. Thank you for your assistance."

Laughter bubbles again, and I have to work hard to suppress the joy trying to escape me.

He turns away from me in disgust, but the eyes of everyone gathered watch as I leave the public area and cross over into the designated dueler's area.

There's no music or noise. In fact it's oddly silent for such a large gathering. It feels official, like I'm finally doing what I set out to show everyone. If a warlock killed me right now, right here in front of everyone, I'd still feel like I accomplished what I set out to do.

And I'm grateful. It is what I wanted to show everyone before. The problem is, now I don't want to just show everyone what women can do. I want to show them a woman can win. That I can win.

CHAPTER 31

My hands are shaking, the one thing I can't seem to control, but I keep them tightly wrapped around my papers. Whether it's the fear or commitment of trying to win causing the shaking, I'm uncertain. I only hope that it was a big enough display in front of enough people to show everyone women can do magic. If it was, I'll be in my first duel in only a few short hours. If not, well, I'll probably be dead before then.

Either way, standing still is my worst option. First, I need to check the schedule and learn where and when my first duel is so I can be ready and check Lukas's as well. Then I have to figure out where both he, Xyer, and Chadwick are. I suppress the growing pit of worry in my stomach and head toward the stone.

A warlock steps in front of me. Chancellor Ryan. Dread clings to me, grappling for me to get away from him and whatever he has planned. But he can't do away with me now, not after everything we've worked so hard on to make my presence accepted. Can he?

"Think pretty highly of yourself, don't you?"

The urge to look down is almost overbearing. Focusing so wholly on keeping his gaze probably makes me look crazed, but any other option is unacceptable. "I only think I'm doing what I've earned the right to do."

He leans closer. "Back out now."

My gaze slips, just for a moment, but enough that defeat seems to cling to me even as I return to holding my stare back on him. "Not happening."

His nose flares, hand flickering toward me. "You will regret it, and so will those you care about."

And he's off, leaving me behind in a wave of emotion. I'm struggling not to regret entering the tournament already. As soon as he's gone, the crowd of duelers swarm in on me. Every jostle and bump as they fight their way by adds to the blow Chancellor Ryan delivered.

One warlock elbows me in the stomach, followed by another jamming into my shoulder. And on and on. I'd like to think that it's because the area is so crammed full of people that there's not enough room to be polite. But the truth is, even with the plethora of warlocks wandering about, there's plenty of empty space. Except around me. When one warlock leaves, another seems to take his place. It's a good thing we aren't allowed to use magic in the waiting area, or I would have been hexed by most of them by now. Did Chancellor Ryan encourage this fray?

Another warlock falls into me, his elbow jamming into my ribs hard enough to leave a bruise. The pain quickly subsides, but my reaction to it doesn't. I grit my teeth, wondering how I'm ever going to make it to the stone when one of them steps in front of me.

I open my mouth ready to let angry words tumble out but realize it's Lukas. My arms ache to wrap around him, both to comfort me and in gratitude that he's fine. "Where have you been? I've been worried about you. Have you seen Chadwick?"

"I've been waiting with him over there." He points to a clear spot where only Chadwick stands Conrad is a ways behind him, keeping an eye on things.

Waiting? Does that mean he saw everything that just happened? The guards? Chancellor Ryan's threat?

As we trudge our way through the crowd to Chadwick, Lukas gives the warlocks surrounding us an angry glare. I've never seen such a look on him before. I don't think I like it, but it's highly effective. The crowd of warlocks eases away from me. Once we reach Chadwick, they eye us but leave a wide circle around us. Chadwick does make an intimidating foe, his thick build looming over all the other duelers. I forgot how much of an impact his presence can make.

"That was something else," Lukas says.

"What was?" The threat or my display?

"The spell you just showed everyone."

"You saw that?" Does that mean the threat went unnoticed? What am I to do about it? "Where were you? I couldn't see you anywhere."

"We both saw it," Chadwick says.

"Not what got you riled enough to cast a spell," Lukas adds. "Just the last part. It was amazing. You did perfect. I don't think the deviation from the plan will matter. You had a big enough crowd that I think things will be all right. But what got you so upset?"

His words warm me and calm some of the frantic worry bounding inside me. I tell them what happened and have to ask, "Do you think they're sending someone to…" I make a cutting sound and fake jabbing at my neck.

"Not now." His hand briefly brushes against my arm, warm and reassuring, but there's doubt in his eyes. "You have everyone worked into a frenzy. People were leaving the scene even as you were still casting the spell. The council shouldn't be able to track them all down. I think you've done it."

"Agreed," Chadwick adds, looking much more certain than Lukas, but his eyes still watch the crowd. They are both nervous and on edge, yet neither said anything about the Chancellor. I should tell them, but what good would it do?

Besides, I've done it. Everyone knows what a woman can do. That we can be strong, and that we can do magic, just like men. No threat is going to stop that from happening now.

But there's not going to be any celebrating anytime soon. Even the small amount of triumph coursing through me is dampened by whatever is worrying Lukas and Chadwick.

"Neither of you ever answered my other question. Where were you this morning, Lukas? And where did you go off to when the law officers were trying to keep me from going in to the waiting area, Chadwick? Why are you both watching the crowd so much?"

Lukas looks at Chadwick, who shrugs one shoulder. Lukas says, "We're almost entirely certain that the council isn't coming after you. Yet."

"Almost? Yet?" I don't like the sound of either of those words.

He leans closer but not close enough that we're touching. "There are no guarantees. The Chardonian council is entirely under the rule of the Grand Chancellor, and we can't predict what he'll do. But we're hopeful."

Guess hopeful is the best I'm going to get. "Then why are you still both on edge and keeping such a watchful eye out?"

Lukas scans the crowd, this time not looking at me at all. "The thing is, I was going to meet you this morning like we discussed, but I was, uh, detained. Physically detained, that is, by some warlocks who intended me harm."

The worry I felt when he didn't show blunders its way back in full force.

"Don't look at me like that," he says. "I'm fine. I called for help and managed to escape unscathed. Though I distracted Chadwick when we found each other, which is why he was missing from protecting you."

"I wasn't missing. I kept an eye out for her the whole time, even if she couldn't see me."

It's nice to know that's the case, though it would have been nice to know sooner. "I'm glad you're both all right, but next time, why don't you wave a giant, bright-orange spell instead of getting lost in the crowd so there's no need to worry."

"Fair enough," Lukas says. "If it's safe for me to, I will."

I resist rolling my eyes and say to Chadwick, "Which means he won't."

He holds up both of his hands. "I'm not getting in the middle of this."

"I will," Lukas reaffirms.

"If it's safe," I counter.

"Exactly."

"Which is great, except for the fact that it's never safe."

"Glad you coul—wait no." The tips of his finger rub against his temple. "I really will do it, if it's safe."

I shrug. Nothing is ever safe in Chardonia.

Lukas squeezes my hand, the gesture more reassuring than his words. "Let's see about your first duel."

Our hands fall apart, and immediately, mine is cold. But it's important to stand on my own here, in front of the other duelers. I can't show any sort of weakness. Really, I probably shouldn't even be communicating with Lukas too much. Or maybe I should, and find other participants with similar values to be around as well. Maybe the more of them I can help to see me as a warlock, the better my casting spells and dueling will be taken. How many more of them exist?

As we make our way to the stone with the schedule spelled on it, the crowd grows thicker again. A warlock elbows me, another pushing his shoulder into me as he moves past. Maybe trying to get closer to them isn't a reality. Magic will have to be the start, I guess.

We get to the line for the stone and wait at the end for our turn. Or rather, I try to wait my turn. First one warlock cuts in front of me, coming between me and Lukas before either of us realizes. Then another. And another. They keep cutting in front of me, not only shoving me farther to the back of the line, but farther from Lukas.

Chadwick stands firmly behind me, not letting their jostling displace him, but it's probably easier to do with his large stature. The crowd's fear of him doesn't last, though. Soon, they're jostling against him. A thin warlock slips between us and slams me forward. I tumble into the warlock ahead of me who shoves me back. Chadwick shoves the thin warlock from between us and grabs a hold of my arm. That firm pressure on my upper arm steels my nerves against the scream trying to claw its way from me.

Where are the law officers now? Except that's a ridiculous thought. They'd only help shove me down. The warlocks seem to be gaining a rhythm to their shoving. The ones that cut me off leave with smirks in the same order they shoved me out of the way. A growly, half-scream spikes from me, but they only shove me harder.

Lukas is on the other side of the crowd from me. He's pushing against the crowd, trying to break through to get to me. While I appreciate the thought, he can't handle all of my problems. He's taught me what I know. Now I just have to use it. Except, there's no magic use in the dueler waiting area. To do so would get me banned. How am I supposed to see my dueling information without getting banned?

Chadwick is still firmly standing behind me, hand tight around my upper arm, so we don't get separated.

I shake my head at Lukas and mouth, "I will handle this." Without waiting to see his reaction, I tell Chadwick, "I have to fight my way there. Can you stay close and help act as a buffer?"

"Do what you need to. I'll follow."

I stare straight at my goal, the stone glowing with today's schedule, take a deep breath, and plunge into the hostile mob. Bruises must already be forming from everywhere they slam into my arms and stomach, but my back is protected by Chadwick's fierce determination not to let me go. When I'm shoved, I shove back. When I'm elbowed, I elbow back. Each step taking me closer to the board, which I refuse to take my gaze from.

Shoving past the last warlock gives me such momentum, I slam against the stone. My face aches with victory. Chadwick turns around and holds his arms out, making it difficult for anyone to get past. Not knowing how long he can last, I quickly locate my name and dueling information for the day.

"I've got it," I tell Chadwick. And it feels good. Really good that I did it without Lukas. Except I still needed Chadwick's help. I always need someone's help.

Together, Chadwick and I make our way out. Going out is much easier than trying to fight in. There are only a few elbows and shoves, until we're almost to Lukas, when a warlock sticks his foot out to trip me. I fly toward the ground, preparing myself to brace for a rough landing in the dirt, but hands reach out to grab each of my arms. Lukas and Chadwick.

Chadwick maintains his stoic expression, but Lukas's jaw is clenched, his free arm raised up in a fist and headed toward the tripper. I grab for his arm, fearing he's about to disqualify himself from the tournament. At my touch, he slows, and after a moment, he shakes his arm free of me. With a look I'm grateful isn't directed at me, he says, "You'd better hope we're not paired up in the tournament."

The warlock has the decency to at least look scared, little good the expression does us.

We walk slower than I'd like but with purpose toward the free area of the clearing that we used before. It's several minutes before Lukas finally calms down enough to speak.

"Are you all right?"

"I'm fine."

His eyes scan my face, which must already be bruising by the feel of it. "No you're not. If we could cast magic in the waiting area, I would heal you."

It's a good thing my clothes cover the rest of what must be bruised. My body is one giant ache. "Don't worry about it. Truly I'm fine."

Lukas looks at Chadwick as if to say, 'she's clearly delusional because it's obvious she's injured' to which Chadwick shrugs back in a way that says, 'what are you going to do?'

A huff escapes me. "I'm really fine. Chadwick can heal me once we're on the field, and everything will be fine. It's not like I'm bleeding to death. Don't worry about it."

Neither of them look like they really believe me, but they don't belabor the point.

"Did you see it? If not, I can go back and look it up for you," Lukas says.

"Don't worry. With Chadwick holding them off I managed. I only have one duel today. I'm at the smaller field in the far corner at eleven."

"Unusual for a first day."

"They probably don't expect me to last through the one duel." And honestly, I'm not sure if I expect me to either. I want to, but am I truly ready?

"You're about to surprise them, then," Lukas says, and I try to believe it. "My first is on the opposite side of the field as you in twenty minutes."

"Guess that means we'll be going our separate ways now."

"Guess so." Lukas turns to Chadwick. "Take care of her."

I want to bristle at his words, but the bruises are still too new and painful for me to think there's not a reason for him to say them. Not only to say them but to mean them.

"I won't let her out of my sight."

"Thank you." He turns back to me and conversation stops. The noise from the participants around us is a dull background noise. Chadwick is kind enough to step back and watch the crowd, though he's still close enough that if we did say anything, he'd still be able to hear it.

I can't help but wish that we were dueling next to each other, that we didn't have to part. Is he going to die today? Am I? The only words I can think of don't seem like enough. The only thing that does seem like enough is to melt into him, to let his arms encircle me and keep me close and tight and safe.

But we agreed not to pursue that type of relationship until after this was all over. Which is just as well. I can't be sure how all these warlocks around us would react to us hugging, but I'm pretty sure I wouldn't like whatever they would do. Instead, we just stare at each other, so close together, yet so far apart, unable to touch or talk. This may be the last we ever see of each other. And if we both do make it out of the day alive, we'll have to go through this all over again the next day and the next, until the tournament is over.

Finally, he says, "Good luck."

I have an overwhelming urge to kiss him before we part. To press my lips against his, to show him what he means to me, what my heart is growing to feel for him. But I settle for a smile, a real one. He returns it with his own heart-melting smile and is off before I can say good-bye.

CHAPTER 32

The array of canopies covering the stands around the field is a varying rainbow of colors. Somehow they seem brighter, splashier than last year. Strolling through the waiting areas on the large field on my way to one of the small waiting areas, I realize something else. There are a lot of stands that aren't covered. People still wear their country's color in some form or another but are crowded together on benches raised up, one behind another. These grow in number the farther I get from the large field and closer to the smaller fields. Save the best for those who can afford their importance, I suppose.

It's good Lukas showed me around so I know where everything is, even if I don't know my place in it all. Chadwick was here last year but stayed in the stands just like I did. Well, I'm sure it wasn't just like me, but he didn't wander around with the participants and get an idea of what duelers do moment to moment. If I had to ask for directions, no one would give the correct answer.

By the time I reach the dueling ring furthest from the center of the action, there are only the benches for sitting and none of the raised boxes, and even these are sparsely populated. Though still enough warlocks speckled throughout them to make me play with my bracelets. Perhaps it's even more fortunate than I first supposed that my display of magic was at the entrance gates and not in front of this small group.

I drum my fingers against my thigh. Usually it's not so hard to hold emotions in, but being nervous is difficult to hide. My betraying fingers only listen to my calls to be still for a moment before dancing through my emotions again.

I keep thinking of Lukas waiting closer to the more important events. The ones I watched last year. Last year. Never would have guessed I'd ever be here competing. I should have been sold off early, like Serena and become a baby maker like mother, always hiding my magic. Always fearing what would happen if it was discovered.

Yet, here I am, about to show everyone what I already showed the early crowd this morning. Only this time my death is even more of a reality as spells are flung back at me.

"We're on the field. Magic is allowed here as long as it's not at another dueler," Chadwick says. "Can I heal your bruises?"

"I'll be fine." What good am I if I can't even take care of myself?

"But not up to what you could be if I don't heal them."

True. And if I did it myself, I'd have less power saved up for later. It's time to let him and others help more even if it isn't what I'm used to. "Thank you. That would be welcome."

The spell is a soothing teal, passing over me with speedy efficiency. Now there's nothing left to do but wait. I watch the few other duels going on nearby. A year ago, I would have been rapt by them. Now they are a measly show of those lacking in skills and not a good distraction.

My necklace pulls tight on the back of my neck as my fingers wind through it. Tight like the growing pressure in my chest.

"Cynthia Stephen's daughter." Finally, they call my name.

I'm so focused on listening for it, I don't even hear them call my opponent. And, naturally, they don't have any sort of title for me, or the decency to call me by just my first name like the others.

No, they have to call me by my old owner, proof to all I'm still my father's daughter, even when he no longer owns me.

I make my way across the waiting strip and onto the field. Grateful that I listened to the instructions being given to the other participants all day, I make my way over to the ring where I think I'm supposed to be. Of course no one is going to tell me. The spelled ring is a bright green, looking almost wrong against the dark grass. A judge and another dueler are already waiting outside it, but the mediator is circling other duels taking place. I force myself to continue on to them, though both men are glaring me down.

Serena, Zade, Bethany, and Waverly are waiting on the sidelines, quiet and steadfast. The fact they made an effort to leave their box to be somewhere they could watch is heartening but nerve wracking. It's enough to know their support is here, though I don't look at them again.

I step to the circle, careful to not cross the line surrounding the dueling area yet. The judge announces something, probably my and my competitor's names, but it's hard to focus on what he's saying. Everything is fuzzier, blurring together in a swarm of nerves. I twist Lukas's ring.

The warlock across from me sneers. "Easiest win of the tournament."

My opponent, apparently. The one they thought would be enough to wipe me out of the competition. He looks scary enough to wipe me out. Eyes dark, almost black against his pale skin. Smirk on his face saying how much he's going to enjoy massacring me. I shiver. Maybe their plan will work.

He steps into the circle, and I do the same, with it flashing bronze as we do so. The instant we're both in and the light is back to green, he zaps an orange arrow hex toward me. Instead of blocking, I dive out of the way my hand landing inches from the boundary.

The pale warlock laughs, and some of the nearby crowd joins

him, quite loudly despite their lacking numbers. "Knew this was going to be too easy. What are you even doing here, little girl?"

My knees are soaked with dew from the grass and burned where they scraped against a rock, but they don't hurt as much as the shame within me burns. Little girl. He's correct. I've spent too many years hiding my skills. It's instinctive to flinch away instead of reacting. At least he's too stupid to throw another hex while I'm down. Fool thinks he has this. I climb to my feet, and the laughing increases.

"You belong in a pigsty, not with world-class warlocks," he taunts.

And it's true. I'm not a world-class warlock. I'm just a girl. Except I'm a girl who learned to tap into her powers when others didn't even try.

"Give up now." He cracks forth another hex, orange, tainted with black.

It slams into my stomach with a pop before I have time to process a defense. The pain sears my skin. I grit my teeth to keep from calling out, grateful it only went skin deep and didn't do more damage. Or worse, kill me.

I fling a yellow hex back at him, meant to puncture him with heat. It misses only inches from his shoulder, enough to wipe the glee from him, though the crowd is still laughing. He zips two more at me, hitting my shoulder and arm. Both take all my effort not to call out, but I keep the pain in and my face determined.

Just barely starting, but I'm already losing, four to zero. I zap an array of mini fireballs at him as quickly as I can, striving to get as many points as I can, even if they're the minor one point attacks. It doesn't help that my mind seems to have gone blank. My spells are weak and slow, most easily blocked with his silvery, translucent shield.

He throws a hex, jagged lights of puce and amber arcing toward me. I ignore my instincts to dive under it or take it while hiding my magic and instead blare a full-force shield that utilizes the spell I used for years. A mirror. The spell reflects back to him, silvers and blues mixed in with a deafening crack as it smashes against his entire body.

There's a sudden hush. His footing wavers. I waver. I didn't want to do this to anyone. Didn't want to become like one of them. It's all too clear as his skin bubbles with thousands of tiny blisters.

Then I remember, that could have been me. It has been me, and thousands of other women. I have to do this. I have to fight back, even if it means becoming like them. For now at least. And both the crowd and my opponent finally understand I'm not playing a game. I will not break.

I hurl several pain spells, angry reds and blacks, aiming for his hands and feet. Three of them hit, causing him to howl with pain and shoot an aqua spell back. I block with a wisp of a shield that comes out in a spurt of pink and pops when hit.

A final pain spell slams into his gut. Is it enough? Have I slipped ahead yet? A final spell comes to me, father's silencing spell. Not really a traditional attack, but I thrust it toward his throat anyway, its clear wavering lines clashing against his throat just as the judge yells, "Time."

It's done. My first duel over.

There's no laughter. No taunting. Only the distant sound of other duels still taking place. Here, all are silent, focused on the judge.

"Cynthia is the winner." His words are begrudging, but it's of no matter.

The eyes of the nearby crowd are on me, watching me. More have come, the crowd growing sometime during the fight, the mediator also watching on with a deep scowl. I wish the duel would have taken place in front of Envado's or Chryos's stands. Maybe then the stares wouldn't be so hostile.

But not all the stares are hostile. Some of the women are

looking at me with something much more complex than hostility. Do they understand that they can do what I've just done?

As poorly as I did, I'm not sure that they will think it's something they want to replicate. I have to be better. Move past whatever it is holding me back, or they'll never wish to try it for themselves.

My opponent spits, barely missing my shoe. His voice is weak and cracking, even if his words are harsh. "Dumb luck, wench."

I paste on my fake smile while inside burning with rage. Partially at him, but mostly at myself. My first duel should have been one that left everyone in awe over my ability, not one that left my opponent skeptical. As he walks away, he pushes his shoulder into me as he passes. I try to stand firm, as he does, but it forces me to stumble back.

I glance at the mediator, who quickly turns his head away, pretending he saw nothing. None of them take any of this seriously. If I slammed into a dueler like that, I'd be disqualified.

At least there are no more duels today. Still, this isn't how I wanted things to go. I turn from the ring and head back to the participant's area, careful to make sure I don't walk past my sisters.

* * *

"THERE YOU ARE," Zade says. "Serena's worried about you."

"Nothing to worry over." I give him one of my fake smiles to defend my words. "Chadwick was just about to take me home."

He lifts a brow. "Without seeing how Lukas is doing?"

I do want to know. Hopefully, he's being much more successful than me. Not only successful, but winning with his life, and body, fully intact.

But hovering at the edge of a field full of warlocks who hate me won't do anything to help him or ease my worry. "I'm sure he'll tell me about it when he finishes."

Zade sighs like he understands. "Maybe I should see you home as well."

"No, don't. Serena and the girls need you, whether they decide to stay or come home as well."

I turn to go, but Zade puts a hand on my shoulder. His words are low. "You've made an impression, Cynthia."

I swallow past the sudden thickening in my throat.

"You may not have seen, or heard it, but people are talking. They want to know what you're doing competing, but more than that, I'm already hearing whispers of other women wondering if they can do what you can."

Which was to barely escape with my life. I'm grateful that they are thinking, but I really made the biggest fool out of myself. There was no excuse for me to perform so poorly, and I'm lucky to have not only won but to have survived. I don't need hooded attackers or other duelers to kill me off. My stupidity is going to do it all on its own. Yet... his words spark embers of hope.

"I'll keep that in mind," I say and then head for home, Chadwick, and probably a few others I don't see, following the whole way. No wonder I need them to constantly follow me everywhere. I'm failing at what I'm supposed to be showing everyone. How could I possibly manage to do something as simple as protecting myself? It's hard to say why, but those embers keep flickering inside me, warming to the hope there is much I can still do, even if it doesn't seem like it.

CHAPTER 33

I can't handle another day in the tournament like this one. It was so much worse than I thought it would be and in more ways than expected.

First duel and I lost my composure. It was nothing like practicing. I only won by a point. A single point. One less spell, and that would have been the end of this escapade. No one believes I can do this, not even me. Those people Zade mentioned were talking of me because it's new and different, not because of any skill level. I'm just another woman. A woman who should be hidden behind some warlock, giving in to his demands. Not allowed to even think as a person.

I smack the thought aside. One hard day isn't worth reverting back to thinking like I was taught for years. The ember of hope inside me proves that, if nothing else does. But there's more. More I'm still learning. More I see inside myself as I look in the mirror.

I am a person. A woman. A strong woman, who can do magic. And everyone will see it. It may have been foolish to enter, but there was a reason I did. There's something inside me that won't settle for inane warlock teachings any longer. Something that drives me to act, to do something I've always wanted to do even before I knew I could do magic.

I stride into my room, grab a pair of scissors out of my sewing basket, and seize a chunk of hair. With a quick snip, the long locks fall to the floor. I stare at them a moment, lonely on the floor. Yet, I already feel lighter.

More snips quickly follow. Dark blond bits flutter through the room as the scissors make their slicing music. With each cluster of hair I cut, I'm lighter. Freer. Each strand is a weight thrust on me by a society unwilling to let me be a person, but not for a moment more. I will no longer be chained down by their rules, by them or myself.

When I'm done, exhilaration is raging through me, bright and happy and absolute.

The door opens, and Serena walks in, startling me from my rampage. "Zade said you wer—" She stares at me and then at the floor and then back at me. Her big eyes grow even bigger. "What happened?"

"I cut my hair."

"I can see that." She gives me the look, the one that says she knows there's more hiding behind my words.

"Don't you ever get tired of not being equal to the warlocks who constantly push us around? I'm sick of it. And then when I try to do something about it, they laugh at me. They think I'm a joke, and really, I am. I almost lost my duel today because my natural instinct is to cower like they trained me to. I can't take it anymore. I'm tired of being trampled on. Tired of not being able to do magic. Tired of these stupid rules that keep us exactly where they want us to be.

"Zade said people were talking about me even though I did poorly, and it sparked hope inside me. Hope that I can be that person they need me to be. The person I want to be."

"So you cut your hair?"

Her words after my tirade seem a little silly. "Well… yes."

She skirts through the pile of hair and wraps her arms around me. "You can be that person. You already are. You've already changed so much, showed us all so much. I should have realized what was going on. I'm sorry I don't understand better."

"I've always been alone in this."

She hugs me tighter. "Not anymore."

I finally give in to her words and comfort, and let my emotions show. She continues hugging me as I cry all over the shoulder of her dress. It's true. I'm not alone any more. Serena and Bethany were watching from the sidelines today. Watching and supporting me, even though Serena still struggles to understand how much good magic can do. They are my support and encouragement. Once I finally settle down, I quickly dry my eyes and wipe my nose with a hanky.

"Sorry, I didn't mean to go overboard."

"It's fine," she says. "Though next time you cut your hair, maybe ask me and I can help."

A giggle escapes me. "It's that bad?"

She cringes and that's all the answer I need. It's what I get for letting my emotions gain control. Nothing good ever comes of letting that happen.

"Should I have you try to fix it before I look at it in the mirror then?"

"That may be best."

"Maybe." After a moment of thinking, I say, "No, I have to know what the damage is. Hopefully I'll never get another chance to see something like this." I let a burst of magic out in a bright flash, growing the silver light into a reflective surface. It was a trick I learned to use when I couldn't tell if I looked good enough to be held up to the standard of the Woman's Canon. Also, it's what I did on a larger scale at my duel earlier today. Doubt any warlock would have come up with defensive spells while making sure they looked proper.

"That looks like a useful spell," Serena says.

I bite my lower lip to keep from squealing. "It is. Maybe sometime I could teach it to you."

"Perhaps so."

Her quiet reflection is louder than any response. If she's this open, I should be able to teach her about magic like Lukas showed me.

The spell in front of me that made her speak up, is shinier than ever. The sight of my curly, choppy hair, all chin length, but horridly uneven and wild, sends me into a fit of giggles. "Maybe I should keep it like this."

"It would certainly startle your opponents tomorrow."

"What's all this—" Waverly stops as soon as she sees me. Her expression still unreadable, she calls out, "Bethany! Girls! You have to see this."

There's a pattering of footsteps, and Bethany hurries in the room, her face wrinkled with concern. "What happened?"

I shrug, calmness chasing away my fears. "I'm done fitting into the council's demands."

CHAPTER 34

Thankfully, Waverly has experience cutting hair. Since she wanted to be a lady's maid, it only makes sense she would have acquired such a skill in Envado. When she's done, it looks surprisingly fantastic.

It's rough and jagged still, hard-edged, but curling in a feminine way. A wild feminine way that isn't permitted to be seen in public. The longest of it is to my chin, but some of the shorter pieces are staggered above that. Now it has texture and purpose that my hack job didn't have before. I look nothing like any Chardonian has ever seen. Good thing I have the status of a warlock. Never again will I spell my hair to keep it in place.

"I love it," Bethany says. "You look as if you're starting a fashion all your own."

"Agreed," Serena says. "Should we show Lukas? He's here talking with Zade."

"No." I'm too scared to see what his reaction will be, but anyone else I couldn't care less. It's time for them to deal with me as I am. But Lukas? I want him to be pleased with who I am as well, but what if he's not? I'm not changing who I am any longer, not for anyone, but it'd still make me happy if he liked it. "He can see it tomorrow. There is one more thing I need, though."

"What's that?"

"Something that Katherine made."

* * *

THE NEXT MORNING, I stride onto the field with a confidence I didn't feel before. My hair tickles my jawline, but I resist the urge to push it back. Hopefully I'll grow used to it soon, but even if I don't, I wouldn't take back cutting it. The feeling of power I get from it is incredible. I didn't know something as simple as cutting my hair could make me feel this way. If I had, I would have done it a long time ago.

No face paint this morning. No sense looking like clownish bed sheets. The black pants and shirt Katherine left for me are sleek and form fitting without being tight. Though the outfit is typically male, but the cut is feminine, fitting my curves. My breeches cling to my legs, sticking to them in a way they don't at home. Yet there's also a freedom of movement. Something that adds confidence to my stride.

When I glanced in the mirror this morning before leaving, it was hard to recognize my reflection. I couldn't help but spell my hair a vivid red to go with the new cut. The overall effect is stunning and strong. I should have donned this look when I first strove for independence. Every speck of me feels like a woman, yet every speck of me feels like me.

The only thing that doesn't fit is the orange band signifying I'm from Chardonia. I'd rather have red. My cheeks burn at the thought, leaving at least part of me the color I want to be. Grateful no one knows my feelings, I head across the field, not avoiding the muddy spots that squelch beneath my boots, straight toward the schedule. I will not fail again. Today, I will show Chardonia what a woman can really do.

Poor Chadwick and Conrad follow right along, mucking through the path I'm trudging. At least no warlocks have bumped into me today, at least not yet. There's not as large of a group around the stone today, but enough that they could still hassle me if they wish to.

When I spot Lukas, waiting off to the side, I let my feet carry me to him. There's only a momentary distraction, one that's polite and wanted, not with just the aim of avoiding what must be done. While I keep my expression at its ever-fake smile, hiding the nerves that are invading, Lukas has no qualms about letting his soft yet powerful smile show the moment his gaze meets mine. I'm lighter than air, yet somehow managing to stay grounded as we near.

Others move around us, but they're a blur. A small part of me wishes they were all gone, that Lukas and I were alone, but mostly I don't care. I'm done caring about what society thinks of me. Instead, I focus on what's important, his smile. It matches exactly how I've felt since waking this morning.

"Your hair looks good," he says. "Real good."

His words send such a glow of happiness through me, past my fake smile to give him a real one. "Thank you."

He leans in closer, his warmth chasing away the chill of the morning. "You should smile like that more often."

Heat rises to my cheeks, and I automatically look down, except his fingers gently reach out and tilt my chin back up. His hand is gone almost as quickly as it came, but my breath still catches in a funny way.

"I already checked the schedule. Would you like me to tell you what duels you have today, or would you like to go find out for yourself?"

The reality of the morning wraps around me with a sudden choking. I don't want to go through another morning like yesterday; it'd be so much easier if he just told me. But I won't show any weakness when I'm just finding my strength. "I'll do it myself. Thank you."

"Good luck then. I probably won't see you again until tonight."

My heart gives a strange little twist as I think that. Once again, this might be the last time I see him. To think I'll have to do this every day this week. Or at least I hope I have to do it every day this week. "Good luck to you, too."

And he's gone. Off to fight his own duel while I need to be off to fight in my own. I glance at Chadwick, who's studying the crowd with keen interest, though he probably knows everything that just took place between Lukas and me.

"I'm going to check the schedule if you're ready."

He straightens. "I'm ready."

I'm not, not really, but if I'm going to be on time, I need to go check anyway. I pivot toward the board, clench my jaw, and walk. At first, nothing changes from when I was just standing there, but then I start to notice warlocks watching me out of the corner of their eye. Hushed conversations are taking place. And the closer I get, the more apparent it is that no one is bumping into me or shoving me around.

Is it my hair, face paint, or clothes that has brought such a drastic change? Or maybe it's all three? Whatever it is, it boosts my confidence all the more. Until I'm almost to the oddly, line-free stone, and a warlock, with broad shoulders and plenty of muscles to support them, steps in front of me.

"What do you think you're doing?" He sneers.

"Checking my duels for the day, just like all warlocks are required to do."

"You think that a stupid slip of paper, a haircut and color while wearing breeches makes you one of us? Think again, wench."

"Watch what happens in my duels today, and you'll know there's more than just a little outward change that makes me someone you shouldn't be mocking."

He laughs. "Oh don't worry, little girly. I won't only be watching. I'm your last opponent of the day, if you manage to live that long."

"Good. You'll see exactly how much more of a warlock I am than you are."

He leans in closer and out of the corner of my eye, I see Chadwick tense, but he doesn't come forward. "I'll see something all right. I'll see you dead before you've cast your first spell."

He leaves before I say another word. A shimmer of doubt forms, but I shove past it, not willing to show all these warlocks watching me just how much I'm affected by it.

After checking over the board and quickly memorizing my more rigorous schedule, I head to the section of the field where I'll be dueling today. Not anywhere important, where Serena's box will overlook, but smushed into some tiny corner. No matter. There are still people there to see me, probably the same ones that laughed at me yesterday. One more incentive to keep moving forward in the competition. Keep working until I am somewhere that not only a few people in the corner will see me but all who attend the tournament.

Those around me seem too quiet as I walk past, but maybe I'm so intent on my destination that I'm letting their conversations fade. I have to focus, and I have to win. I can't come as close as I did to losing last time. If I do… Well, I just won't. I will make them see what I can do. What a woman can do.

A strand of hair blows in my eyes. Instead of brushing it aside with my fingers, I go against that screaming instinct since I'm not in the forbidden magic zone anymore, and brush it back into place with a wisp of air in the form of a blue spell. The spell glitters as it passes by. Why is it glittering? Please tell me it's not my nerves, but I'm sure that's why. I lengthen my stride and keep my shoulders back. Maybe anyone who saw it will mistake it for confidence.

They call my name, and I move forward, leaving Chadwick behind on the sidelines. Serena and the others aren't watching today, at least not where I can see them. They must be in one of the boxes or stands to watch, and no one wants them anywhere around here. Hopefully someone will soften toward them soon, though it may just be more nerve-wracking to have them watch than supportive. It'd still be a nice thought. Conrad isn't anywhere to be seen either, though I know he's keeping an eye on things from somewhere. He always is there somewhere protecting me.

The chatter grows louder as I walk toward my duel. I ignore them all as I stride to my dueling ring. When I stop at my spot, the judge doesn't say a word but just stares at me.

"Um, what are you doing?" He finally squeaks out.

I give him an icy smile. "Getting ready to fight in my duel."

His eyes widen. "Cynthia Stephen's daughter?"

"Just Cynthia." I maintain my cool demeanor, but all this attention is making me itchy. "Are we starting now or do I need to come back later?"

My wiry opponent says, "Can she do this?"

"I don't know," the judge responds.

"It's not hard," I say. "I have the status of a warlock. I can style my hair and clothes as I please."

"I don't think she can do this," my opponent continues as if I didn't say anything.

The judge ignores me just as much. At least they aren't laughing?

"I don't know. We'll have to check the rule book."

"There's a rule book?"

Idiots. They know less about what's going on than I do, and it's my first experience out in a warlock's world. I yawn and spell my nails different colors and patterns while they putter around, using as little energy as I can while showing proof of why I belong. The first flash of color has them eying me like an Envadi, but if they can ignore me, I can ignore them right back. Or at least pretend to as I take my time coloring each nail.

Through my nonchalance, I keep track of every move they

make. The nonchalance gets harder to fake when another warlock joins us, not the mediator of this area. Oh, no that would be so much the more preferable.

"Chancellor Ryan," the judge says. "We're honored you'd attend to this issue yourself."

Not him. This can't be a good sign. I stop spelling my nails, leaving the pinky on my right hand uncolored, but continue to examine them like I don't care what these men are doing.

"What seems to be the issue?"

"Well, this…" The judge screws up his face and points to me. "…this *warlock* is dressed as well, a warlock. And her hair and face paint are most unacceptable."

The Chancellor doesn't even look at me as he lets disdain coat each of his words. "This contestant is sadly within regulation. I'm afraid there's nothing I can do about it at present. We are working on changing things so this will not be an issue in the future."

What is that supposed to mean? It can't be good. But at least it sounds like, for now at least, I'm going to be able to compete in my duel, which is what I want. Except the Chancellor leans over to my opponent and whispers something in his ear before giving me a smug glance.

I brush a finger across Lukas's ring. Inside, I'm quivering with dread, but I give him the same cold smile I've used for everyone else this morning. It does the trick of morphing his smug features into a scowl.

"Go ahead and begin, Judge Manes," the Chancellor says.

The judge opens his mouth as if to protest more, but the Chancellor's jaw tightens, making the judge instead wave at the glowing ring. "Enter."

I step into the circle the same time as my opponent and immediately throw a shield up. It's a good instinct because a spell crashes into it almost immediately. Nothing is holding them back from taking me down. Nothing except me.

I fling a sharp spell, silver with razor edges of gold. He throws an aqua shield up, but not fast enough. The golden edge of light slices into the side of his abdomen as I lift my hand to send another from up high. While it's in the air, I spread my hands out wide from my sides and shoot two more at him. The one from above whips across his cheek and one of the side spells slices his arm before he strengthens his shield, the last one crashing into it, breaking into dust-like pieces before dissipating.

An icy blue ball erupts from him, bigger than me. I dive to the ground, but instead of just getting out of the way, I shoot an icy spell back at him, angled from the ground. It slams against his thigh, sinking into him. He rocks onto one foot with a hiss, but it doesn't stop. A black light bounds out of him, heading straight for my vulnerable spot on the ground.

No time to move. A blaze of power storms out of me as I think on it transforming into a wall, thick and unmovable. Its transparent iron color holds as the black splats against it, saving me from whatever fate it held.

I flick out a dozen mini arrows, nothing hard to block, but enough to give me time. A few nick his arm as I bounce to my feet. I send two arrows, this time big—both in size and punch—but he had the same thought, sending three blue darts after me. I block the first two, but the third hits my shoulder with an icy stab.

Instinctively, I throw up a shield, giving me a moment to recover only to discover I jumped up much too close to him. If I advanced just a bit, I could reach out and touch him. He seems to realize this, too. As I throw the first spell at him that comes to mind, I take a step back. Only he steps forward as well, his shield spell in place, effectively blocking my useless silencing spell.

Before I can out pace him, his fist crushes my stomach. Pain and confusion over the illegal move pollute my thoughts. Something rips across my chest, a brass-colored spell flickering out of sight. I throw my magic at him, ineffective for points, but giving me a moment to step back, almost to the ring line.

Cheater and the judge hasn't called him on it. No surprise, but

I can't hold anything back. I fling spell after spell at him, blocking any that come my way except for one that nicks my right hand. Ignoring the pain, I keep flinging my magic until the judge calls out, "Time."

I look to him, waiting to have him call my opponent out. Instead, he mumbles, "Stephen's daughter is the winner."

"It's Cynthia." My voice is as loud as the frustration boiling inside me. I round on my opponent, "Cheat much?"

He just sneers and shoves his way past me. At least I won this duel.

* * *

I WANDER on the edge of the field, wishing it was my turn for the next duel of the day. It's still a long ways off, though. The field is a bit squishy beneath my feet, the rain-soaked grass fresh from last night. Someone has erected a giant shield over the fields, protecting everyone from further downpour. Rather, several someones I'd imagine. It's massive enough to cover everything.

As I roam, I study it, trying to decide how much power it would take to make the pale blue protection. Then something odd catches my eye. Everyone seems to be staring in one direction. I follow their gazes and can't but help stare with them.

Serena is alone in her box, dark locks flowing forbiddingly to her waist.

My breath catches. Will she be punished for this even though she's free? Will someone find a way to punish her? Why did she do this? It's hard to notice anything else about her except her dark hair, sharply contrasted by her pale complexion. I've seen her hair down before. I used to help her with it all the time. But to see it flowing free like this in public?

The crowd begins to talk, their noise growing by the second. What did she think she was doing, coming out here like this? It's one thing for me to cut my hair when I'm fighting in a duel, but leaving hers down? Somehow, it seems like a stronger statement than me cutting my hair. Like it's something the general public isn't meant to see.

I want to talk to her, but I don't want to make things worse by going over there. Who am I kidding? Things are already bad for us. How is talking to her going to make it any worse? What are they going to do? Try to kill us even more? Doubtful that's even possible.

I hurry to her box, bringing memories of last year, and march up the stairs. The guards Zade set up for her let me pass without question. When she sees me, she doesn't look surprised, but calmly sits in her chair, a warlock's chair of comfort, and motions for me to take the one next to her.

I don't sit. "Why is your hair down?"

"I—I..."

Her fingers worry her skirt. I reach over, take her hand, and soften the shock from my voice. "It's all right. It's just me."

But her eyes drift to those surrounding us. We are right next to the Grand Chancellor's box.

"I can cast Zade's spell so they can't hear us if you'd like. We could lower the curtains so they can't even see me do it."

She straightens her back. "No. We don't need to hide anymore. You taught me that."

I squeeze her hand before letting it go. "Then will you tell me what's going on?"

"I wanted to support you, but I couldn't bring myself to cut it. I'm sorry. It would have made more of a point if I could, but I like my long hair."

"So you wanted to cut it, but didn't want to lose it, so you let it down instead?"

She worries her skirt again. "I'm sorry I didn't do more."

I laugh, all too aware of the many eyes on us, yet still unable to help myself. For a moment, she looks startled, but then she relaxes.

"You might not have cut your hair," I say. "But you made your statement nevertheless. Maybe even more of one than if you had cut your hair."

"I hope it leads to good things and not trouble."

"Coming here to talk to you, I realized something. We're already in trouble, and nothing is going to change that. Whatever we do from this point on, sure, it might make things even harder, but it can't change our situation very much. They already want to kill us, and they probably want to make a public spectacle out of it since what I've done is proof of what women can do. It's not as if they could kill us twice."

"I suppose this year it's your turn to be the morbid one."

"Is that why Bethany isn't with you?"

"Things started getting a bit rowdy for a while, and I tried to send her home. But she's starting to take more after you and insisted on staying." As Serena continues, I can't help but wonder if that's a good thing or a bad one. "She's doing a good job of keeping a low profile, at least."

"A low profile where?"

"Headed toward the food, but that was a while ago. She's probably on her way back. And don't look at me like that. She has a guard with her. She'll be fine."

Maybe if things hadn't been so hostile toward me this week, I'd believe that as much as Serena's trying to convince us both. "I'm going to see if I can find her. Would you like to join me?"

She hesitates, glancing around at the boxes surrounding us. "No. I think I need to be here. But please tell her to keep safe."

"I will." I stand. "And thank you for everything."

Her smile is stiff as her eyes glance at the others watching us, but her voice genuine. "You're welcome."

"There's something I want to show you tonight." If I'm still alive.

She lifts a brow but doesn't question me. "I'll be there."

I give her a tight smile, unable to say what I really want, that I'll be there too.

* * *

IT TAKES ALMOST twenty minutes of searching and I still haven't found her. But there is a man, a servant I think, who looks vaguely familiar coming my way. I want to dodge him, but this isn't my past life anymore. Besides, Chadwick is here.

"Excuse me," the man says, and finally I realize who he is. The scar on his right temple reminds me, sending a wave of fear through me though I try to hide it. "You probably don't remember me. I serve Master Edward. I was there when he freed you."

My words can't get past my closing throat. Does this mean Edward finally told someone how I forced him to free me? It's all going to come to an end. My magic bounces restlessly inside me but I keep it wrapped tight. At least I have shown my magic in public before it came down to this.

"I just wanted to let you know." He steps closer, lowering his voice. "Master Edward isn't here. He hasn't left the house since he freed you. It's rare for him to even leave his rooms. You're safe from him."

Despite trying to keep my emotions hidden, a sigh of relief escapes me. "Thank you for letting me know."

"It's the least I could do. You've given many of us hope." He hurries off before I can say another word to him.

Doesn't matter. I'm too stunned to say anything. Given many of who hope? Edward's servants? His household? Someone else? That's not the most shocking part of all though. It's that a man was the one to tell me. I've given a Chardonian warlock hope.

I continue my search for Bethany in sort of a haze. The fog in my mind finally dissipates when I finally find her hidden in some corner, her face glowing as a warlock is leaving. I can't tell who it is from the back, but something about him seems familiar.

"You've done very well," Bethany says the moment she sees me.

I cast Zade's spell to prevent eavesdropping, not trusting that whatever warlock is leaving or someone else, is out of hearing distance.

"Who was that?"

She gives a little half grin and shakes her head.

"What?"

"You're so like mother sometimes."

I'm appalled to think I could ever be compared to my mother, whom I love, but does so many things I wish I could change. But then I realize what I'm doing, my hands fisted on my hips, using mother's scolding voice. Immediately, I drop my hands and lower my tone.

"What's going on Bethany?" It's unlike her to willingly be around warlocks, let alone smiling about it.

She sighs. "You're not as fun as you used to be."

Letting go of a little worry, I stick my tongue out, and she laughs. "I just want you to be careful. This is dangerous for all of us. I don't want anything bad to happen to you."

Her smile is still so innocent, even after all the years of being punished by father. "Even if something bad happens, I have you for a sister."

Unfortunately, much of the bad stuff comes from choices I make. "It's time to get to my next duel. Make sure I'm there well before it starts."

"Even if you don't see me, I'll be watching and quietly cheering you on."

"Be careful," I say before leaving, her words adding a strut of confidence to my step.

CHAPTER 35

I f I'm forced through another day like this one, and survive it, I may never be able to move my arms again. They ache something fierce. Or maybe it's the stress of what I want to show Serena. Either way, my arms are like stiff, giant logs. I'm rolling my shoulders, trying to ease the strain, when Serena walks in.

"Long day?"

"Battling warlocks will do that." I shake my arms out. "And you? Facing them down while defying their rules isn't easy."

"Easier than doing magic in front of them."

"About that…" Please don't be scared off by this. "I found a way that may help you understand what your magic feels like."

She runs her hands across her skirt. Of course she does. Serena never wants anything to do with magic, whether she wants to admit it or not. At least she's trying, even with her discomfort.

"What do I need to do?" she asks.

"Nothing. Just stand there. I'm going to send my magic to you so as to coax your magic to the surface temporarily. It should help you to recognize the feeling so you will be able to understand what it is inside that's part of your magic."

"Oh. That sounds sort of like…"

"Like what?"

She looks away. "Nothing."

"It was clearly something, and it sounded like something that might help me explain it."

"It's something from the engagement ceremony, which I can't talk about. Zade still hasn't found a way around the spell that forbids me from speaking of it."

"I see." Stupid warlocks. I can't even have a proper conversation with my own sister while we're alone without them interrupting.

"Where did you get that ring? It doesn't look familiar?"

Her words make me realize I've been twisting the ring Lukas gave me. My face heats. "It was a gift from Lukas."

Her eyebrows raise. "A gift, huh? Things are getting pretty serious between you two."

My face grows hotter. "I'm hoping they will once the tournament settles down."

"Well, then. I suppose I ought to get to know him better."

I clear my throat. "You're getting away from learning about magic."

"And you're avoiding talking about your good-looking Chryon."

A giggle escapes. "Most definitely. But at least magic is something we can work on now. Lukas isn't around."

"We don't have to do this. You probably should be doing—" She waves her hand around in the air. "—something to get ready for tomorrow."

She just doesn't want to have to do this, but I'm not going to let her out of it. "There's not much more I can do to prepare. Besides, I want to help you with this. It's important and may prove as useful as learning to use a gun." And if I don't do it tonight, there's always the possibility I'll die tomorrow and won't be around show her another time. This possibility of dying at any time thing is getting old.

Her expression tightens with resolve, and I know I've said the right thing.

"You only need to stand there," I say. "It won't hurt. It will add my magic to your own temporarily so that it will be easier for you to feel. Hopefully, then you'll be able to recognize what you're sensing."

"Sounds, well, terrifying, but I'm willing."

Willing is something she hasn't been before, hopefully it's enough. I let my magic ease from my core like Lukas taught. Thinking of him tints the white light pink, making my cheeks heat. At least Serena hasn't learned yet what the different colors mean. I always wondered how she could miss so much from the spells going on around us, especially at the tournament last year. But now's my chance to teach her.

The more I let my magic relax toward her, the more focused I become and the pink tint lessens until the spell is pure white. I let it slowly move toward her, even slower than Lukas sent it to me. By the look on her face, Serena probably is thinking it's too fast, but if I go any slower it might as well hover in place.

When it finally reaches her, she leans away. I don't push it forward, instead giving her a moment to collect herself, to become accustomed to the idea that she's actually going to do this. After a shorter time than I expected, she straightens right into the light and lets it in. Gradually, her face goes from one of confusion to one of delight.

"That's what magic feels like? That warmth inside me?"

I grin. "That's it."

"I thought it was something everyone has."

"Most people do, just in varying degrees. Only a few lucky ones, like us, have very much of it. You even unconsciously use it at times. Like when we went in Zade's room to see what furniture he'd need, and you canceled out his spell without even realizing it."

After pulling my magic back, the room seems gloomy without its bright presence, but I think it did exactly what we were all hoping it would. I wait, not doing or saying anything, letting her absorb the knowledge of the power she holds. She's quiet for several minutes, and when she finally speaks, her words are faint.

"I didn't know."

"But now you do, so what's to be done about it?"

She bites her lower lip. "You know how magic has always been in our lives."

It's burned into my memory all too well. "Harsh and painful. But it doesn't have to be that way. I made it much different in my own life. And you can't always say anymore if you're referring to father's hexes. What has Zade done for you, just with your carriage sickness?"

"I know. I really do know. Not just about that, but everything. Like how our ball gowns were beautiful in a way I've never seen. But that night didn't end with all the enjoyable spells he cast."

Now probably isn't the time to mention to her that Waverly did most of those spells. Or maybe it is? "You're right. It ended with the attack."

"Zade could have died." Her voice cracks. "He'll forever have a limp the rest of his life from that night. Magic can't fix that."

"No one may have enough knowledge or power to fix his injury, but I think your fear of magic is making him feel worse."

A stunned expression crosses her face. "I— I never thought of that before." She pulls at her fingers and then seems to realize she's not wearing any gloves and huffs. "Do you really think he's upset that I don't care for magic?"

I try to choose my words carefully so as not to hurt her but remain truthful. "Zade loves you. I don't think he'd let your dislike for magic break that, but I do think your disdain for it makes it hard for him to be himself around you."

"Oh." She shuffles to a chair and plops into it. "I never thought about it like that. It was just my disdain for magic all along causing problems. How do I fix it?"

Relief fills me. "Ask him to teach you some spells. He'll be thrilled at your interest, and you'll be safer. The more ways you can defend yourself, the better for you and the girls."

She nods. "Maybe I will."

CHAPTER 36

The next morning I'm on my way to check the schedule when Lukas pulls me over to an empty tent. His grip is tight but not painful. With his free hand he takes off his glasses, holds them with his middle finger, and pinches the bridge of his nose.

"What's wrong?" I ask, my magic skittering about inside me.

He huffs, puts his glasses back on, runs a hand through his hair, and paces the tent. It's the first time I've seen him without any hint of a smile and definitely the first time I've seen him pacing like Zade. The whole process has me skittish. Something must be seriously wrong for him to act like this. My sisters were fine when I left home. Zade was with them. Chadwick is with me, now waiting outside the tent, and Lukas looks, well, he looks as distractingly good as ever. Which is not the point. The point is that something is seriously wrong.

"Please tell me what's going on. All this pacing is making me nervous."

"Sorry, I just—" His hands open and close. "If we both make it through our first two duels of the day…"

"Yes?"

Finally, he stops, turns to me, and grabs a hold of my shoulders. His touch sends a thrill through me, but the touch is tainted with fear because of how tight his fingers grip me. It's not painful, but urgent. "They've paired us to fight each other."

Air rushes out of me, taking my grasp on remaining calm with it. I knew this might happen, knew it was a possibility, but was hoping it wouldn't happen. There are many other warlocks in the tournament from all over Chardonia and other countries. It's day three, so many duelers have been eliminated but still, the odds of us being paired against each other shouldn't have been against us. Did someone set us against each other on purpose?

"I'll forfeit."

He's serious. But not only would it leave me feeling guilty, it'd make him miss out on his chance. "You can't. You didn't come here to give up on everything. And having me win by default is not winning at all."

"But we can't fight against each other."

I most definitely don't want to kill him, but we have dueled together many times. "Why not? We do it all the time."

"Practice is different. I won't risk hurting you."

"And I won't hurt you either, but we can't just give up. You said yourself that in Chryos they don't allow you to kill each other. This is something we can do. Not only that, but we need to see it through. Fairly. You refusing to fight me is just as bad as those who won't let women fight in the first place."

His hands slide down my arms and take a hold of mine. "I'm sorry. You're right. I just don't want to hurt you. I don't want anything bad to happen to you."

Tingles start from where his hands touch mine and spread through me. "I promise I won't cast any life-threatening spells. You can do the same, but other than that, we shouldn't hold back. They need to see what I'm capable of, and they won't be able to see it if I'm not truly fighting."

He leans his forehead against mine. "I am overreacting."

"It's a normal reaction." One that is actually kind of sweet, even if a little misguided. "No matter which of us wins, it will be fine. Even if you are victorious, I'll support you. Though I'd like to see you try. Thanks to the past month and a half, I know all your spells."

The corners of his mouth twitch. "You only think you know all of them."

I giggle. Darn that boy-obsessed girl taking over again. Except with him, I don't mind, not really.

"It may do them just as much good to see us fighting as it would be for them to see you supporting me after I win."

His grin is finally back to its usual sunny self, easing some of the strain from his revelation. "It will do them even more good when they see me defeat you and how I'll still follow you around like a puppy."

I laugh and shake my head. Even with our best efforts to keep distance between us, whenever possible, he has been trailing after me. A very attractive addition to the usual view. A most promising reason to look forward to next week.

CHAPTER 37

Despite what I told Lukas, the very last warlock I want to see standing across from me right now is him. The ring, glowing its vibrant green, is separating me from him, just not for long enough. The crowd seems antsy, noisier than usual. Many have come to watch, though we're on a smaller field. They stand because there is not enough room to sit. Chancellor Ryan is there, too. Not with the crowd, but not with the judge either. He's standing close enough to be seen, but still part of the background, a sneer on his face directed wholly at me.

"Enter," the judge says, yanking my attention away from the threat and back to the problem.

Across from me, Lukas steps into the circle. It feels so wrong to join him, but there's no other option. We agreed to this, and it's really for the best. Still, I don't want to fight him. Once I join him inside the ring, we both stare at each other. There are no spells I wish to cast at him.

Suddenly, his hand jerks up and a murky blue spell flashes toward me. I deflect, but I'm too late. As pain stings my shoulder, I know he's not going to hold back. Which is exactly what I want, but blast, it hurts.

There's no time to dwell on the pain. I flash the same spell back at him, aiming for his torso, but he deflects, and flings a maroon one back. I throw a silver wall spell in front of me, which his spell breaks against, hurling bits of maroon everywhere until they dispel.

As our spells cross, sometimes hitting a shield, falling short, or cringingly hitting their mark, I mentally keep track of the score. We stay fairly even at first, but I slowly stretch ahead of him. Is he letting me win? I pull my hand back, waiting to cast another spell so I can see what he'll do. A dull yellow slams into my chest, sucking the air from me. I gasp for breath. Nope. Not holding back, and now we're even again.

Another spell flies at me. I race to throw a shield up before it can reach me. After it crashes against my barrier, I quickly thrust two spells back at him. One aiming straight for him, the other a faint, pale lemon-colored spell which should cause a stomach ache that sneaks around the side.

He blocks the first, but the second crashes into him. I cringe as his face crumples with pain, and he groans. The judge calls time.

I want to sprint to Lukas, make certain he's not seriously injured, but I refrain. Not that it stops me from subtly watching to make sure he's not going to pass out at any moment. That was the longest two minutes of my life.

"Stephen's daughter is the winner."

"Cynthia." I glance at Lukas, who is trying to force a grin past a grimace of pain, but it only makes my chest twist more. Have I permanently injured him like what happened to Zade? Why did I agree to this? I don't feel like a winner. I feel like father, using magic to hurt others.

CHAPTER 38

Being able to move onto the next round tomorrow is good, but not as fantastic as it felt yesterday. It's tainted by my actions, my becoming increasingly like a hexing warlock. Like father. The thought haunts me as I continue to win duels using more hexes. I watch as the last duel of the day finishes, with Nathaniel as the winner.

Will I be paired against him? I can't see the Grand Chancellor being happy about his son fighting against a mere woman, though I don't know how much the Grand Chancellor has any control over it. I suppose even if he's not in charge, they will still give him whatever he wants. He always gets what he wants.

My thoughts are interrupted when I realize that Nathaniel has left his duel and is headed my way. He must need something or someone that's over this way instead of the adoring Chardonian crowd on the opposite side. I glance behind me, but there's only Xyer. Maybe Nathaniel needs him for something? Or, more likely, he's simply going in that direction.

Except when he gets close to me he stops. "You're doing very well."

Where is this coming from? Bethany and Serena have spoken

with him a few times since he helped Serena at her ball, but why is he talking to me? Is his father trying to leverage him closer to us? I finally manage to say, "Thank you. You are as well."

"We'll see if tomorrow brings continued good fortune for us both. I hope it does. I'd be honored to duel against you," he says before walking away.

I'm still contemplating the odd scenario and understanding the compliment he gave when Lukas strolls to me, arm protecting his stomach. Has he seen a healer?

"Are you ready?" he asks.

"To join you at the healer's tent?"

"Already did that." Great. I did give him a permanent injury. "They healed me up just fine, though it will be a while before it's not as tender."

There's no hiding my relief. "What do I need to be ready for then?"

"Thought I'd accompany you home tonight. If that's all right?"

It's so much more than all right. "That would be outstanding." A whole lot more outstanding if there weren't other guards with us, and I didn't need to ride in the carriage.

The walk to the carriage and from the carriage to the house is silent but not awkwardly so. The house is dark and quiet when we enter. The girls must have found something peaceful to do, and mother is probably sleeping. The last part of pregnancy makes her sleep often.

I lead Lukas to the kitchen. He sits, and I open the pantry, a familiar ritual between the two of us by now. But while I'm hungry, nothing appeals to me. What does one eat after injuring a man she thinks she's fallen for?

The thought freezes my actions further. Fallen for? Before, men were always just a game, something to hide my true interest, but this is no game. No game at all.

Gripping a shelf with one hand to hide the shaking, I rummage around with the other, even though nothing is appealing. If I pretend hard enough, and long enough, something is bound to sound good. Maybe. Probably not.

After a minute, there's a creak behind me.

"Are you okay?" Lukas asks.

I spin around, finding he's within touching distance. The pantry shrinks, like the walls and shelves are suddenly crowding in on me. On us. There's not enough room for him and me and my guilt next to all this food.

He reaches out to me, his hand like a peace offering, but I just can't. Not only are we supposed to be keeping things light between us until after this is all over, but I feel too much like father. A warlock that hexes others for sport. I step back, knocking into a shelf with a clang. His hand falls away.

We avoid looking at each other. Instead, I stare at the space that, a moment ago, felt so small and now which feels too big. Wide and impassable.

"Why don't I whip us up a little something tonight?" he says. "My turn is long overdue anyway."

He reaches toward me again, and I press harder against the shelf, expecting him to touch me. Except he doesn't. His arm moves past me and to the side, grabbing a tin of sugar before exiting the pantry. My hands are shaking. Why am I disappointed if I was the one to step away? Why is it so hard to control my emotions tonight?

A few deep breaths later, I still haven't managed to calm myself down. When he returns for more items, the pantry shrinks further with each of his movements. This time when he leaves, I scurry after, unwilling to let the pattern go on. I take his usual place at the table and watch as he continues bringing things out of the pantry. His slow but methodical movements helps ease some of my tension. By the time he has a bowl out and is dumping ingredients in, I'm fully in control of myself again.

"I didn't know you could cook," I say.

Using the back of his hand to push his glasses up leaves a

dusting of flour on his cheek. "There's not a lot I know how to make, only my favorites."

It's hard to look away from that bit of flour on his dark skin. "And what are your favorites?"

His attention shifts to me a moment, just long enough for a small, but full of life smile before turning back to what he's making. "I know you like hot chocolate. Have you ever tried it with a little spice?"

"I've only had a few spicy things. They were… different."

"In a good way or bad?"

"Good, I suppose." Where is he going with this? "Am I going to be inflicted with some sort of spicy concoction?"

"Nah. You'll like it, so no inflicting needed. But, if for some strange reason you don't, I'll have something to revive you if it does too much damage."

Revive me? "That's reassuring."

He grins and continues mixing things together. It's mesmerizing to watch. The way his hands move and work, as if he's done this enough times that the movements have become perfected. Somehow, the quickly multiplying bits of flour on his face only add to the effect. Is this the same reason he likes to sit and watch me while I cook something up for him? I can see the appeal.

Long nights of practicing and early mornings of getting to the tournament are catching up with me. My eyelids blink heavily as I observe. When he focuses on the stove, I give in and rest my forehead on my palms, closing my eyes. The sound of him working creates an unpredictable rhythm. Metal clanging against metal. Scrapping. Sizzling. The smell of something yeasty and familiar but not familiar enough to place, mixed with a hint of chocolate. And spiciness. My mouth waters as I doze.

The clink of two items being set in front of me pulls me from my lull. I lift my head to find a mug of steaming hot chocolate and a plate of, well, I'm not sure exactly what. They're golden brown, long and crinkly-looking with brown spotted sugar coating them.

"This looks fantastic."

"Emma, the woman who is like my mother, calls it Spiced Delight. I call it Flamin'."

"That's reassuring."

He chuckles as he takes the chair next to me, a second helping in front of him. He takes the long, stick-like bread and dunks it in the hot chocolate before taking a bite. Sort of like we do with biscuits, then. I follow suit. I sip the hot chocolate. It's good. Warm and thick. More sweet than flaming. Fantastic. A burn tickles the back of my throat. A burn that's growing. I cough.

"Take another bite of fry bread."

I cough harder before managing to take another bite of the bread that helps ease some of the tickling. He wasn't kidding about the spice.

"Are you okay? Do you want me to make you some chocolate without the spice?"

"I'm fine. This is good," I say. "Different. But good. Thank you."

"Glad you like it."

The bit of flour dusting his dark skin is difficult not to touch. "You've got something, I'm just going to…" Leaning closer, I rub my fingers across his cheek, brushing the flour off with a tingle racing up my hand.

He doesn't move. Doesn't say anything. My fingers stay, lightly touching his warm cheek, gaze suddenly focused on his lips. What am I doing? Not only should we not be doing this, but I hurt him.

I jerk back and take a swig of chocolate. The cinnamon from dunking the fry bread mixes with the sweet heat. It's so much like him. I pour all my focus on it, enjoying the creation while the jumbled feelings inside me settle.

"So," Lukas says. "Are we going to talk about what's upsetting you?"

"Nothing is upsetting me."

He shakes his head. "It's more than that. You always play with your jewelry when you're upset."

"Sometimes I just like playing with my necklace," I scoff.

"True, but you only rub your ring when you're really distressed. You've been rubbing it all day. Something's up."

"I do that?"

"Only when you're trying to keep something in. Or something more than usual, I should say."

"Oh."

"Is this because you defeated me in the tournament?"

I want to brush him off when suddenly I realize I'm rubbing my ring again. Why does he have to know me so well? "Now you've got me all flustered."

He grabs my hand. "It's me, Cyn. There's no reason to be anyone but yourself."

Does he really mean that? And if he does, can I really be me? I'm not even sure I know who I am, except that lately I feel more and more like blowing apart. I thought that doing this, getting my freedom, and casting spells in front of anyone was what I wanted, but it's exhausting and terrifying and overwhelming. Everything is just so hard. And I'm making things with Lukas worse. He came all the way here for the tournament, and I just dueled him out of it.

He must sense something of my feelings, because he takes his hand away, but even with everything I'm feeling, I don't want to be apart. I snatch it back in mine and hold it as if it's the only thing keeping me from completely zapping apart as the words spill out.

"I've become what I always feared. A hexing warlock who hurts others, just like my father."

He grips my hand tighter. "Is that what you think?"

Unable to speak, I nod.

"Your father hexed people not out of anger, but out of a desire to show Chardonians what they were capable of?"

"Well, no. He was cruel for his own pleasure." Too many memories plague me of pain, torment, and fear that he caused

Serena and sometimes me or another sister. Of how I'm reaching inside myself and doing similar spells to others. "But I am hexing others."

"And how do you feel about it?"

"Terrible. Like I shouldn't be hurting them. Like the guilt of it will kill me as much as any warlock could."

His hand brushes against my cheek. "And that is what makes you different than him."

It's true. Father always did it with the intent to cause pain and that's the last thing I want to do. Not the first time I've heard such words, but they settle deeper this time, perhaps because I've actually dueled now. Seen for myself how I feel and behave during the fighting. "I sill don't like it though."

"Which is more proof you're nothing like him."

The words soak into me, easing the worries I've had since I started hexing others. It does nothing to calm my other fear.

"You're still rubbing your ring, is it still bothering you or is there something else."

If things weren't so somber, I'd laugh. Even with one of his hands still gripping mine, I am reaching out and twisting it. He helped with the big problem, maybe he can help with the more personal one. The one that could come between us. "I think I'll grow used to the idea of hexing for duels but…

"Go on," he encourages, voice gentle.

"I know we said it would be fine. That whichever of us won, we'd support the other. But I defeated you, not just a little, but hard. I mean, I injured you." He starts to say something, but I press on, not willing to hear that he's fine now. "Even if you're almost better, I still did that to you. And you came for the tournament, and I just ended it. Your chance is gone because of me."

He waits a moment then says, "Is there anything else you need to add to that?"

"No," I say. "Yes. I'm going to eat the last fry bread. Now I'm done."

A chuckle is followed by him giving my hand a squeeze. "Good. Now no more self-pity. I meant it when I said it'd be fine if you won. Honestly, it's better."

What can he possibly be speaking of? "Better?"

He smiles, brighter than I've seen since we started training. "I wanted to let you win, but I knew you'd hex me silly later if I didn't give it my best."

"But that's why you're here."

"You know it's just an excuse, especially now." His gaze is filled with something stronger than I've ever seen, directed right at me.

Oh. My. Suddenly I'm as hot as my cup of chocolate. "I thought we weren't going to talk about this until next week."

"Do you really think one week is going to make a difference?"

My hand tightens around his, betraying my true feelings on the subject, but I still say, "I thought we agreed it was distracting."

"When we were training, yes. And if this is going to distract you for the few days you have left in the duel, I won't say another word. But, Cynthia, what I feel isn't going to suddenly disappear after the tournament. I can hide it, but being with you has taught me that my feelings aren't fleeting. They grow with each moment I spend with you, each moment I see you growing and trying to show others. You are an amazing source of strength. Should I wait until next week to tell you more?"

"No, don't." The words escape before I can stop them. Not that I want to stop them, only maybe I should.

He leans close, taking my hand in both of his. "Good, because I don't know what the next few days are going to bring. I don't know how much time we're going to have together. But there's something I do know is true more than anything else I've ever known before."

I inch closer, touching my finger to his cheek, smudging some of the flour. "What is that?"

"I love you."

He brushes his thumb across my chin. I tilt my head toward

him, the strength I gain from him pulling us together. My heart is so full, but it still continues building and building until it swells so much that it forces tears out of my eyes. Lukas shoves his chair back, stands and pulls me up to him, his arms encompassing me, encircling me as I press my face into his neck, breathing him in.

Maybe it's not about being a distraction when we're together. It's distracting being apart. Being together is better. It's not tearing us apart, not distracting us from our responsibility. Not tearing us from our duty. Being together makes us stronger. His strength fills my weakness, and my weakness fills his strength. Together we are more than we could ever be apart.

CHAPTER 39

It's difficult to concentrate on much, remembering my time with Lukas from last night. Did he really say he loved me? Never before have I heard those words, not ever. I know my sisters love me, and maybe mother as well, but to have Lukas say those words to me, to know I feel them back? It's hard not to skip down the street since we left it behind a few streets ago. In only a few more minutes, I'll be at the tournament, and Lukas will be there waiting for me. I can't help it. I start skipping.

I glance back to see if the guards are paying any attention to my silliness. Fear scratches at me, trying to pry its way in as I stop moving. They aren't there.

Where could they be? Never once have I been left alone since this started, though I haven't always been able to see them. Perhaps that's all it is now. They're hiding somewhere out of sight... even though no one else is around. Hiding when danger is pricking at my senses? The time Chadwick, at least, usually sticks the closest to me? Right.

"Chadwick? Xyer? Conrad?"

There's no response. What do I do? When did they stop following me? Why did they stop? Why did I have to go and get so distracted to the point where I'm not even paying attention? Something is very wrong. Love should have waited until next week to warm my life. Because I let it distract me, I'm chilled through my core.

"Chadwick?"

A clatter echoes, making me jump. Where did it come from? I doubt it was Chadwick or another guard. Do I try to find them, or go for help? If they were attacked, I don't know how many warlocks have them, or if we just somehow got separated. *Somehow.* Right. The best thing to do is go for help. Lukas will know how to find him and get others to help. I quickly turn and jog toward the field.

What if Lukas isn't there? I banish the thought. It can't be allowed.

There are footsteps behind me. I turn, hoping to see Chadwick or someone familiar, but there's no one. I almost call his name again, but fear clogs my words from coming. Something is really wrong. I have to get out of here and get help finding my guards.

No time to just run. I zap several message spells to Zade, Lukas, and Chadwick, though with Chadwick missing I don't know if sending him one will do any good. Once they're out of my control, I turn and sprint for the field.

Before I've taken more than a few steps something gray smears the corner of my vision before smashing into the side of my head. Pain explodes through me. Hands grab me. I try to call out, but the world is going black...

CHAPTER 40

My head hurts. Everything looks blurry.

"Make her swallow it while she's still waking up."

Something is jammed against my lips. I tighten them, not allowing anything past.

"She has to drink it, idiot. Make her!"

"I'm trying."

The words help to clear my mind a little, but my skull still feels hexed. There are enough thoughts working to know that this isn't a good thing. What are they trying to make me drink? Poison?

I buck against the arms holding me, keeping me down. They give a little, but not enough to break free. My efforts are weak and wasted. My head buzzes. I open my eyes to find hooded figures above me, faces hidden within the folds. A cup moves toward me. Whatever they're trying to force me to drink smells of dirt. Why would anyone care if I drank something disgusting? It must be poison. They're trying to kill me since nothing else has worked.

But then a memory comes to me, distant from the ache in my head but still close enough to have the details I need. Details of Serena telling me never to drink the stuff. Something to do with not being herself and unable to control her actions.

The man squeezes his fingers into my jaw, trying to force it open. My best efforts aren't enough. I fail to stop him, and it pops open. I try to squirm away, but it's not enough to do any good. The earthy-smelling liquid spills into my mouth. Can't lose control of myself now. Panic closes my throat. I try to spit it back out, but he smashes his hand over my mouth. Still, I refuse to swallow it. Instead its foulness sloshes around my mouth.

"Hurry it up. Someone's coming," the unseen voice says.

Even if it is someone they want to get away from, it's doubtful it's someone that will want to help me, either. Unless it's someone I sent a message to, but I can't be sure. I can't be sure of anything other than I need to do everything I can. Starting with spitting out this liquid dirt.

My attackers look up, and I take advantage of the moment to envision punching the man holding me in the stomach. Once the vision is clear in my head, I gather my magic and thrust it toward him. Red hot light burns from my hand straight for him. The moment it hits, the man lets go in a howling rage, flying away from me.

I spring to my feet, spitting out the foul drink. My head pounds as I spit again and again, trying to clear it from my mouth. The other man, the one I wasn't able to see before, is already on the run, not stopping to help his cohort. Better than coming for me. I spit again, keeping an eye on both the retreating warlock and the unconscious one.

The footsteps they were so worried about stroll closer. When I turn to see who they're coming from, hoping for Chadwick, the heaviness in my chest sinks further. It's a warlock I don't recognize. The attackers didn't want to be seen, so he must not be with him. It would be nice if he stopped to help, but he'll probably find something to curse at me for.

When he brushes past us as if nothing was amiss, shock leaves me unable to move. Blast him. At least if he would have stopped, it would have brought some sort of attention to the situation and hopefully Zade or Lukas would have heard about it. Shouldn't be surprised, but after spending so much time with decent warlocks, the real world no longer seems real.

I check the man on the ground. He's moaning in a ball, while clutching his stomach, thankfully still unconscious. Probably sent too much power at him, but there wasn't time to better control it, and if I hadn't, I wouldn't have been able to stop them. Besides, it's hard to feel too bad about it. The man attacked me and was trying to force me to drink something bad. I refuse to feel guilty. If only someone would tell my guilt that.

What to do now, though? If I stay here, I'll be late. But the man, attacker or not, needs help. I may have hexed him like father, but I won't turn all the way like a vicious warlock and hex without mercy. Even if he was trying to do, well, whatever it was that drink would have done to me.

Also, I need to find out what happened to the guards. Did these men do something to them and that's why they weren't here? Or did the men come because we got separated somehow? It couldn't have been five minutes since I last saw them. But I still don't know where to look. Besides, they should have gotten my note by now. Why aren't they here?

Moving much slower than I want, I turn toward the tournament field. There's no telling how long I was out for. I doubt it was very long. The sun doesn't seem any further up in the sky, but it could still be late enough that I've forfeited my spot if I had an early fight. Is anyone wondering where Chadwick and I are?

I run as fast and hard as I can, breezing by the man who so completely ignored me a moment ago. I hope he trips over a rock.

The closer I get, the more crowded it becomes. People everywhere, not just warlocks but more women than I'm accustomed to. It's definitely later than I usually arrive. I can only hope I'm not too late. Finally, I spot Lukas and Zade talking, both look agitated.

"Where have you been?" Zade asks.

"And where's Chadwick?" Lukas adds.

I'm gasping for air too hard to let out words, sharp pangs in my chest with each breath. I grasp the sides of my stomach and bend in half, trying to catch my breath. As soon as I'm able, I say, "Don't know. Attacked."

Lukas and Zade exchange a quick glance and then Lukas pulls me off to the side, away from the crowd of people while Zade takes off as fast as he can with his limp.

"Is he going to find Chadwick?"

"Yes. What happened?"

I explain as quickly as the words will come without leaving out any details, making sure to let them know about the attacker that needs help and may offer clues. Except I do leave out the detail about being distracted by thoughts of him and that's why I didn't realize my guards were gone sooner.

"I'll see what we can do about it after your duel, but you've got to go now or you'll be disqualified. Middle field, right corner. Run. I'll follow."

And I do. I pump my legs as hard and as fast as I can. There's too much running going on this morning. I bump into a few warlocks standing between me and where I'm supposed to be. I don't even have time to apologize, though. I feel bad. They may treat me horrid, but I don't want to do the same to them. Don't want to be like Father. I only want them to respect me. But there's not time.

The dueling ring I need to be at is in sight. The judge and the other dueler are already there. The dueler looks bored, but the judge waits next to Chancellor Ryan, both with victorious looks gleaming their faces. Stupid warlocks. Despite what they think, I'm not going to be late. I push myself the last stretch and come to a crashing halt just outside the ring.

The smirk wipes from the judge's face, but Chancellor Ryan's grin grows. "Glad you could finally join us." He strides to me and leans over. Lukas tilts closer, but doesn't interfere. I'm scared of what the Chancellor is going to do.

"Now," the Chancellor whispers in my ear, "you are not going to cast a single spell during your next duel."

I lean away from him and say loud enough for everyone to hear. "Excuse me?"

His forehead wrinkles, but he repeats it again, a little louder.

I don't know if anyone else can hear him or not, but he's clearly expecting me to comply. And why? Is this a threat of some kind, or am I just supposed to listen to him because he's on the council?

"I don't think so."

"But you're supposed to—" He stops himself and scowls.

"Supposed to what?" The drink, the one that makes me lose control of myself. He knew about it, probably set it up. What a surprise for him. "I think the only thing I'm supposed to do right now is defeat another opponent. If you'll please excuse me."

I brush past him, trying not to think about the vicious scowl on his face, and focus on the duel. The judge looks unhappier than ever, eyes darting between me and the chancellor.

"Enter," he says.

I wish for more time to clear my thoughts and to find out if Zade found my guards. But there's not time for a reprieve, even if worry for them is trying to distract me, I have to push the thoughts aside. I step into the ring. My opponent no longer looks bored. His eyes gleam as he takes me in, raising his hands toward me with a smirk.

I block before I even see the spell coming. Whatever the spell is, the look in his eye says it's deadly. A black light, with red and orange twisting through it, hurtles toward my silver wall, and doesn't just crash into it. It sinks into it, becoming part of it. My power stumbles, shield weakening as my power does.

Umpf. I shove my power into the shield as hard I can, but it's not enough. The black spell continues seeping into my shield, getting closer and closer, tugging more and more power away from me. Draining me and destroying my shield.

The magic that usually dances within me is growing dim. I try to rein my power back in, to call some of it back to me, but it's sluggish, as if it torn between being drained away and heeding my directions. My heart races with the certainty that if I can't figure a way out of this, it will never beat again.

While keeping the ever-weakening shield up, I ready another spell to throw at him. But his spell is attacking from all around. Maybe he saw me sneak a spell around before because he hasn't left an opening to do that now. I'll have to surge through. Sweat beads on me. It's risky, opening the shield up enough to let my spell out may let his in, but if I don't, his spell is going to get through, and I don't know if I'll survive it.

I reach deep inside, but focusing while keeping the wall up is difficult. Death is nearing. Being out of breath from the jog here, I'm just tired. So tired. Exhaustion is weakening my limbs and magic. Making everything heavy. Which gives me an idea.

I gather the magic together, but focus on how weak I am, how my limbs drag and my arm struggles to stay raised. When my thoughts and magic are drenched with fatigue, I thrust it out with the last of my energy as fast and as hard as I can, leaving a spot in my shield open just big and long enough for it to sneak by. My opponent is so focused on his spell, he doesn't even react to the dark blue and silver -glittering spell flying straight at his head. The instant it hits, he collapses to the ground.

His spell dissipates and I let my shield fall and sink to the ground. His spell never hit. I did, though. I hit him and effectively used a shield against his power sucking. I've won.

But my muscles ache. What little power is left inside me is bobbing weakly. Someone is booing, at me, certainly. Others are crying out. Something about death. They think I killed him. It's possible, I suppose, though I shudder to think it. I've never tried a spell like this before.

Thoughts are struggling to surface. To make sense. Whatever

else the case may be, I hope he's still alive. I don't want to lose, but I don't want to kill someone either.

It's getting harder and harder to care. To push past the darkness oozing over me. The world sways as I struggle to maintain myself. I sink further to the ground, and further. Everything is thick, weighty. Then the world once again goes black.

CHAPTER 41

I'm lying down. Somewhere soft, but cold, except my right side, which is warm and welcoming. I shift closer to the warmth. It pulls me near and a sigh escapes me. Peace drifting through me. Then I realize the warmth smells spicy, sort of like Lukas. Why does it smell like Lukas? I open my eyes and see Lukas brushed up against my side. I jolt into a sitting position and turn away so he won't see the heat flushing my cheeks.

The cold replacing his warmth is sudden and brisk from the slight wind that's picked up in the waiting area, but does nothing to ease the heat in my cheeks. It would be so much less trouble-some if he hadn't been the cause of my not paying enough atten-tion to my surroundings this morning. The thought rids the heat in my face.

"Did Zade find them? Are they well?"

"He found Chadwick and Xyer. They'll both be fine. Though your attacker was gone by the time he got there." Answers from him would have been nice, but the wellbeing of those helping me is more important. Tension relaxes from me as he continues. "Someone knocked him unconscious, but he doesn't remember who, or why it happened. Only that one moment he was following behind you, and the next, Zade was waking him up with a spell. He'll be fine though. Just really embarrassed that he let his guard down."

I know how he feels, though I'm sure his excuse is different than mine. It's a really bad excuse. Finally, I face Lukas. "I'm sorry."

"It's not your fault."

"But it is."

"You are not the one that attacked him or the one that can't handle seeing a woman take control of her life. None of this is your fault."

I almost stay silent, but it's Lukas. "I didn't notice anything happen to him."

"It's fine. He didn't see it coming either."

"Except I didn't see it coming because I was thinking about last night. About you and me."

"Ah." He nods his head like he understands but then leans closer so I don't think he does. "And if you weren't thinking about us, you would have noticed someone sneaking up on a trained warlock even when that highly-trained warlock didn't notice?"

"When you put it that way…"

"I know you're scared to let yourself feel. I know this life hasn't been easy. It hasn't allowed for love that's good and true. But, Cyn, it's not a bad thing. I'll give you the time and space you need, but I hope you soon learn that bad things happen whether or not you love, but it's love that can help pull you away from those bad things. And when you do learn, I'll be here."

I turn back away from him, not because of blushing or because of not wanting to see him, but because there's so much tumbling about inside, it's hard to focus on my feelings.

"How long have I been out?"

"Only about five minutes."

Much shorter than I thought. "The duel. What happened? I won, correct? My opponent, is he…dead?"

He's silent a moment. "No. I don't know what you did to him, but he's alive. Just still unconscious."

A tension I didn't realize was sprung tightly inside me eases, leaving me feeling like I'll topple. "I tried a sleep spell on him."

"Ah. Lunk should have known to block it. Did you put much magic behind it?"

"Everything I had left. Didn't feel like much, I was really worn from being attacked this morning, and his spell was eating through my shield like nothing I've ever seen."

"It was enough. He's out cold. They haven't been able to wake him."

I hope he wakes soon. "Do you know what spell he cast that would eat through my shield like that? It felt like death, but the other death spells haven't felt like that."

"I don't know. Maybe he found a way to focus the spell on draining someone else's magic, but he'd have to be strong to do so."

"That's comforting. Next time I duel, someone's spell may try to gnaw through my shield while draining me of my power."

"Don't worry, Cyn, you only have to tap them with your sleep spell and they'll be out before that can happen."

The tone of his voice makes me smile despite myself, but it doesn't last. "You don't think my spell did any permanent damage, do you? Is he truly going to wake and be fine?"

"More so than he deserves. Don't worry about him. Worry about you. You still have more duels to take care of."

Speaking of more duels. "I shouldn't be this aware. I was exhausted, both physically and mentally, after running and fighting. Never have I been so drained before, but I feel fine. If I haven't slept the day away and missed all my duels, how is that possible?"

"That uh, may have been me."

I lift my eyebrow at him. "What's that supposed to mean?"

"I may have healed you." He rubs his forehead. "I know you like doing things yourself, but you were unconscious, and I wanted to help."

"No, thank you. I appreciate you helping me." If only he could rest my magic up as well. It's not as sluggish as before but not jumping about either. "Wait, you said Xyer and Chadwick. What about Conrad?"

He presses his lips together like he doesn't want to tell me, and then he gives a sigh. "He's missing."

"Missing?" Fear clenches my muscles. "We should go find him."

"Your next duel starts soon."

"Blast." Am I to have him on my conscience as well? Please let it not be so!

"Let's get to it, then. Others are looking for him, I'm sure he'll be fine." He stands. "May I walk you?"

"Please. And I'll do better at paying attention so if someone sneaks up on you, I'll at least realize it happened. I'd prefer to still be alive at the end of the tournament, and well, if I have to die, it'd be better if it happened during a duel. To be killed off before then would be disappointing, to say the least." Much more disappointing if they don't find Conrad, though. If something bad happened to him…

We start walking together toward the duel, and Lukas says, "We should probably see if we can get you more guards."

"More? I already feel bad enough that Conrad is gone, and there's so many others watching over me. Is it really necessary?"

"I know it's hard, but if they're going to sneak attack to the point where we're getting knocked out and missing, we need someone else to make it harder for that to happen."

"They're still going to try." If I had known my actions all those months ago would have led to this, would I still have made the choices I did?

"I can't stop the attacks, but at least you can have more protection. Plus, it will be safer for the guards," Lukas says. "Do you remember any more details from this morning?"

I sigh. "Nothing that can help."

He stops, takes me by both shoulders right in the middle of the field, close by where my next duel takes place, a spot where everyone can see. "There is something that can help. Me. I will do everything I can. Understand?"

The depth of feeling behind his declaration pushes into me so strongly, it takes a moment to respond. "Yes."

"Good. Now, let's go over everything again, and we'll figure out what to do about it."

I tell him what I remember from the attack, my voice shaking with memories and fear over the fact that Conrad is still missing. Will a day ever come when I, and those around me, won't be persecuted?

CHAPTER 42

Soon it's time for my next duel. Lukas stays close, along with Xyer. It's difficult to concentrate, difficult to have enough energy. Somehow I win it and the next two, just not by much. My final duel of the day is only a few minutes away, and I'm slumped onto the wet grass. Lukas keeps prompting me to eat something, but food has no appeal. Just sleep.

But Lukas is here, prodding me to my feet.

"It's time already?" My voice feels thick, as if tainted by an entire bowl of honey.

"Afraid so."

"Don't think I can."

He grabs both of my upper arms, steadying me. "You can do this. You'll find the strength."

Usually the words would boost me, stir my magic, and make me eager to fulfill his belief in me. Now, I want to plop my head onto his shoulder and doze off. My magic barely stirs within me, a faint trickle of its usual power. I'll never regain enough of it by tomorrow to win, let alone have enough to win the next duel.

"I think it's time to admit defeat." My head bobs toward his shoulder. If I could just rest a little longer…

"No." His hands wrap around the back of my neck, supporting me, lifting up my head, his face only inches from mine. "Don't give up. Not now. You're so close. Where's that fire? The spark in you I love?"

"It's sleeping."

"Tell it to wake up. You're not giving up when you're so close."

I glance at the ring I'm to duel at next. The judge is already there, as is my opponent. A well-built younger warlock, feet so firmly planted on the ground it looks as if he's already won the tournament.

"He'll have so many points on me in the first ten seconds, I'll be lucky if I don't need some major healing afterward."

"Though I sure hope not, it's a possibility." He softens his voice, drawing my attention back on him. "How will you feel if you don't even try?"

"Like I should have never asked Serena to sell me." I sigh, wishing the sound would drain my exhaustion and not make me want to lay down all the more. "Be prepared to patch me up."

He gives my arm a squeeze before letting go. "I'll be here. I'll always be here."

The words fill me with warmth, if not energy, as I stumble on toward the duel ring. There's still a few minutes before start time, but if I don't drag myself there now, I don't know if I'll be able to force myself to.

The judge pays me no attention, but my opponent looks me over, head to foot, sneer growing with each inch he scrutinizes. "This is the girl everyone's been talking about."

The condescension in his voice flickers my magic, stirring it, no matter how small. It dances within me like a dozen mini explosions. "The name is Cynthia, and at least everyone is talking about me."

"Only because you are an abomination in the world of men. An enchantress trying to doom us all, not a warlock. Not someone for generations to remember and revere." Though we're separated by the entire ring, he straightens and leans forward some as if to loom over me even if it has little effect on my bleary mind. "And everyone is talking about me. The great Saban Wright, future of Chardonia."

"Funny. I haven't heard of you."

Except the name does sound familiar, as does his voice. Where have I heard it before? Somewhere dark and cold and—oh gross! This is the warlock that relieved himself in the alley. Everyone probably is talking about him, talking about what a flop he is. Except he did make it this far in the tournament. It can't be without reason.

He must be strong, or perhaps well trained. Whatever it may be, I'm in no condition to beat anyone but the weakest. But the time is here. Soon the judge will start the duel. How can I defeat him without power? There's nothing.

Enough time to back out. I could do it. Better that than end up dead. I take a step back, but then I think on Lukas's words. He's right. If I don't even try, I'll always wonder and never forgive myself. Too many years were spent giving in under the pressure of what's hard. No more.

"Enter," the judge calls out.

I step in, confidence in my choice bolstering my stride, if not my energy. At least my magic is dancing around again, albeit a soft tap instead of a blaring rhythm. I focus between his hands and eyes, keeping track of what I think his intention is going to be.

The first two spells come with a lazy, dull-yellow. The first one I block with a small grayish shield, but the other shield misses blocking, the spell worming its way to my stomach. Nausea builds, gradually filling me. The churning in my stomach makes me grateful there's nothing in it.

An orange spell is already coming at me. There's not enough power to continue blocking and attack. The nausea ripples through me as I send another shield spell, just big enough to block his. I need to throw something at him, but what is there that won't take the rest of what I have? Only pure magic would do that. That's it!

The silence attack spell I did before still gave me points. I only need to touch him with spells, they don't have to do damage. I don't have to be like them to win. Don't have to hex to gain points. And it's within my power. Instantly, I gather what magic I'm not using to block another of his spells, and shoot out my magic in pure rays, like what I showed Serena, only this time they're white muddied with a dull gray fear.

They zip across, already to him when he throws up a tan shield. The pure magic spells slam against him, covering him in a shower of light. Some hit his shield, but many hit him, gaining me points while not injuring him. He howls in anger, a growling, terrifying sound, or at least it should be. Yet when it means all I need do is block most of his spells and I've won, it's the sound of victory.

The attacking spells he casts come faster and harder. More than I can withstand. I give in to my heavy, sick body, and plop down on the ground, curling myself into a ball. Smaller target, less energy. A ruby spell pounds into me, burning my shoulder. A scream rips from me.

With my hand the only thing out of the ball I've curled myself into, I envision an impenetrable wall and release my magic. A dome forms around me, a white so thick I can barely see through it.

There's nothing left of my magic. All of it is depleted. The shield fades until there's nothing but Saban's face, glistening with a growing smirk. He lifts his hand, pointing it straight at the heap I've become. This is it. The end.

"Time," the judge calls out, his voice faint, but clearly distinguishable. "Stephen's daughter wins."

Saban howls, hurling a black ball at me, purple glowing within it. I flinch away, but it won't be enough, it's streaking straight for me. I try to summon my magic, to pull any last scrap together. Nothing is there. It's going to hit.

Suddenly a shield appears before me, its dark gray sheen marbled with maroon. The black spell slams against it, purple and black tingeing the gray before both spells dissipate. The noise of the crowd is growing. Saban's face is contorted with rage, but no longer directed at me. He's staring at Zade.

"I believe," Zade says, "once time has been called, you're no longer allowed to attack your opponent."

"It doesn't matter. She's just a woman."

Zade's brows lift, and he motions to the crowd. "Think so? Try telling them that."

I scan the crowd, a huge mass of people, some in their boxes, many sitting or standing wherever they can. Colors from every country greens, reds, white, and even Chardonian orange. All watching the scene with rapt attention. I force myself to sit up but can carry myself no further.

"I don't believe the crowd heard who won the duel," Zade says to the judge.

The judge scowls but says, "Certainly, Chancellor." His next words boom across the silent field. "Stephen's daughter is the winner."

A murmur passes through the crowd, growing louder and louder, but I can't tell what they're shouting. Saban scowls a moment and then gives me a fake smile as the sound grows, like he's trying to pretend he never attacked me.

And the chanting, it's taking shape into something familiar. It sounds like… like my name. They're chanting my name. For me, the woman! The chanting boosts me, though it's doubtful it will last, it's enough to haul me to my feet. I pump my fist in the air.

"CYNTHIA!" The crowd roars my name, my legs steady before me, my arm firm in the air. This is it. This is everything I was trying for. The crowd knows it. I know it. And the council knows it. The Grand Chancellor. I glance his way, and my fist wants to sink, though I keep it steady in the air and don't let a trace of fear cross my face. Not even a hint of the chill soaking through me.

The crowd may support me, many from other countries, and even some orange-banded Chardonians. But the Grand Chancellor and Chancellor Ryan look on from their box, eyes boring into me with unrestrained hatred.

CHAPTER 43

Serena's box is crowded, full of guards, Serena, and me but the eyes on us make it feel as if the entire crowd is crammed in the box with us. Many are probably actually staring at the Grand Chancellor's box directly next to us, just a little higher than ours, but it feels like too much attention is stifling us. Stifling me, sticking to me like a sweltering day as I slouch in my chair.

Except Conrad still isn't here. What have they done to him? First thing we have to do after this is search for him. We shouldn't even be here wasting time, but I need to show everyone I'm still here. That I'm a part of Chardonia, especially now that I'm moving on to the last day. As mother so worriedly told me over a year ago the day with the most deaths. Won't be told to drink any soothing tea through them this year. So far there has been only a handful of deaths. Not as many as last year. Either many are coming today or this year won't be as bad.

It's all too much to think on. Even with the crowd cheering me on, I've no energy left to even sit straight. My magic is muddled, weak, and in need of a long night of sleep to perk it back up. Not to mention food. At least there will be some of that at the feast. I close my eyes only to have to open them again when someone approaches.

"Annabelle is here to see you, if it's all right?" Serena asks me.

"It's better than all right."

I begin to stand, but Annabelle ushers me back into the chair. "Don't you dare spend any more energy on me when you've been working so hard. We're all so grateful to you."

My ears perk up even if the rest of me is still melted into my chair. "We?"

She scoots to the side to reveal another female, unmarked though, so not married like Annabelle, probably about my age. Her vivid green eyes stand out against her pale skin and dark hair pulled back in the usual bun.

"This is Nelly, a friend of mine who wanted to meet you."

Nelly steps forward, a flash of perfect grace they used to always try to press into us at class. "You are amazing. I'm so grateful Councilman Daniel convinced my Father to bring me to the tournament. I will always remember what you've done here."

Heat burns my face so hot, it feels as if I could start the entire box on fire. Praise is not something I think I'll ever grow used to. "I'm glad you were able to be here to see it. You know, this is something most women are capable of if they have magic within them."

"Oh no, I couldn't do such a thing."

"Why certainly you could," Annabelle says, linking arms with her. "It's something we should all learn to do."

"But quietly," Serena adds.

"Yes, just not while we are in my house." She winks. "We should let you rest now, though. And get to our own box before... We should get going."

We give our good-byes, and they go off, leaving me with a lot to think on. Hearing everyone chant my name was invigorating, having a specific person talk to me like that makes me want to get back out on the field right now and continue showing them what they can all do. Only it's also paired with worry over failing. Silly thought since I've already proven I can do it. Except, what if I do let them all down tomorrow?

I close my eyes and doze while the thoughts continue pulsing through me, Nelly's sweet face behind them. Sometime later, when I'm not feeling myself, but much more rested, Xyer leans forward from behind Serena and me and says, "There's someone here that says they know you, a tarnished who's quite insistent."

Serena jolts toward the steps before stopping herself and strolls toward the edge of the box. Is it Katherine? I hurry toward the stairs, weaving my way through the guards until I can see a familiar bald head trying to peek over the shoulder of a guard I don't recognize.

"Let her up," I call down to him, yawning.

He moves to the side, and Katherine bounces up the stairs, her tattoos glowing a muted orange today. Against the darkening night, the glow is almost eerie.

"A friend came with me. Can he come up?" she says.

"He?" I give her the most playful smile that can curl my lips. "Of course he's welcome." I motion the guards to let him through. A male tarnished comes up the stairs behind her, with his ink glowing orange as well, but a strength about him that makes me wonder if the guards would be any good around him if he were an enemy. Luckily, he seems to be a friend.

I wave Lukas over, introducing him, a grin involuntarily escaping me just at the sight of him.

"Lukas, huh?" She gives me a knowing smile. "It is very, very good to meet you. This is Charles."

She motions to the tarnished with her, though from the adoring way he watches her, and the protective stance at her side, he seems more than just a friend.

"I don't mean to sound ungrateful because I'm thrilled to see you," I tell her, "but it's just before the feast when the Grand Chancellor makes his sacrifice."

"We know." Her voice is heavy.

"They shouldn't be able to do this."

Serena nudges me, glancing at the box all too close to our own. The Grand Chancellor and Chancellor Ryan are talking about something, both pairs of eyes flitting to our box.

I lower my voice. "We have to do something to stop it."

"I wish we could," Katherine says.

"We all do," Zade adds, stepping closer to our conversation. "But we're not in a place to do anything about it yet. If we step in, we'll be breaking the law. We'd be lucky if the punishment didn't include losing our lives."

"But everything I've been doing all week, it's nothing." My power roils inside me, building my frustration more than if it would settle. "My magic is nothing. Nothing. Not with what they do to these girls, what they always do."

Lukas squeezes my hand. "Everything you're doing isn't nothing. It's what will help others, both in this country and from other countries. It makes them all realize that women are people, that they need others to stand up for them, too."

The Grand Chancellor stands, motioning the crowd to quiet as he brings in what I wish could be stopped. I step closer to Katherine, not letting go of Lukas's hand. Zade puts an arm around Serena. We're all silent as a tarnished girl willingly lowers herself on the torch lit altar.

Chancellor Ryan sneers at me as the Grand Chancellor says a few things. My stomach knots around itself, making me wish I could throw a hex at him. His sneer turns to a smirk as if he knows just what I want to do and, more so, at the fact that I can't.

As the Grand Chancellor moves from his box to the altar, I focus on him instead. I force my eyes to stay open, unlike last year when I couldn't bring myself to do it. Though it's wretched, I need to understand what's happening. But with each step forward the Grand Chancellor takes, the urge to turn away builds.

When he's standing next to the altar with the tarnished staring blankly at the sky, a silvery spell slithers from him, forming a knife. My free hand curls so tightly into a fist that my nails bite into my skin. I want to look away, to watch the blood pool from my own palms instead of from this innocent girl, but I don't let myself.

The crowd is silent as a stench grows stronger. The knife-like spell darts to her neck, crimson flowing, immediately gathered up by a second spell, clear from this vantage, save for flashes of bright red. It wastes no time pulling the blood from the girl toward the Grand Chancellor.

My fingers push harder, enough that they become wet with my own blood. I can't stop myself any more than I can stop him without finding myself in her very place.

The Grand Chancellor directs the spell, pulling the helpless girl's blood toward his wrist where he's opened up a cut in his own arm. He uses the spell to pull the pure, untainted blood into him. How much magic did this tarnished girl have in her blood? Odds are, a lot. My hands ache, but not nearly as much as my chest.

The Grand Chancellor's mouth turns up at the corners, framed by his beard as the spell continues sucking out her life force and magic. Moving her blood to him while she becomes paler under the strain. He is glowing though, as if the magic he has stolen isn't fully absorbed into him, the light of it taking time to meld with his.

A moan escapes me. Hands are on me, pulling me toward them. Lukas, his spicy sweet scent fills me as I curl into his shoulder. Why can't we do anything? Why?

CHAPTER 44

The nightmare is over. For the tarnished girl at least. The sight of her motionless body. Of it being drained of life while I just stood and did nothing will terrorize me for a long time.

"It doesn't matter what sort of hold they have over us. We can't keep doing nothing."

Serena glances around, eyes watchful of the crowd, but Lukas doesn't take his gaze from me. "We will do something."

"And we are," Katherine says from behind me, coming to my side. "We're doing as much as we can. It just takes time for people to realize this is something they need to fight for, that they need to believe in."

"Still wish I could throw a fireball at him."

"Don't we all," Bethany mutters.

And I can't help but smile, even if it's not for the best of reason. I'm no longer alone in wanting to do magic.

"We should leave," Serena says.

"You and Bethany go ahead. There's something I need to do," I say, trying not to think on how soft my bed is.

"I could stay with you," Bethany says.

"Not this time. Katherine, you and Charles are welcome to go with Serena and Bethany, or to come with me to the feast."

Serena shivers, no doubt remembering her experience with Thomas at the festival last year. Just thinking on it makes me want to shiver as well, but I turn my gaze on Katherine and keep steady. She and Charles exchange a look, one that seems to speak in a language I don't understand.

"We'll join you," she says.

We see Serena and Bethany off with Zade and their guards. Lukas, Chadwick, and Xyer remaining behind. The rotten stench invades my senses as we near the feast. The revelers are already loud, laughing and shouting at each other. Women and men watch me closely as I near, though none speak with me.

The crowd grows as we move within it. Somehow I feel more alone here than when no one was around at that first house. At least the others are close by, but I try only to think on them as a support. Mostly, I just need to be seen here. Show I belong here as much as the other duelers. More so even. I am one of the few going on to the last day.

"What is that stench?" I finally ask my guard.

"Traditional Chardonian tournament fare," Chadwick answers, knowing more about my country, even though he's from Envado. "Week-old, twice-boiled cabbage."

"What brilliant person came up with that idea?"

Lukas snickers, but Chadwick replies with a lowered voice. "The Grand Chancellor. His favorite, apparently."

"Ah." And I have to keep my own laughter in. No wonder he's so foul when that's his favorite food. "Does anyone know what a mime is? Some women talked about them last year, but I've never been able to figure out what they are."

"There's one over this way that I spotted earlier," Lukas says, placing a hand on the small of my back.

We weave through the crowd, drawing attention from almost everyone. I lean in closer to Lukas, not because I need the support but because I want them all to know how I feel about him.

We reach a crowd surrounding a man, but not just any man. He's wearing all black except for his hands, which have white gloves, the kind only women wear. What's more, his face is painted, sort of like a woman's, but his features have been exaggerated toward happiness.

"Why does he look like that?"

Lukas quiets me. "Just watch."

The man pulls a black bag out of his pocket, takes a ball out, and throws it into the air. Then he does it again, but I realize there is no ball. He's only pretending to throw it and catch it behind his back. As he looks at the imaginary ball, he pulls his mouth to the side, his features appearing extra stretched with the black lines drawn on his face. Then he proceeds to throw his imaginary ball at a warlock's head and catch it as it bounces back.

Laughter escapes me, as it does many others in the crowd. He continues his performance, doing all sorts of tricks that grow funnier each time. It may not be a restful way to spend the evening, but my magic is responding anyway, bouncing happily through me even if it's not at full power.

It's all splendid until I recognize a familiar face next to another, more dreaded familiar face. The laughter and magic with me freezes into icy points.

"Is that Conrad by Chancellor Ryan?" My mind is blank, struggling to process why my missing guard, the one who worked so hard to protect me, is by a warlock I loathe.

Lukas glances where I point, and his hands immediately fist. "Not just by him, but smiling and talking to him like they're old pals."

Never have I wanted to throw a hex as badly as I do now. The crowd around us, laughing at another of the mime's antics, seems to blur as I focus in on him. I shove my way past them all, not caring about anything but getting to him. Getting to someone who swore to protect me, who we've all been worried about and had other guards out looking for. Someone who is about to feel my wrath.

"We've been looking for you."

"Stop looking so hard. I've been right here." His gaze flits to Chancellor Ryan, smile uneasy.

"It would seem Conrad and I have the same goals," the Chancellor replies, much more confidently.

"Harassing women?" The words spit from me and make me realize the laughter is dying down, the crowd focusing in on us.

"I wouldn't," Conrad says, finally having the decency to look a little guilty. "We've been working on better trade between our countries."

"Which includes giving up your oath to protect those who need you," Lukas says, voice bristling with even more anger than mine. He leans in closer, words taking on a deadly whisper. "And what did you give up to secure better trade? Setting the trap for Cynthia?"

Conrad takes a step back, looking away.

"You did, didn't you?" My voice is small, betrayal shocking a larger reaction from flaring out. "You set up me, Chadwick, and Xyer."

He takes another step back, enough that Chancellor Ryan puts himself between us, eyeing the crowd. "Conrad is an honored tradesman between our countries. If anyone threatens him, the consequences would be swift, I assure you."

Magic and anger seethe through me, a riot of emotion struggling to let loose. Lukas grabs my hand, making me realize I had lifted it up, readying to hex them both. The crowd around me is wide-eyed as they take in the scene.

I clench my teeth, struggling to rein my power in before speaking. "Consequences for disloyalty may not be as swift but will still haunt any who follow that path."

Though the Chancellor holds his sneer, Conrad pales. Good. I hold myself rigid and confident as I stride away, trying to think of anything but what just happened. The crowd parts before me, many giving me a nod of encouragement but others looking away. As soon as we're away from the crowd, I don't give up my act but let more of my true emotions sink in.

"I'm so sorry," Lukas says. "If I'd known he was like th—"

"Stop. You couldn't have known. None of us could have. He was too good at pretending for that."

Lukas doesn't say anything, only clenches his jaw.

"Let's go home." The weariness in my voice shows that it's almost as drained as I am.

Without a word, Lukas puts an arm around me and leads me away.

CHAPTER 45

Today is the last day of the tournament. This is it, and I've gotten farther than I ever thought I would. I spell my hair a muted brown, nails black, jewelry minimal, only a single necklace and bracelet and Lukas's ring. The ride over to the grounds and checking the schedule are somber and silent. Magic, not fully restored, lumbers through me, but hopefully it's enough to get me through the day.

Everything is heavier with Conrad's betrayal. After telling Zade, no one has spoken of it, but it still hangs heavy on me like a hex, keeping me under the weight of a house. Save for my family, Katherine, Zade, and Lukas, those close to me can't even be counted on to stand by my side, let alone Chardonians.

I press on anyway. The fights are tough, but I don't die, and somehow manage to win. There's not much left in me for the last fight. My magic is weak, struggling to respond to my commands. I lay on the ground, trying to rest, trying to gain back as much of it as I can while Bethany and Serena hover near with water, and more importantly, their support.

The ground is just beginning to feel welcoming enough to sleep when Lukas joins us. "Your opponent just won his duel."

"Who is it?"

"Nathaniel."

The Grand Chancellor's son. No one besides him was likely to win, just like no one else is likely to win the entire tournament. Though he's been kind, the news fills me with a sort of dread. Thick and heavy, it presses the magic regaining strength within me into a tight ball.

The rain crashes down on the protective spell above us. I don't ever remember seeing it rain so hard. It's probably a sign of how vastly I'm going to fail. A council member always wins the tournament, and since the Grand Chancellor's son is participating, he might as well be the most important councilman even if he is not, in fact, a councilman.

"It's good I made it here." The sky continues its incessant splashing into the dome overhead as Lukas leans into view. "It should be enough."

"But?" he says.

I close my eyes and give a defeated, "I want more."

"You can have more."

"You're sweet, but look at me, sprawled in the grass, trying to do everything I can just to let some of my magic recharge. It's ridiculous for me to want what's clearly not going to happen. Chancellor Ryan was sure to make me have to duel so much more than the others over the past two days so this would be how I ended up."

"Maybe, but it doesn't mean you have to give up."

"What else am I supposed to do? I'll go out there and fight, certainly, but there's no way to win."

"Not if you think like that, there isn't." He reaches a hand down to help me up. "You made it this far when many didn't think you could. Now you just need to believe in yourself to make it through the last step. Many hope you do."

I take his hand and stand. How to win the impossible, I'm not sure. If no one else before me was able to defeat the Grand Chancellor's choice for a winner, why should I be any different?

I am different, though. I am a woman. I am a warlock. I am going to win. And if not, if I die, I won't go without flair.

Giving Lukas's hand a squeeze, I let go. He nods at me like he knows just what I'm thinking. I don't leave it at that. If I'm going to win or die today, I'm going to do it with the memory of him. I wrap myself around him and kiss him with everything I have. All my longing and hope. All my struggle and sorrow.

He responds in kind, his mouth moving with mine, his hands gripping me tighter, holding me close and fierce. Everything has been worth it, but I only wish there was time for us to simply be like this before my probable end. He tastes spicy, just like the first time we kissed. The intensity of the kiss gives way to something sweet and tender. Tender, yet filled with heart-broken passion. Something that brings tears to my eyes that I don't blink away. Something I hope he will remember, even if I'm no longer with him.

When our lips brush apart, he holds me close for another moment, places a peck on my forehead, and lets me go.

With my lips aching, I turn to Bethany and Serena.

"I need to go." I motion to the crowd that's just out of sight. "They need me to." I hug her, tight and fierce. "Everything will be fine. If not—"

"It will be," Bethany says.

"If not," I persist, "Serena and Zade will take care of things."

Serena's face is tight as she nods.

Chadwick says, "You're being called."

And indeed, my name sounds close by, around the stands, just out of sight. I wish there was more time, time for more good-byes if nothing else. I turn to Lukas "I—"

He puts a finger on my lips, stopping me. "Tell me after your duel."

"But—"

"After."

He presses a final, swift kiss to my lips, and then twirls me around. It doesn't matter that there may not be an after. It only matters that my memory will live on long after I am gone. Bethany has her back to me. I give her another quick hug. "Tell all the girls I love them."

She nods, her lips tight, her eyes blinking back tears.

And I'm off, striding to the field that will either bring a new freedom or my death.

CHAPTER 46

The others hurry to their box while I stride around it and onto the field. It's dim with the storm overhead, despite the lit torches surrounding the field. The judge and the mediator stand by the glowing ring, Nathaniel is not yet in sight, so I wait, close enough they can't say I'm not here, but far enough that I will still need to walk there when Nathaniel does.

The box next to the Grand Chancellor's—Serena's box—is ethereal. Bethany, Serena, Waverly, and Katherine stand regally side-by-side. My short locks rustle in the small breeze that's managed to break through the spell. If the breeze is starting to break through, how long until the rain does as well? Hopefully not until after the tournament ends. By then, it probably won't matter to me anyway. It's hard enough dueling without adding bad weather.

The Grand Chancellor rises. I have an overwhelming urge to punch a spell at him. Thrust the pain at him that he's put an entire country full of women through. Course it wouldn't do a bit of good. If someone else didn't stop it before it got to him, he'd be sure to, and then I'd be killed as an outlaw instead of dying in the final duel of the tournament.

Nathaniel appears across the field from me. I stride onto the field as he does. Thunder rumbles in the distance as we meet in the middle, both stopping on our own sides of the dueling ring. The torches go dim, leaving them the only faint light. My ribs feel as if they're about to break from the frantic pounding of my heart. The stands are quiet. I grip my hands together, Lukas's ring reminding me both of him and the strength I need to have.

"Enter," the Grand Chancellor calls out.

Though my magic bounces, as much as is left, my skin is icy. Nathaniel is different. He's changed. No longer the quiet, unassuming man who just happens to be the son of the Grand Chancellor. His face, bland as life without magic, except for his focus on me making his eyes the only part of his face with expression. Eyes that are strong and harsh as if he wants to kill me. So much for being honored to duel against me. My stomach becomes a pit of dread, filled with hexes. This is the face of my death.

We step into the circle at the same time, flashing it vivid orange as we cross. His spells are immediate and with such intensity, they crack every shield I shove at them. Both spells dissipate, but with my magic already so depleted, it won't last long.

I continue throwing up shields as a slew of colors fly at me, trying to think of a way to draw this out, to show everyone that I am fighting for everything, that I have this power, and I'm willing to die to show it. A bit of wind tousles my hair. I glance up. That's something he won't expect. Hopefully something he's not prepared for.

He zaps another spell at me. I fling two block shields to replace the ones he's pummeled through, and then zap a spell at the dome above us, not strong, but pointed. Just a spot of icy cold focused exactly on the dome above our dueling ring. A resounding crack echoes through the field, quickly followed by howling wind. Within a second I'm soaked, the ground quickly growing slick with mud.

I crouch down, making myself as small of a target as possible, the mud sloshing as Nathaniel slips to the side. But it doesn't stop the attack. Two violet shocks of light stream close but pass over my head.

Thinking of the sunniest day I can remember, I give my eyes a quick shield of darkness and flash pure light at him. The brightness still makes me squint, even with the graying shield. He grunts and screws his eyes shut against the light. Leaving the light spell blinding, I dart a dozen tiny bits of pure magic straight at his torso. Points. Even if I die, I will be remembered as having the most points, the almost winner.

Only three touch him before a thick emerald light encompasses him, creating a sort of full-body shield. Once the shield is in place, I keep my magic centered in me, ready to shield as I scan for cracks in his.

Something puffs from his hands, the deepest black, though my gray eye shield is still up. It puffs bigger and bigger, quickly taking over the area and surrounding my light spell. I rip the shield covering my eyes away just as there's a yank on my magic. He's attacking my spell.

I focus on releasing it, letting it dissipate, but as soon as I do, the puff of black whirls toward me. There's no room to move. I'm already crouched as low as I can, and the ring is just behind me. It creeps closer and closer, snaking past my usual shield. I crouch lower, trying not to let panic overwhelm my senses.

His hands stretch toward me, pushing the cloud spell on. That's it! His hands. Gathering the bits of magic left inside me, I shove it out at his hands, twisting them back so they point at his chest just as the cloud wisps against my forehead. The center of my forehead goes numb, but the spell fails with his hands now pointed back.

He howls, neck arching back as he struggles against my spell. I sway to my feet, keeping my spell at full force, mud and rain soaking through me, filling the air with their scents. Almost over now. Just have to last a little longer.

Spells fly from him, blood-red and sooty-black. They flick backward toward the crowd, smashing against the protective shield.

His nostrils flare, teeth bared toward me. "Must. Kill. Her."

Before I think on it, I step back, hands shaking, but the spell holding steady. Then I realize I'm right against the line. Any farther and the ring will change colors, forcing me out. I have to move closer, and give myself some leeway.

Nathaniel continues struggling against my spell, yanking on the last of my energy, growling and snarling like a mad man, but not moving any closer. Taking a ragged breath, I force myself to take a single step forward.

Another howl screeches from him, scraping across my ears. I hold the last of my magic steady, but it's not going to be enough. Between my weakening state, and his fighting against it, he's going to break free.

A burnt orange spell rips from him, breaking through the last of my magic. I totter, but stay standing firm as my magic is depleted, his hands free to do their damage. There's no gathering glee in him like other warlocks would have, just a hex, black and dark silver with flickers of crimson. It slams against my leg, collapsing me to the ground. It's as if my leg is no longer there, even if I can still see it.

Another comes hurtling at me. Twenty seconds to go, but it's too long. I'll be dead.

Desperate, I scream, "Stop!"

And he does.

CHAPTER 47

The moment passes and then another. Did he really just listen to me? Not that I didn't want him to, but why would he? His expression is bland, nothing of the snarling man from moments ago. I stand and wipe the mud from my face.

"What's going on?" the Grand Chancellor yells. "Keep fighting." Though the raging face doesn't return, Nathaniel zaps a crimson hex. I throw myself in the mud, it squishing beneath me as the light flashes overhead, just missing me. I turn my face toward him and yell again, "No, Nathaniel, stop."

Again he listens, though I can't fathom why or what's going on. Except, wait. Maybe there is something. Something that makes you lose control of yourself and have to listen to others around you.

Swiftly, I whirl toward the crowd and yell before the Grand Chancellor can speak again, "Someone has tampered with Nathaniel. He isn't under his own control. He does whatever anyone says. Whoever did it… is forcing him to fight me to the death and not in line with the tournament rules."

The crowd is against me enough without my pointing out that the Grand Chancellor set this all up.

"Absurd," the Grand Chancellor calls out.

But already the crowed is doubting. Their chatter is growing, hopefully wondering if my words could be true. Even though I am just a woman, they can tell something is wrong. That Nathaniel has been stopping and starting at my and the Grand Chancellor's words.

I yell as loudly as I can from my muddy spot on the ground, "It's easy enough to figure out. Have several people tell him to do something simple and harmless, but something he wouldn't do on his own."

"We aren't going through such a charade," the Grand Chancellor says.

But I ignore him. What's worse, I turn my back on him, at least as well as I can without being able to feel my leg. I hope, with every fiber of my being, that he doesn't zap a spell at it. "Nathaniel, put your hands on your head."

He promptly complies, placing both hands on the back of his head. My shoulders sag as the final murmuring of the crowd goes silent. It has to be the Califrasum tea. If that's truly the case, I should be able to find out.

"What happened to you?" I'm grateful my voice sounds strong and firm. Never before have I so desperately needed it to be so.

"When I refused to illegally increase my magic, Chancellor Ryan forced me to drink something. Once it took effect, he made me take blood magic from five tarnished women."

A gasp escapes not only me but the entire crowd. Chancellor Ryan! I should have known. At that instant, the time expires, the moment a winner should be declared. It only distracts me for a moment, though. Five women were killed in order for Nathaniel to beat me. I roll to the side, my dead leg flopping to the ground, and vomit atop the dueling ring.

CHAPTER 48

My stomach still churns as I finally turn back toward the Grand Chancellor. Did he know about this? Would he have permitted Chancellor Ryan to do something like this to his own son? Everything about this is so wrong, I can't bring myself to speak, but it's no matter. My point has already been proved, and everyone here saw it and knows something is going on.

The only sound is the pattering of rain and the howling of wind. Everyone seems just as focused on the Grand Chancellor as I am. The way his eyes pierce into mine, I don't relish what's to happen if he should ever come upon me alone, without the crowd he depends on to keep both his leadership and his sources of trade intact.

He waves his hand. I want to flinch but make my last moments firm and steady. Instead of slamming into me, his spell rises to the crack in the dome and repairs it. How many warlocks did it take to make that the first time? The rain stops, though I'm still soaked and covered with mud. At some point, I started shivering.

The Grand Chancellor's lips thin. His fingers flex. I don't like where this is going. "Perhaps there's been a misunderstanding."

"It didn't sound like a misunderstanding." Lukas's voice sounds from behind me.

I glance behind me to see the field filling with not just him and my other guards but other duelers. And the boxes, people are standing in them, coming to the front. Even in Serena's box next to the Grand Chancellor. Every person is standing with their focus directly on him.

"No mistake at all," Councilman Daniel adds from his box.

And soon the air is full of voices in support but not of anything I ever expected them to be in support of. Me.

The growing number of people calling out grows the feeling within me that I've done exactly what I wanted to. Most of these people are no longer what my existence represents. They are standing up for me. A woman who does magic.

The Grand Chancellor holds up a hand, but the crowd doesn't silence right away. The voices take much longer to fade and show proper respect. When they finally silence, he leaves them hanging a moment before speaking.

"It would appear that she is... correct." A tick in his eyes is the only hint at how strongly he disagrees with this. "I will question my son upon his returning to himself, and the matter will be investigated. Ryan will no longer be part of the council and will remain in my custody until the entire matter has been dealt with appropriately."

At the back of the Grand Chancellor's box, Ryan shows no emotion, doesn't give hint one way or another as to how this makes him feel. Likely nothing too bad will befall him if it was what the Grand Chancellor wanted. The thought makes me want to seethe, but there's no energy left for it. At least he won't be on the council and out torturing girls.

The Grand Chancellor starts to turn, but I can't entirely leave it at that. "And the tournament," I call out. "Since Nathaniel is not able to finish his participation in the duel..."

I let my words trail so that everyone knows where they are

going and what they mean but let them come to the conclusion themselves.

The Grand Chancellor snaps back around, his face not guarded against the hatred he feels toward me for a brief moment. He quickly schools his features, but not quickly enough. I know how strongly he detests me, but at least a few others have to have seen it as well. His crisp veneer is beginning to show flaws.

"Forgive me, this business with my son and the Chancellor has rattled me." Then something seems to change, his lips curling into a smile. "Cynthia is the champion. Her reward shall be given in three hours."

He whisks away faster than the crowd can cheer. But cheer they do, or at least many of them, much more than I would have expected. Both men and women, Chardonians and those from other countries, are cheering me on. Everyone has seen what I can do, and now I know what I can do as well. I am no longer the girl who forced herself to always hide everything. I am Cynthia. A warlock. Champion of the Chardonian tournament.

But even with all those wondrous, unbelievable things, the Chancellor's smile and quick getaway have me worried.

"Do they usually wait to reward the champion?" I ask Zade when he reaches me.

"No. It's always done immediately."

It's good my leg is dead and I'm stuck on the ground. Otherwise I'd have trouble staying steady on my feet. What does the Grand Chancellor have planned for me?

CHAPTER 49

Moments later, several warlocks arrive to take Nathaniel away. Their hurried departure heads in the same direction the Grand Chancellor left. Will anything bad happen to him because of this? Does it even matter? Before today, he seemed all right, but now it's difficult to think of him without seeing his face snarling, his voice growling.

"Cynthia."

I jump.

Lukas places a hand on my shoulder. "It's over now."

That's right. It's over. I don't have to think on him anymore, though I'm certain my nightmares will still try.

"Can we take you to a healer? Or bring one here?" His gaze is hovering on my dead leg. The one completely lost of feeling.

"That probably would be wise."

"Yes, it would," Zade says, reminding me of his own permanent limp. "Chadwick is already on his way to fetch one to come to you."

"What if…" The dead weight of my leg is heavy.

"Don't start down that road until we know," he says.

The dead weight of my leg grows more burdensome as the minutes tick by. I slump more and more with each passing minute, only Lukas's coat keeping me out of the mud. The crowd is gathered around, giving some space between us, but pressed tight together. Fears creep in, pounding against my skull. What has this path I choose cost me? I glance at Zade wondering if he regrets the choices that lead him to have a permanent limp. He stares at the ground a moment before looking up at me, regret fueled by something I don't understand burning in his eyes.

"I was wrong." Zade's voice is so quiet, I have to strain to hear him. "I was so wrong."

"What do you mean?"

"Showing your magic like this. It was foolish and dangerous, but it was right." He glances over those gathered around us. "They needed this and you were brave enough to give it to them."

His words settle deep inside, spreading warmth through me. "I couldn't have done it without your help."

He gives my hand a squeeze and I can't help but think how glad I am that he came into Serena's life. Into my life. If I had a brother, I hope he'd be like Zade. My thoughts dwell less on my injury and more on Zade's approval while we continue to wait. Chardonians may have needed to see my magic but I needed to show it to them as much as they needed to see it.

When the healer finally arrives, he kneels down beside me, quickly going through the motions of restoring me to health. He works quickly and efficiently using a soft blue spell to probe my injury followed by a bright yellow one. Thankfully it mends my leg, though not without pain. It's nothing compared to what Zade has to live with or how I might have not lived at all. The pain affects me very little and quickly leaves.

"You're going to be just fine," the healer says. "Try and get some rest when you can."

Relief fills me as I thank him and he moves back through the crowd. As time passes, I feel better physically, the exhausted state of my magic leaves a gaping hole. A few days will help, but until then, there's nothing I can do to help myself.

We hover around the field, waiting for the Grand Chancellor to return. Chadwick, Lukas, and Xyer stay close by as people come to talk to me. There's only a few at first, including Councilman Daniel and Annabelle. But as they come, it seems to bolster the confidence of others, and soon I'm conversing with more people than I ever have before.

Not everyone is excited or curious with my victory. Some leave or stay in the stands and boxes giving dark looks. The few from Envado seem pleased, though. Those from Chryos seem a little more mixed. I hear one tell Lukas, "This isn't going to keep our coal trade open. It's going to send them into a civil war."

War? Is that really what I've started? I hope not. I only wanted to do magic and to show other women that they could do the same. War would bring uncertainty and death.

The chattering stops slowly, like a wave of silence rushing toward me. I turn around to see that the crowd has parted for the Grand Chancellor who is striding forward, his eyes bright with accomplishment. And there's someone behind him. Someone I can't make out, but whose bulk sticking out from behind the Grand Chancellor seems familiar. As soon as the Grand Chancellor sees me watching, he shifts to let the person behind him show as they continue toward us. My breath catches. A boulder lodges in my chest. Father.

My mind stays blank for too long. By the time it starts working again, they are almost to me and there's no time left to think. Only time for icy cold to permeate through me.

The Grand Chancellor stops a few feet from me. Father stays behind him and to the side a little, his expression completely blank. What is this? What is he doing here? Are they punishing him more? Or is he here to punish me?

I keep my face impassive, but inside I'm like fire and ice, a burning cold that threatens to overwhelm me.

"Cynthia Stephen's daughter," the Grand Chancellor's gleeful voice carries through the field, making the iciness stab through me in ragged cuts, though I refuse to let them show. "You, my dear, are the champion of our tournament, and it is time for your reward."

My lungs squeeze painfully. I slowly take a breath, using it to help keep control of the facade that's desperately trying to break.

"I thought it would only be fitting to have Stephen here. You see, he very recently completed his sentence and has showed the proper remorse for his... mistake," the Grand Chancellor says. "Because of his sincere remorse and desire to right his wrongs, I've forgiven him and reinstated him to the council."

This is bad. This is very bad.

"Since he is a member of the council again, he can give you your reward. I thought it would be fitting, would it not? To have a parent delivering the reward like I was so fortunate to do in years past." His eyes are sharp with anger, but brightened with glee. "If you please, Stephen."

Father steps forward, a trophy larger than my head in his hands. I clench my hands together but don't make a further move. I should pretend that this is good and fine. That the Grand Chancellor has done nothing to bother me. But I can't bring myself to pretend Father's presence is a happy one. No, not Father. He is only father, the man that helped give me life, but nothing more. He no longer owns me.

"Hello, father." I purposefully make his name sound lower case, fitting of what he's earned even if he always demanded more.

"Cynthia." He hands me the prize, heavy as his stare, and leans closer, his voice so low I doubt anyone else can hear him. "Freedom is temporary."

I plaster a big, fake smile on my face. If there's one thing I know how to fake my way past, it's father and his threats. "Only your own freedom is fleeting." I quickly pull away and hold up the trophy, straining against its weight. "For all Chardonian women!"

The crowd around me breaks into cheering. The Grand Chancellor's face tightens, but only for a moment. I may have the moment, but he is still our ruler. He will do whatever he can to smash the hope I've given to our people.

CHAPTER 50

"Does she really have to go?" I ask Zade.

He answers patiently, though we've already been over this a plethora of times since the tournament. "She promised our mom she would only stay as long as things were fairly safe. They aren't anymore. She should have left before the tournament. You should all be going with her."

"Maybe we should," Serena says, "but we're needed here to help women see the road we've started them on."

"The Grand Chancellor isn't taking his son's disgrace and defeat lightly," Zade says. "Repercussions are coming. I just want you all safe."

"Serena's right," I say. "We know you love us and don't want us hurt or back under father's control, but we are needed here."

"But you've got your foul wish with me, Zade." Waverly turns her back on him and wraps me in a hug.

Emotions try to clog my words, but I force past them. "I will miss you."

"We all will," Serena adds as she gets a hug of her own. The other girls have already said good-bye, Bethany keeping them inside while we see her off. I step closer to Lukas and lean into him as he puts an arm around me.

"Be sure to write us and let us know you're safe," Serena says.

"Only if you promise to spell back your replies."

A fierce look of determination crosses Serena's face. Her eyes narrow, and she holds up her hand. A dark blue spell splutters out, slow and broken, but determined. Big enough for all of us to see as it forms the words "I will." My sister is finally embracing magic. Even with the threat of father and the Grand Chancellor, there is hope.

"I'll look forward to it." Waverly turns toward me. "From both of you."

Unable to give a reply for the emotions clogging my throat, I nod.

"Good then." She turns to Zade and he quickly picks her up into a hug, tight and fierce. "Don't you let them do anything to my sisters, or to you. You keep everyone safe, including yourself. Do you understand me?"

"You know I'll do everything I can."

She hangs on another moment before letting go. After taking time to say goodbye to mother, whose rounded belly makes the hug difficult, Waverly moves toward the carriage, and Chadwick steps up to her. I feel like we should give them a moment alone, but I don't want to miss seeing her off.

"You stay safe, too," she tells him.

"I'll do my best."

"Even if it means not staying safe."

He doesn't deny it. "Tell everyone I said hello."

"I will." She pivots toward the carriage.

"And Waverly?"

"Yes," she calls over her shoulder.

"I'll be thinking of you."

Her back stiffens a moment before she turns and says, "I'll think of our friendship, too. Good-bye, everyone. I'll miss you."

"We'll miss you, too," I say.

With that, she's in the carriage, door closed, and it's pulling away. Most likely with the way things are here, it's uncertain if I'll ever see her again. We all watch it until it's out of sight, a few tears escaping. Chadwick is the first to leave, skirting out back around the house. Serena tells Zade, "I know you want us safe, and I love you for it."

"Just not enough to leave."

"You came here to help. Let me stay here to do the same."

He closes his eyes and pulls her tight against him. "I know. I know. I just don't want to lose you."

"You won't."

Zade gives me and Lukas a quick glance, his gaze taking in Lukas's arm around me before turning back to Serena. "You're right. I don't have to. I've been looking at everything all wrong. Relationships as weights instead of anchors, but Cynthia and Lukas have shown me so much more." Suddenly he gets down on one knee, clutching both of her hands in his. "I need you by my side. You are my anchor, my strength. I want to always keep it that way. Serena, will you marry me?"

My breath catches, and Lukas pulls me closer.

Serena says, through her tears, "I will. Oh, yes, I will!"

He stands, pulling her all the way up to him in a fierce kiss. I blush and, though I'm brimming with happiness, turn away from them toward Lukas. He nods at me, and together we stroll around the house.

"Do you think that will be enough to keep Serena safe from your father if he ends up carrying out his threat?"

This isn't something I even need to think about. "If the Grand Chancellor is helping father, he'll make it so father can get whatever he wants. No, if we want things to really change, the Grand Chancellor will need to be knocked from his position."

"Zade said he's been hinting at political change, something to do with not needing Chryos's coal anymore."

"I thought the Grand Chancellor was in love with his electricity," I say.

"He is." Lukas's mouth pulls into a grim line. "That means I'll have to keep working at undermining him however we can. I wouldn't want to lose relations with your country."

He lightens a moment, enough to wink at me, sending a thrill through my magic. "I'll do whatever I can to help defeat him, not just for our countries, but to stay with you."

"You know how powerful the Grand Chancellor is. He's taken more tarnished blood than any other. Is anyone strong enough to knock him out of power? Even if we combine strength, it seems doubtful."

A shudder runs through me. Lukas stops walking and wraps his arms around me.

"This isn't what I meant to cause when I left home."

"I know."

His chocolate eyes keep steady on mine as I say, "As much as I'm scared for what the future brings, I'm glad I did."

"I couldn't agree more."

It feels good and right, being here with him.

An aqua-colored light crashes to the ground right next to me, bringing a wave of cold. Lukas pulls me back for I've frozen, not from the spell but from the sight behind it. Father stands almost within touching distance, Edward next to him.

My breath catches in my throat, still frozen, hands propped up in the air from the defensive spell I was readying before spotting them, which is now useless. And father knows it. His grin brightens the anger in his eyes.

"I told you freedom is temporary. And look what I found. Seems your last owner didn't give up your ownership by his own free will. Seems he was threatened. The Grand Chancellor didn't like that news one bit."

Oh no. Oh no, oh no, oh no. Why is this coming up now? Why

is it coming up when things are going so well? It can't be like this. It can't.

Lukas isn't frozen like me. He grabs hold of my arm, his hand clenched tight around me.

Edward doesn't look like he wants to be here either. In fact, he keeps looking at the ground, father, the grass, anywhere but me. Father must have scared him into coming. That must be why he didn't come forward sooner. Why I was able to compete and win the tournament without being punished in a way worse than anything I've been through before? In a way that's going to happen now. Unless I can do something to stop it.

"It appears you've been busy since you got out of jail."

"And it seems you were busy while I was in jail, thanks to your wenchit sister. But I've got you. It won't be long before I find a way to get her and the rest of my property. Especially my pregnant wife," he growls. "You're all in need of some drastic changes."

"We are. But not the type of changes you want."

Frozen no longer, I shove a barrage of fire at them and zip a volley of air at the ground beneath Lukas and me. He clings to me, swearing as we soar into the sky from the blast.

Hexes dart after us. Mostly reds, but some gray ones as well. One nears Lukas. I push the air to the side, dodging them. I shove all my magic into the air, propelling us higher. Father and Edward grow too small to see. The attacking spells don't stop, but they grow wider,

"Afraid of heights?" I ask Lukas as he continues clinging to me, and I cling to my magic.

"Afraid of your magic running out."

Right. The strain is already wearing on my newly built-up state, but we can't go back down. I push the air at us, move us toward the side as far as I can before letting it ease. The strain pulses through me as we float toward the ground. We've covered a lot of ground, enough that they're no longer in sight, but I can hear the faint sound of father screaming.

"Can you take over if I set us down?" My body is exhausted, the sky growing spotted with black. My magic never fully recovered from the tournament and now this. It's too much.

"You've saved us. Now it's my job to keep us safe." The way he clings to me, the way he's supported me, I know it's true.

We're almost to the ground. It's coming. Coming closer. Fast. Much too fast. But tired. Too tir…

* * *

MY EYELIDS ACHE. They want to stay closed forever. But they can't. Something happened that—I jolt up, my head pounding with the action.

"Ow."

"Take it slowly," Lukas says. "Don't worry. We're safe."

"Where are we?"

"A safe house for now. We'll move to a more secure one in a few hours when you're feeling well. Just rest."

"My sisters?"

His frown deepens, making my heart twist. "They are all safe, but everyone is back under your father's control except Serena."

This is it then. Serena and I prepared the way for change, or at least have got people thinking. Our choices brought us here. Hers proving that women can have freedom. Mine to spell as well as any warlock. Now everyone in the country knows what women are capable of. What we can be.

And because of it, father's struck back, using my own actions against me. Despite him, and how he always treated me, I found my own way, showed others what they can do. As I enjoy the feel of Lukas's arm around me, my sisters are even worse off. I can't help but think of father's attack. Of the Grand Chancellor and what else he has planned. They've taken what's mine.

And I want it back.

AFTERWORD

Look for Waverly's story in the next book:
MINE TO FEAR

If you enjoyed reading this book, please consider helping the author by leaving a review where you purchased the book and/or on Goodreads.

You can sign up to receive newsletters from Janeal Falor at www.janealfalor.com on the Works in Progress page. Or talk to the author directly at janealfalor@gmail.com

See where the story all started with Serena in YOU ARE MINE or with Katherine in the prequel novella, MINE TO TARNISH

ACKNOWLEDGMENTS

When I first published YOU ARE MINE, I was expecting very few sales but I was happy that it was finally out in the world. Then it became a bestseller and reached many more people than I ever thought possible. To each and every one of you who has bought and read my books, THANK YOU! Every single time a book sells, a review is left, a comment is made, or an email sent, I'm in awe of you.

This whole journey wouldn't be possible without a phenomenal group of book bloggers. Each and every one of you that accepted my review request, took the time to read, and then share your feelings with your blog readers and friends helped make my dreams a reality. My gratitude for all of your hard work and enthusiasm is boundless. Thank you so much for your continued work and support.

A big thanks to Karen C. Eddington for always pushing me forward, making my day, having such good insights. I would have given up on writing long ago if it wasn't for her. Not only the best sister ever, but a comedian that can keep me laughing for hours.

RaeChell Garrett not only helped me fix big problems but chatted with me about things that needed to be worked on with insight on how to fix them. It was such a joy to finally talk to you! Plus, you really do rock at seeing things I can't, like people having more than two ears. My thanks to Loralie Hall, for reading a very messy draft and giving me the confidence to keep working on it. You are so The Awesome. Your emails always make my day. The best two critique partners and friends an author could ask for!

The super sweet and phenomenal Michelle Paskett has a way of catching things no one else can see and making my words so much prettier than I could do on my own. Such amazing talent I'm blessed to work with. And thanks to Kenneth Paskett for always being our courier and never giving into the temptation to use my manuscripts as kindling.

My editor, Kathy Middlemiss at Kat's Eye Editing. She not only helps to polish my words and teach me things but gave an amazing one sentence suggestion that made the ending pop. And my proofreader Yesenia Vargas for being so wonderful at not only helping clean up my grammar mess, but going above and beyond. My book is so much better for having passed through your hands and as a writer, I'm beyond fortune to have found you.

The wonderful Jennifer Graves won the Woman's Canon contest with the rule: A woman must tend to the needs of a son before that of a daughter. Part of her prize was naming a character for this book: Saban (Say-ben)Wright whose character may be my creation, but the name is all hers. Thanks Jennifer!

My beta readers are seriously fantastic. Naomi Bawden for being willing and enthused. I'm so grateful you offered and were willing to put up with my crazied author ways. C.M for many wonderful insights, including keeping Cynthia from eating an entire cake. Sarah Canning for her helpful comments, and, what's more, ones that made me smile, laugh, and fist pump because of the parts I'd finally got right. And Lisa for helping me find and correct mistakes after the book had been published.

Writing is fun. I wouldn't feel complete without it, but it does take a lot of time away from family *cough*and cleaning*cough.*

Even so, my family supports me. My kids are always so patient when mommy's working and even make up fun jokes like, "What did the U say to the R? You are mine." Yeah, my eight-year-old is cool. I could not ask for better, more incredible kids. Big hugs, kisses, and thank yous from mommy!

And Erik, what words are there left to say that you haven't heard me ramble on about a thousand times before? You're the best, most amazing, wonderfully fantastic, superbly awesome, unbelievably patient, insanely good-looking, incredibly supportive husband a girl could have. Which you have heard before, but with the eighteen months it took to get this book from first draft to published (and all the crazy life stuff we had to deal with during that time), it's all the more true. Thank you for everything. I love you.

Amazon best selling author Janeal Falor lives in Utah with her husband and three children. In her non-writing time she teaches her kids to make silly faces, cooks whatever strikes her fancy, and attempts to cultivate a garden even when half the things she plants die. When it's time for a break she can be found taking a scenic drive with her family or drinking hot chocolate.